Willis O'Brien

McFarland
Classics

1997

1. Michael R. Pitts. *Western Movies*
2. William C. Cline. *In the Nick of Time*
3. Bill Warren. *Keep Watching the Skies!*
4. Mark McGee. *Roger Corman*
5. R. M. Hayes. *Trick Cinematography*
6. David J. Hogan. *Dark Romance*
7. Spencer Selby. *Dark City: The Film Noir*
8. David K. Frasier. *Russ Meyer—The Life and Films*
9. Ted Holland. *B Western Actors Encyclopedia*
10. Franklin Jarlett. *Robert Ryan*

1998

11. R. M. Hayes. *3-D Movies*
12. Richard West. *Television Westerns*
13. Ted Okuda *with* Edward Watz. *The Columbia Comedy Shorts*
14. Steve Archer. *Willis O'Brien*

Willis O'Brien
At age 33, in 1919

Willis O'Brien

Special Effects Genius

by
Steve Archer

McFarland & Company, Inc., Publishers
Jefferson, North Carolina

Front cover: Willis O'Brien, 1933.
Back cover: Willis O'Brien (right) with Irwin Allen during the
making of *Animal World* (1956).

The present work is a reprint of the library bound edition of
Willis O'Brien: Special Effects Genius, *first published in 1993.*
McFarland Classics is an imprint of McFarland & Company,
Inc., Publishers, Jefferson, North Carolina, who also published
the original edition.

British Library Cataloguing-in-Publication data are available

Library of Congress Cataloguing-in-Publication Data

Archer, Steve, 1957–
    Willis O'Brien : special effects genius / by Steve Archer.
        p.   cm.
    Filmography: p.
    Includes bibliographical references (p.   ) and index.
    ISBN 0-7864-0573-2 (paperback : 50# alkaline paper) ∞
    1. O'Brien, Willis, 1886–1962.   2. Motion picture producers and
directors—United States—Credits.   3. Cinematographers—United
States—Credits.   4. Cinematography—Special effects.   I. Title.
PN1998.3.O25A73   1998
791.43'024'092—dc20   92-50950
                                                                            CIP

Manufactured in the United States of America

McFarland & Company, Inc., Publishers
    Box 611, Jefferson, North Carolina 28640

For my father Harvey Archer
and
in memory of
my mother Winifred Archer
and Mrs. Willis Darlyne O'Brien

Acknowledgments

All the photographs and much other material and information regarding the life and work of Willis O'Brien, and advice in the writing of this book, came via the generous help of the following: Dave Allen, Kevin Brownlow, Jim Danforth, Mike Hankin, Ray Harryhausen, Donald E. Hughes, Murray Glass/Glenn Photo, Darlyne O'Brien, Paul Mandell (who gave permission to use information and photograph from his "Of Beasts and Behemoths" article), Stephen R. Pickard, Neil Pettigrew, Don Shay (who provided information and advice on Willis O'Brien and Marcel Delgado), Harry Walton and the British Film Institute.

Table of Contents

About This Book

This book is divided into three major parts. The first part deals with the films of Willis O'Brien and contains a brief synopsis and reviews of each film and interviews with the people who knew and worked with him. The second part deals with O'Brien's story ideas and illustrations for proposed film projects and ideas for television that were never realized. Except for some minor spelling and grammatical corrections and minor editing to enhance readability, the stories are presented as O'Brien originally wrote them. The third part covers key people who worked with O'Brien or were connected in some way with his world.

The final sections of this book contain a Willis O'Brien filmography and a list of the sources from which I drew most of the information for this book.

Although the book is designed to be used as a reference book, there is some biographical information about O'Brien, albeit brief. For those who wish to delve further into O'Brien's life and technical work, or wish to know more about the special effects processes he used, I suggest that you consider consulting some of the writings mentioned in the Bibliography. I have described some of the techniques that he used in his films, but they are presented in lay terms.

O'Brien was a bloody genius, you know.
He could sketch anything you wanted.
He was the best trick man in the
business. Nobody in his class.

—Merian C. Cooper

Part I. Films

Chapter 1

Silent and Sound
(1915–1936)

You know a conjurer gets no credit when once he
has explained his trick; and if I show you too much
of my method of working, you will come to the
conclusion that I am a very ordinary individual
after all.—Sherlock Holmes to Dr. Watson, in Sir
Arthur Conan Doyle's *A Study in Scarlet.*

Conjurers, like stage magicians, never used to show the public how
their illusions were achieved. In fact, the articles written about the technical work of both *King Kong* and *The Lost World* steered clear of going
into any detail concerning how the effects were achieved. Even the codirector of *King Kong*, Ernest B. Schoedsack, wrote an article about the
film that said, "You'll be certain at any rate to wonder how the scenes
were filmed and how they were recorded. I'm afraid I cannot reveal all
of the secrets—they are hugged tightly in the breasts of the technical ex-
perts actually responsible for them," adding later in the article that "the
animals themselves were made under the direction of Willis O'Brien,
who is, in addition to being an artist of merit, a well-known expert in
natural history."[1]

For a long time, it was thought that *King Kong* was a man in a gorilla
suit. It wasn't until the late 1950s that the real truth about the special
effects processes used on the films became known to the public. The mystery that surrounded the special effects work in films gave its practi-
tioners the aura of magicians. Willis O'Brien, or "Obie" as he was known
by his friends and associates, was the film equivalent of these stage magicians. Among the early pioneers of "trick work," as it was called, Obie
specialized in "stop motion animation," a technique of photographing

miniature models — such as a model puppet of a man or dinosaur — one frame of film at a time and readjusting their position between frames, thereby giving the final impression, when the film was shown, that the model moved by itself.

It was this method that Obie devised and developed which created the dinosaurs and giant ape for *King Kong* and almost a dozen other feature films, beginning with *The Lost World* (1925) and ending with *The Giant Behemoth* (1959). Despite the huge success *King Kong* achieved both artistically and financially, O'Brien struggled in a life and career filled with personal tragedies and aborted film projects. With the demise of the elaborately planned *War Eagles* (1938–39), O'Brien was less and less involved in the film industry until his death in 1962.[2] To "keep the work coming in" during the lean periods, he would initiate film projects by creating story ideas and presenting them to prospective film producers with the hope that they might be developed into movies. Many of his ideas were purchased. Two of them — *The Beast of Hollow Mountain* (1956) and "Emilio & Guloso" — actually made it to the screen, although in a somewhat altered form. Unfortunately most of his ideas were unproduced. How did he enter the film business, where did his ideas come from and what was he like?

Willis Harold O'Brien was born on March 2, 1886, in Oakland, California. He worked in a variety of jobs (cowboy, newspaper cartoonist, and prizefighter) before discovering the technique of model animation quite by accident in 1914. His experimentation with clay models and photographing them one frame at a time — like cartoons — led him to create the successful short "caveman comedy" entitled *The Dinosaur and the Missing Link* (1915). This film was followed by a series of similar films O'Brien made for the Thomas A. Edison Company, such as *The Birth of a Flivver* (1916), *Morpheus Mike* (1917), *R.F.D. 10,000 B.C.* (1917), and *Prehistoric Poultry* (1917). O'Brien's animation for these silent shorts contained similar "acting mannerisms" that later appeared in his animation work in *King Kong* (1933). All his work displayed this humorous style, which helped humanize his characters and broadened their appeal to the movie audience. He made other shorts, but the ones already mentioned are the only shorts that have survived. After leaving Edison, O'Brien made *The Ghost of Slumber Mountain* (1919).

Directed, written, photographed and with special effects created by O'Brien, *Ghost of Slumber Mountain* is his first film using animation to create the realistic appearance of prehistoric animals. His earlier shorts were meant to be seen purely as animated puppets (although he apparently

The Lost World (1925): Bessie Love is menaced by a dinosaur. This could be another posed shot because this scene does not appear in any of the available prints of the film.

had made a short film before *Ghost* that combined animation with live action that appears to have been lost). *Ghost* is his only surviving film before *The Lost World*, which combined animation with live action. It also has the distinction of being the only film in which O'Brien supposedly appeared as "Mad Dick," an old hermit who beckons author and amateur artist Jack Holmes to look through Dick's telescope to see the prehistoric animals.

Unlike the earlier surviving short films—available prints of which show a clear picture—the only surviving print of *The Ghost of Slumber Mountain* appears to have been derived from a 16mm negative, which unfortunately reveals poor picture quality. This is a big problem with viewing films from the silent period. Films were not expected to make any money after their initial release, so they were later stored—not so future generations could see them, but to be forgotten and to disintegrate slowly to unviewable dust. The films now available from those days were derived mainly from actual cinema projection prints; few original negatives of these films survived. This unfortunate situation creates the impression that silent films were badly photographed and edited because some films, like *The Lost World* (which lost many scenes), have not survived complete. Films from later periods, such as the 1930s and 1940s, also suffer from these problems, due mainly to the neglect, indifference and sad lack of foresight by the film studios. According to some sources, the original running time of *The Ghost of Slumber Mountain* was considerably longer than it is today.

Nevertheless, this film signposts the turn away from puppet animation and the beginning of O'Brien's use of animation to create realism in all his work that followed. After *Ghost*, O'Brien created the special effects for his first feature film, *The Lost World,* in 1925.

The Lost World begins in London, where Edward Malone (played by Lloyd Hughes), a young Irish journalist, earnestly proposes to his girlfriend Gladys Hungerford (Alma Bennett). "I will only marry a man of great deeds and strange experiences—a man who can look death in the face without flinching!" she states. Thrilled by the demand, which challenges the man in him, he asks his boss at the *London Gazette* to send him on "some mission for the paper. Anything, just so it's dangerous!" Malone is sent to interview Professor Challenger (Wallace Beery) at the Zoological Institute, who has recently returned from South America with strange tales of prehistoric monsters. Although the professor has instructed that all reporters be barred from his talk at the institute, Malone gets in and meets Sir John Roxton (Lewis Stone), the famous, big-game hunter "here to check up on Challenger's cock-and-bull story."

Amid catcalls from the audience, Challenger appears on the platform, evidently unpopular—and aware of it and resenting it. "Show us! Bring on your Mastodons! Bring on your Mammoths!" yell the audience. "I will—if any of you worms, you insects, are brave enough to go up the Amazon with me!" he replies. Professor Summerlee (Arthur Hoyt) accepts this challenge, along with Roxton and Malone. "And your occupation?" Challenger asks Malone. "Reporter, sir. *London Gazette,*" Malone splutters nervously. Infuriated by Malone's reply, Challenger comes hurtling down from the platform like a heat-seeking missile and chases Malone out into the London fog. After they fight, the two become friends and are later joined by Roxton. Challenger shows them a tattered and water-stained notebook of Maple White. "Is this all?" Malone asks. Then Paula White (the actress Bessie Love) enters the room, eyed by Roxton. "Miss Paula White— the daughter of the unfortunate scientist whose notebook you hold in your hands," Challenger says. Malone is interested. "My father left me in our camp on the plain when he ascended to the plateau. He would go in spite of what . . . what we had seen," she tells them. Convinced that her father is still alive, the men undertake a trip to the Amazon, backed by the *Gazette*. But Colin McArdle (George Bunny) requests that Roxton take command of the expedition. Challenger's eyes blaze at this, and he orders Austin (Finch Smiles), his aide, to "leave Sir John Roxton's gun here—and come ashore with me."

As the ship casts off, Challenger secretly chuckles to himself while watching McArdle waving. Soon, the group arrive at a trading post in the Amazon, where a pretty girl, Marquette (Virginia Browne Faire)—half–Indian, half–Portuguese—sits at an open window strumming a love song on a battered guitar, while Indians and half-breeds, under the direction of Zambo (Jules Cowles), gather up a great deal of scientific paraphernalia. Outside the trader's hut, Malone is busily thumping out a letter to Gladys on his portable typewriter. "In half an hour, we will open the sealed envelope containing Challenger's secret map that will guide us from here on," he writes. Malone joins Paula in the hut for breakfast and opens Challenger's envelope, only to find nothing but a blank piece of paper. Summerlee's face is full of scorn. "The jungle rivers branch in a thousand directions. We are absolutely helpless without Challenger's maps," Roxton says. With perfect timing, Challenger enters with boots caked with mud and wearing a jaunty straw hat that looks like it originally belonged to a 14-year-old boy. Perched on his shoulder is "Jocko," a little monkey. "I think it is now established that I am the logical leader of this party. Is it agreed?" he states.

The party leave in three canoes and make their way up river, watched by a naked Indian hidden in the dense shadows of the woods. Along the riverbank, Challenger points out a reedy spot among the unbroken vegetation. "Those green rushes mark my private doorway into the unknown. We turn here." They go through a narrow channel, alert and on guard, as war drums begin to rattle in the distance. At night they make camp and huddle round a small fire. The drumbeats continue. "They are merely signal drums of the Cucuma Indians. Degraded savages with scarcely more intelligence than the average college professor!" barks Challenger to Summerlee. Suddenly, a bearer staggers into the camp with a poisoned arrow sticking out of his shoulder. "Cannibals, Zambo. But I'm told they prefer white meat," Roxton says. Meanwhile, Malone and Paula become close. Roxton sees them and asks Malone to join him to "scout about a bit." Challenger goes with them, and they come across the savages dancing

A 16mm filmstrip showing the battle between the brontosaurus and the allosaurus at the edge of the plateau in *The Lost World*. This series of frames suggests that this scene may have been shot on "twos" with several "holds." Sometimes in animation, when the character makes a simple move from one position to another, the animator can shoot a series of 8 or 10 continuous frames without having to move the model. Care has to be taken in doing so because with too many 8- or 10-frame "holds," the action may look stilted.

Opposite left: Another 16mm strip of frames showing the allosaurus from *The Lost World*. This shot also shows the figure "breathing." Breathing can be achieved by using either a football bladder and inflating or deflating it, bit by bit, or a mechanism that expands and contracts inside the rubber exterior of the model and is part of the figure's "skeleton." This mechanism normally has to be constructed by a skilled engineer. *Right:* A 16mm filmstrip that shows the frame-by-frame progression of the animated dinosaur from *The Lost World* (1925). The speed at which the film was projected in the silent days varied from 16 frames per second (FPS) to sometimes 18 or 20 FPS. Today, films are shown at 24 FPS. The amount of animation that can be shot in a day depends largely on the speed of the animator and the complexity of the animation shot. About five seconds of footage a day is normal. Most animation is shot "single frame," which means that the figure is moved for each frame of film. Shooting on "twos" (two frames of each movement, instead of one), helps create more animation footage, but makes the figure appear to move stiffly. Another thing to consider is that when the figure walks — as the dinosaur appears to be doing in this scene — a few frames will require the figure to balance on one leg. This leg is usually bolted from beneath the table and into the dinosaur's foot, to ensure that the model doesn't fall over.

under the white moon to the sound of drums. It's their war dance in full swing. "These chaps 'ill keep this up until daylight — and we'll all be miles up the river by that time!" Roxton says to Challenger.[3]

However, when they return to the camp, they find Paula, Austin and Summerlee bound hand and foot, Zambo wounded in the arm and their supplies gone. "Poor Zambo tried to prevent them from stealing the canoes," Paula says. They leave the camp and head upstream, making camp at the foot of the plateau. A great pinnacle rises beside the plateau, its perpendicular walls paralleling the walls of the plateau itself. A shadow passes over them, and they look up to see a great pterodactyl landing on the pinnacle. "Gad, what a trophy. If one could only bag that!" exclaims Roxton. Challenger views the creature through his glass and says, "This is the greatest moment of my life! I have seen a living pterodactyl!" The next day, they bridge the chasm between the plateau and the pinnacle with a fallen tree. "As leader of this expedition, it is my privilege to be the first to cross into the Lost World!" Challenger states importantly. They make their way across. Now some distance away, they turn in amazement to see a brontosaurus turning the tree over and hurling it down into the canyon below.

Cut off from the outside world, they make camp near a huge ginko tree, while Challenger works on a thorn-bush barricade. That night, they are attacked by an allosaurus, "a meat-eater, and the most vicious beast of the ancient world! To think that we should actually see it!" whispers Challenger gleefully. Malone drives the beast back into the darkness with a flaming torch. The next day, the group move to a lake, where they witness a fight between an allosaurus and a trachodon. The allosaurus wins and then fights and kills a triceratops that appears. Meanwhile, a cave is discovered in which Roxton finds an old rifle with its steel barrel bent and a partly clothed skeleton with an old-fashioned watch monogrammed M.W. on the back. Challenger and Summerlee go off to stalk a brontosaurus and "observe its habits!" But Summerlee forgets his pipe, unaware that it lays smouldering in the dry ferns. The ferns catch fire, which spreads rapidly, bringing out an allosaurus that attacks the brontosaurus, driving it backward off the edge of the plateau into the marsh below. Malone finds Challenger and Summerlee and leads them back to the others in the cave.

The group finally escape the plateau by climbing a rope ladder from the cave back to their world — almost stopped in the process by an apeman (Bull Montana), whom Roxton shoots — and see the mired brontosaurus slowly rolling around in the mud, trapped. "Ah certainly hopes

The Lost World (1925): **The allosaurus invades the encampment as the group prepare to fight it off with rifle and torch.**

dat mud holds!" says Zambo. Horsemen approach, led by Major Hibbard (Charles Wellesley) "of the Brazilian Geodesic Survey." All look at the beast. "I'd give anything to get that creature to London and throw it in the face of my critics!" Challenger says. The major feels their enthusiasm. "I'll send for men to dredge out this stream, and build a raft—and when the big rains come next month, we might float your 'rat' out!" Confined in a huge steel cage, the brontosaurus is carefully floated downstream on a big raft with Challenger standing just outside of the cage, triumphant.

At the hall of the Zoological Institute in London, huge crowds pour in. Challenger and his group—except Malone—are sitting with major Hibbard on the platform beside the speaker's table. "Tonight, you will not jeer—for I have brought back living proof of my statement!" Challenger declares to the audience. "A live brontosaurus nearly sixty feet long from the nose to the tail!" But he receives bad news from Malone: "As we swung the cage out over the dock the cables broke—the fall smashed the cage—and it got out! We haven't been able to catch it!" Challenger is stunned. He cries in tense tones to the audience: "My brontosaurus has escaped!" The audience reacts furiously, shouting "Fake! Liar! Charlatan!" as Challenger curses the infuriated crowd—now a mob gone out of control.

The brontosaurus goes on the rampage in the streets of London. Challenger and his group follow it to the Tower Bridge. The bridge collapses under the weight of the brontosaurus and it swims downstream, heading for the ocean and freedom.

Challenger and his group gaze at the site as Gladys and a young man rush up to join them. She introduces the young man as her husband—Percy Bumberry. Bumberry extends a limp hand and smiles vacuously and conceitedly at his defeated rival. Malone gets into a taxi with Paula, closes the door and pulls down the blind. "She didn't wait for me—she's married!"

Based on the 1912 novel by Sir Arthur Conan Doyle (the creator of Sherlock Holmes), "The Lost World" was the first of five adventure stories to feature Professor Challenger, the others being "The Poison Belt," "The Land of Mist," "The Disintegration Machine" and "When the World Screamed." In Challenger, Doyle designed a marvelous bombastic character, who was played excellently by Wallace Beery. Lewis Stone gave a subtle and sensitive performance as Roxton with Bessie Love in a rather thankless part that gave her little chance for character development. The same can be said for the rest of the cast, in that O'Brien's special effects tended to overshadow them. Reviews of the day praised O'Brien and his special effects. One review said, "It is probable that chief honours for its success should be awarded to Willis O'Brien, the research and technical director. The prehistoric monsters which are the leading feature if not the raison d'etre of the production are marvels of ingenuity both in design and in the method of animation . . . in many cases they are doubtless small models, but their movements are so supple and natural that it would be easy to believe them to be huge living creatures."[4] Another review said that the "settings of *The Lost World* are very good and well photographed," but recognized that "London scenes are well faked, although London bridge appears very unfamiliar."[5] Critics of the time were, in general, unsure of how the dinosaurs were created. One stated that "whether they are really as large as they appear, and are worked by mechanism or even concealed men as in the case in *The Nibelungs*, they are the most startling and intriguing monsters who have ever invaded screenland."[6]

Even as late as 1976, the film was recognized for its "engaging simplicity" and seen as the "godfather to a whole genre of fantasy cinema and the first major demonstration of Willis O'Brien's stop-frame animation process," with the critic concluding that "once . . . the dull direction of Harry Hoyt . . . gives way to Willis O'Brien's special effects . . . things rapidly improve."[7]

When the original script is compared with a present-day copy of the film, it appears that a considerable number of scenes either were not shot or were edited from the film. Scenes, such as the expedition being loaded on to the ship, the trading post sequence and the loading of the brontosaurus into a cage in the Amazon, are missing, as is footage of Alma Bennett and Virginia Brown Faire.[8] There appears to be no camera negative or complete print of the film that survived. The version that is available is five reels long (just over an hour) and seems to have been edited down by Kodascope from the original 10-reel feature. Prints that I have seen of this film have poor picture quality.

However, in 1925 the public saw the full version, and the film was a great success. The technical aspects of the film marked a major step up in O'Brien's career and away from the shorts. But, perhaps more important, it also marked the first of eight film projects that O'Brien would make with model maker Marcel Delgado. As Delgado remarked:

> At first, O'Brien had an assistant named Cliff Markay. I don't know what he ever did for Obie. I never saw anything being done by him, although he talked a lot about it. He was supposed to be making the models with Obie for the picture. He was there for many months, I discovered later on. And all he did was talk. O'Brien was funny that way. He hired people he didn't know, like me. I had a job at the grocery that paid $18 a week and I wasn't about to give it up. Then Obie insisted that I should work for him. I must have turned him down fifteen or twenty times. When I saw the studio, I immediately changed my mind! Obie didn't know me from Adam. He was just taking a chance. I never did see the other guy again. And Obie put me on salary for $75 a week. I was never taught how to make models. I did them on my own. There were no instructions; I had to rely on my own imagination. And, by God, I produced the first ones, and they looked good to me! O'Brien didn't have any complaints.[9]

After *The Lost World*, O'Brien worked on a follow-up project for First National entitled *Atlantis* (which was canceled) and later on *Frankenstein* (also canceled).[10] At RKO (Radio-Keith-Orpheum Corporation), O'Brien joined director Harry Hoyt to make *Creation* (1930–31),[11] the first of many films that used variations of *The Lost World* storyline. A year was spent planning *Creation*. O'Brien and artists Byron L. Crabbe and Mario Larrinaga created artwork for the project, and two test reels were shot — one of a yacht in a storm and one showing a triceratops chasing a man. The latter test film is the only one that survives today. Unfortunately RKO was in financial straits at that time, and its vice-president, William Le Baron — who had given the go-ahead for *Creation* — decided to go to Paramount, leaving his position to be filled by David O. Selznick (later the producer of the monumental *Gone With the Wind*, 1939). To assess the value of the projects in production at RKO, Selznick chose Merian C. Cooper, who decided to abort *Creation*, along with a number of other films, but to retain O'Brien and his technical crew for his own project.

With *Creation* "in the ashcan," Cooper got O'Brien and his artists to make a series of drawings for a story he had about a giant ape. Then he hired the English thriller writer Edgar Wallace to write the script, calling his story project "The Beast." But on February 10, 1932, Wallace died. Cooper continued with the project, now calling it "The Eighth Wonder," and began shooting a test reel that contained O'Brien's animation of a giant gorilla shaking men off a log and fighting a tyrannosaurus, using the miniature sets and dinosaurs that were originally built for *Creation*. Writer James Creelman (whose previous RKO writing credits included *The Vagabond Lover* (1929) and *Half Shot at Midnight* — a Wheeler and Woolsey film of 1930) was hired to continue work on the script.

By May 1932, Cooper gave the go-ahead to *The Most Dangerous Game* (1932) and brought director Ernest B. Schoedsack to codirect that film and *The Eighth Wonder*. Both productions would use an elaborate jungle set built specially for *The Most Dangerous Game*. By this method, Cooper cleverly managed to spread some of the costs of *The Eighth Wonder* into the budgets of other RKO films that were in production. Schoedsack had worked with "Coop," as he was known, on three earlier films: *Grass* (1924), *Chang* (1927) and *The Four Feathers* (1929). Both had served during World War I, and both were tough devil-may-care adventurers who were ready for a challenge. Cooper showed the test reel and drawings for *The Eighth Wonder* to Selznick, who gave the project the OK, and production started with the title now changed to *Kong*. The use of many of Cooper's and Schoedsack's real-life experiences during the making of *Grass* and *Chang* gave the film the feeling of a Cooper-Schoedsack expedition. The final title of the film was *King Kong*.

King Kong tells the story of reckless film producer Carl Denham (played by Robert Armstrong, based on Cooper's personality), about to leave on a "crazy voyage" to an uncharted island. Denham needs a girl for a film that he wants to make there. "The public, bless 'em, must have

The 1942 poster of the reissue *King Kong*, crediting Obie as Willis J. O'Brien.

a pretty face," he says, as he goes off in search of such a girl among the unemployed. He finds out-of-work actress Ann Darrow (Fay Wray, based on Schoedsack's wife, Ruth Rose, who accompanied Coop and Monty on their real-life expeditions), who agrees to join him on a "thrill of a life-time . . . and a long sea voyage."

On board the ship, Denham shoots a film test of Ann, watched by

King Kong (1933): **Put on display in New York, Kong breaks free from his chains and goes on the rampage, searching for Ann.**

Captain Englehorn (Frank Reicher, also in Schoedsack's *Dr. Cyclops*, 1940) and Jack Driscoll (Bruce Cabot, based on Schoedsack). Driscoll asks Englehorn, "Do you think he's crazy, skipper?" referring to Denham. "No, just enthusiastic!" Englehorn replies (in a dialogue that describes Cooper to a T). Denham's idea is to take Ann and the crew to an uncharted island and photograph "something monstrous, all powerful, still living, still holding that island in a grip of deadly fear!"

  This "God or spirit or something" is worshipped by the island's gorilla-crazed natives. Denham and his group arrive on the island in time to witness the natives' sacrificial ceremony in full swing. "Oh boy! What a chance! What a picture!" enthuses a bewitched Denham. But the native chief sees Denham and his group and starts getting unhealthy ideas about Ann. He asks to swap six of his gals for the golden dame. "Yeah, blonds are scarce around here!" quips Denham. But it's no deal, and Denham and his group return to the ship. However, the natives don't take no for an answer; later that night, they kidnap Ann and take her back to the

King Kong (1933): A posed still in which Kong battles the tyrannosaurus rex in a vicious fight to the death.

island. With flaming torches "looking like the night before election," the overenthusiastic natives prepare to offer Ann to Kong, the giant ape. Jack alerts Denham and the crew, who go to the island to try to rescue Ann.

Almost a third of the way into *King Kong*, with Max Steiner's pounding music building to a thrilling climax, the real action of the movie finally begins! With the zombielike natives yelling and jumping about, Ann is taken to the sacrificial altar, revealed by a track-in camera move, which shows the great gates opening. After tying her to the altar, the natives become quiet, and a huge gong is sounded. From out of the darkness of the forbidden jungle, Kong emerges. After a few roars and a bit of chest beating, Kong snatches Ann and disappears back into the jungle with her, watched in stunned silence by Denham and his recently arrived crew. Denham brushes aside the natives, orders the gates reopened and goes into the jungle with the crew to pursue Kong. In the dense jungle, they follow Kong's huge footprints ("Yeah, there's his mark all right!") that lead them to encounter and kill a stegosaurus ("Something from the dinosaur family!") and find a brontosaurus, which drowns some of the crew in a swamp and bites two others, chasing the survivors onto a log that bridges a chasm. As they cross the log, Kong appears on the other side and picks it up, shaking most of the men off it to fall to their mysterious fate below. (In the original film, the crew are devoured by spiders and other creatures in this "pit," but this sequence was cut out and has never been found.) Kong is about to grab Driscoll, when his simian ears are alerted to the sounds of a tyrannosaurus approaching Ann, whom Kong has left perched high in a tree.

Kong shakes his head at Driscoll (as if to say, "I'll be back for you later!") and goes off to defend Ann from the approaching dinosaur. The fight between the two giants is a marvelous and engrossing study of savagery, which shows Kong and his leather-faced opponent growl, lunge and swipe paw and jaw as they try to tear each other apart. What makes this sequence so great (and helps support the argument that animation is usually more effective than any other method in creating an imaginary creature) is that both monsters show character. From the beginning of the fight, Kong's character comes through. At first Kong shows anger at the interloper's appearance, then caution as he tries to figure how to tackle the monster and later sheer animal cunning (like a lion stalking its pray). O'Brien's experiences as a prizefighter and his sharp observation of the way animals behave brought to the screen a fight whose actions have been often copied but never surpassed. After killing the tyrannosaurus Kong beats his chest in victory and carries Ann off to his lair, high atop Skull Island. Meanwhile, Denham—the only other survivor along with Driscoll—returns to the gates, and Driscoll secretly follows Kong. Inside Kong's headquarters, the ape bashes to death a snakelike monster that threatens Ann, as Driscoll watches in hiding.

After this brief encounter, Kong carries Ann to the highest point of his mountain headquarters. After a quick defiant roar, Kong goes to the business at hand, tearing Ann's clothes off. Just as things are getting interesting (he's down to her slip), Kong is rudely interrupted by a pterodactyl that swoops down and tries to take Ann away. During Kong's fight with the creature, Driscoll takes Ann and escapes back to Denham and safety at the natives' village. After killing the monster, Kong goes after them and breaks open the massive gates—a marvelous bit of action (you can see Kong straining to push open the gates) and goes on a rampage, killing every native he can in his search for Ann. Finally Denham stops Kong in his tracks by throwing gas bombs at him. "He'll be out for days!" Denham yells triumphantly. Back in New York, Denham prepares to exhibit Kong chained to a massive wooden cross to a paying audience in a theater (the Shrine Auditorium in Los Angeles).

Crowds of people file into the theater. "What is it anyhow?" asks one man. "I hear it's a kind of gorilla," replies another. A woman overhears this answer as a man shows apelike rudeness by treading on her feet. "Ain't we got enough of them in New York!" she says. After a brief introduction by Denham, the curtain goes up to reveal Kong on the stage, chained up. Newspaper reporters start taking photographs, but Kong doesn't want his picture taken, and roars at them.

"Oh let him roar! It's a swell piture!" the cameraman barks back. But Kong has had enough. He breaks his chains and smashes his way out of the theater, going after Ann, who has been taken away to safety. In his search, Kong wrecks a train (a situation that would later appear in *The Black Scorpion*) and throws the wrong woman to her death thinking she is Ann. He finally finds Ann and carries her to the highest building in New York—the newly built Empire State Building. "That licks us!" Denham says to the police. But Driscoll suggests airplanes: "If he should put Ann down . . . !" Immediately a squadron of four biplanes takes off, swooping down at Kong from the sky, rattling their machine guns at him.

Kong snarls at them in defiance, as one by one they dive at him, gradually weakening him with their bullets. The whole battle is stacked high in favor of the pilots winning. Like the blind Samson helplessly trying to fend off the dwarfs before he's killed, Kong struggles in vain to fight against his flying foes. He knocks one plane out of the air, which crashes against the side of the building. Finally, when he is too weak to fight, he gently puts Ann down safely beside his feet.

Bleeding and near death, he wipes his brow, gives one last roar and falls off the building to his death below. A crowd gathers around his inert body. "Well, Denham, the airplanes got 'im," says a policeman. Denham looks sadly at the dead body, shakes his head and says, "No. It wasn't the airplanes. It was beauty killed the beast."

"This fantastic stuff," said one review, was "obviously influenced by *The Lost World*."[12] The review recognized that the real heroes of *King Kong* "are the technicians who, by back projection, the use of miniatures and other processes, have worked a year giving the monsters sufficient illusion of reality to wring gasps from all but the most critical." Most critics were taken in by *Kong*'s magic, praising the film for "an astonishing technical tour de force [that] marks a distinct advance on anything in the same tradition which has yet been attempted."[13] Words could not be found to describe the excitement that the film contained. "It is too bad that 'Colossal' and 'super-colossal' have been bandied about so freely," said *Photoplay*, "for here is a real hair-raiser to which those terms are appropriate."[14] Another critic agreed, stating, "No, you just can't believe your eyes—but it's true. Why it's colossal—and don't laugh—for here, really, is a picture that is colossal."[15] "Fantastic Thriller—Mechanical triumph; *King Kong* . . . is simply awe-inspiring" said still another critic.[16] "An astonishing conception" said the *Evening News*. Even the *Star*'s critic warmed to it: "If there are people who cannot be thrilled by this I am sorry for them."

King Kong was the same kind of success as later films like *Star Wars* and *ET*. It was so popular in drawing both cash and affection from the entertainment-hungry public of the 1930s depression that it was successfully rereleased in 1947, remaining unchallenged or undated. *The Cinema* said of the film's rerelease in its January 22, 1947, issue:

> Hailed in its day as the screen's most brilliant technical achievement . . . for a picture close on fifteen years old . . . may indeed be classed as a worthwhile revival, the passing of time has done but little to impair its startling melodramatic spectacle.[17]

On March 8, 1983, *King Kong* received its 50th-anniversary showing at Grauman's Chinese Theatre, where the film was originally premiered in 1933.[18] Three years later, it was revived again in London's West End to rave reviews:

> Modern special effects have not impaired the impressive nature of the old beast, who uses arrows as toothpicks and swats bi-planes with his fist.[19]

> *King Kong* . . . proves just as ripping a yarn now as it was then. There's an indestructible quality to Edgar Wallace's dense story, and the delights of dialogue such as "Let me on board, I'm a theatrical agent" rank alongside the later line from *Ghostbusters*, "back off man, I'm a scientist."[20]

King Kong was a triumph for all who were connected with it. It helped put RKO on its feet and established the successful team of Cooper, Schoedsack and O'Brien. For O'Brien, it represented an everlasting monument to his genius and talent. David Hogan observed that O'Brien was "one of the towering figures of the fantastic film, a pioneer in the articulation and frame-by-frame filming of small, jointed models," adding that, "O'Brien's work is not flawless, but his understanding of personality is impeccable."[21]

Willis O'Brien ropes his second wife, Darlyne Prenett, on a ranch near lake Sherwood, circa 1936.

Did O'Brien ever write a script for his animation? According to his second wife, Darlyne O'Brien,

> he just sought of filled those things in as he went along. He would think that this was the natural thing to do, and he always got those little touches in, and this is why people say you can see *King Kong* over and over again and each time you see something different about it, and it's true, because of all these little touches, that's what was so typical of his work. He just got those little true-to-nature things in him.[22]

To cash in on the film's outstanding success, the team made a sequel, *The Son of Kong*, which retained much of the original film's cast and production crew, but not much of its budget. With less money and more laughs, *The Son of Kong* was an entertaining film that the audiences found disappointing.

The Son of Kong starts where *King Kong* left off. Hiding from press men and lawyers who are seeking to sue him for the damage that the killer gorilla caused in New York, Denham (Robert Armstrong) decides to escape from his boardinghouse hideout and join his old associate Captain Englehorn (Frank Reicher), who proposes an idea to Denham. "What is it? Gonna get a couple of mega-phones and run site-seeing trips around the harbor?" Denham asks. Together, they set sail again in the *Venture* in the hopes of drumming up work shipping freight. They land in Dakang and go on shore to see a circus act called La Belle Helene, which features a singer Hilda (Helen Mack) and her monkeys.

Later, Hilda's father accuses his drunken friend Helstrom (John Marston) of losing a ship to "get the insurance." Helstrom knocks the old boy unconscious with a bottle of booze and accidently sets fire to the circus tent. In an exciting sequence, Hilda goes into the flaming tent to rescue her father and free the animals. But moments later, he dies. Helstrom is now in a big hurry to escape Dakang and reveals to Englehorn that it was he who sold the map of Kong's island to Denham. "But didn't you get the treasure?" he asks as bait to lure Denham and Englehorn back to the island—and to take him with them. With the shifty-eyed Helstrom as their guide, Denham and Englehorn agree to return to Skull Island, aided by a not-so-loyal crew. During the voyage, they discover Hilda on board, secretly stowed away, intending to take revenge on Helstrom for her father's death.

Helstrom has other ideas, however, and encourages the ship's crew to mutiny and to throw Denham, Englehorn, Charlie, the cook (Victor Wong, also in the first film) and Hilda off the ship into a small boat. Thinking that he is now captain, Helstrom is dumbfounded at the crew's rejection of his kind offer to take over. "Do you think we got rid of a good captain, so that we could have a bad one?" a rebellious sailor asks.

The crew throw Helstrom in the small boat with Denham and company, who cast off and head for the island. "When they see us," Denham says, "they'll throw a party!" But their arrival is greeted by a spear thrown at their feet by the chief. "Hey! Did you throw that, you rat!" Denham exclaims. "Muko. Muko Nasee Boga! Wahta tee Goofa! Noola tooga Kong!" the chief replies. "He said, 'Yes, he did!'" Englehorn translates. In short, the chief politely refuses the group permission to land, so they sail to another part of the island and enter a large cavern. Here, the happy group split up into two parties. Hilda joins Denham; to their surprise, they discover a white-furred ape trapped in swamplike mud. With no dramatic music or exciting introduction, the star of the film is shown. "Well, if it isn't a little Kong," Denham says. They free the ape from the mud, only to

Top: Willis O'Brien, Jr., on the set of *Son of Kong*, 1933. *Bottom:* William O'Brien visiting the *Son of Kong* set. He was blind and the eldest of Obie's two sons from his first marriage.

Little Kong fights with a dragonlike reptile in the temple.

be surprised by a big cave bear that engages in a comically staged fight
with Little Kong. The 12-foot-tall snowball wins. Just before that,
however, Helstrom and the other group encounter their own problem in
the shape of a styracosaurus that chases them in a short but exciting sequence. Later, Kong junior leads Hilda and Denham into a hidden cave,
where they find the treasure. After Denham takes some of the jewels,
they are suddenly interrupted by a dragonlike lizard that enters the cave
and fights with Little Kong.

Little Kong kills the creature in a fight (which contains action similar
to the Kong-Tyrannosaurus fight in the first film) and follows Denham
and Hilda out of the cave, just as Helstrom and the others arrive.
Helstrom nearly has heart failure at the sight of the white ape and makes
a mad dash for the boat, just in time to be eaten by a sea monster rising
out of the water. Next, an earthquake erupts on the now-sinking island.
This sequence is well staged, with fissures opening in the ground beneath
the feet of the fleeing natives, rocks crashing down, and the bubbling
seawater rising, flooding the island. During this holocaust, Little Kong

saves Denham's life by holding him above the fast-rising waves, to be rescued by the three remaining survivors. In the raging storm, Little Kong is pulled to his death beneath the water. A few days later, they are rescued by a ship. Hilda and Denham decide to split the treasure among all four of them, resulting in a happy ending. O'Brien was far from pleased with the finished film. As Darlyne O'Brien said:

> Obie was unahppy about the making of *Son of Kong*. He felt it was too soon to follow *King Kong* and then there was not going to be enough money to make it good. He asked them to not put his name on it and he didn't do any more than put in appearances each day, so that he would get his check. He did no animation and was a little unhappy with some of the humor—supposedly that was put in to it, and especially laughed at the idea of bandaging the little finger of a big creature like that. He never wanted to do anything that would make *Kong* or *Joe* look ridiculous.[23]

The disappointment O'Brien must have felt over *Son of Kong* was nothing compared to the personal tragedy that affected him during the film's production—the loss of his two sons. As Marcel Delgado recalled:

> I had occasion to meet the former Mrs. Hazel O'Brien just after *The Lost World* was finished along with their two boys. At the time I met her, she gave me the impression of being under high, nervous tension. She didn't seem to act as normally as an ordinary person would do under normal circumstances. I never saw her again after this meeting, although I did see the boys a couple of times after that at the studio, shortly before they died. By that time, the older boy was totally blind. A few days after that meeting, the tragic end came. In a case of illness, despair, despondency and a troubled mind, their mother committed an act of matricide, shooting them and also herself, in an attempt to commit suicide, but she failed. She was rushed to a hospital where she was treated and kept alive for, approximately, one year after the tragedy. The end came for her in 1934.[24]

The following year, O'Brien married his second wife, the former Darlyne Prenett, who recounted their first meeting:

> After the release of *King Kong* and the first time I met him, I didn't know who he was at all, and he asked me if I was a movie fan, and I said "Oh somewhat," and he said "Have you seen *King Kong*?" and I said "Ooh no! I hate those horror pictures!" and he said "Oh, I don't think you'll hate Kong." And it wasn't until after that, that I found out what his work was, and I didn't see *King Kong* until after we were married. I [didn't see] *King Kong* at all for about six months or so, but I did like it when I saw it. So I didn't know—I had never been inside a studio. I lived in Santa Barbara, and I didn't visit the studio . . . until . . . I met him in November and the following March—

Robert Armstrong binds Little Kong's wounded finger with a strip from Helen Mack's petticoat.

> I think it was that year I came down and went to the studios and visited him and he showed me around. So . . . I had no idea what his work consisted of.[25]

After *Son of Kong*, O'Brien's next major film assignment was *The Last Days of Pompeii* (RKO, 1935). In May, Cooper decided to resign from RKO, but agreed to produce personally two films for the studio — *She* (RKO, 1935) and *The Last Days of Pompeii* (RKO, 1935).[26] Cooper had wanted to make *Pompeii* in Technicolor, and some 16mm color tests were shot on the set, but the film was finally made in black and white, with O'Brien as effects supervisor and Schoedsack as sole director.

Pompeii tells the story of Marcus (Preston Foster), a beefy blacksmith who lives with his wife and son in Pompeii. One day, a slave trader stops by. "This smith should be in the arena," he says. "No," replies Marcus, "I couldn't fight a man who never harmed me," adding, "I have enough money." The trader leads the unhappy slaves away to the arena, as Marcus reflects: "A man in chains, going to his death like a caged animal. Makes a man count his blessings."

However, things change for the worse when his wife and son are

Willis O'Brien, aged 47, in 1933 during the making of *The Son of Kong*.

knocked down by a chariot. To find extra money to get a doctor and pay the taxman, Marcus reluctantly goes into the arena to fight for prize money as a gladiator. He wins the fight, but it's too late. Both his wife and son are dead. "I lost all I love, because I was poor. Money is all that matters. It's easy to get money . . . all you have to do . . . is kill!" Guilt-ridden

The poster for *The Last Days of Pompeii* (1935, RKO).

and driven, Marcus returns to the arena on a slaughtering spree, wiping out his opponents with a vengeance, and literally strikes it rich.

   With plenty of money in the bank, Marcus spends his winnings; adopts a young boy, Flavius (David Holt), after killing his father; and buys a Greek scholar, now a slave, to teach the boy. After getting wounded in the arena, Marcus goes to Judea for work and seeks out Pontius Pilate (Basil Rathbone), who sends him on a mission to steal horses from his enemy. On his return, Marcus finds Flavius near death. "There's a young man — a wandering healer — passing on his way through to Jerusalem. All the poor call him master and Lord," says the tutor. Marcus doesn't get it. "What can he do?" he asks. "Perhaps he can help. What harm to ask?" replies the tutor. Marcus takes Flavius to the healer, who saves him. Later, Pilate sentences the healer to be crucified. "Poor man," laments Pilate, "I found no fault in him. But I must keep the peace." In the streets, a beggar pleads with Marcus to save the healer. "You have a sword . . . they'll crucify him!" But Marcus doesn't want to know, takes his son, and leaves town. "Don't look back, Flavius," he says (in a beautiful biblical-style landscape shot). "Look ahead. Think how happy we're going to be, rich," encourages the money-minded Marcus.

Back in Pompeii, Marcus becomes manager of the arena and hints that he might like his boy — now a grown man (John Wood) — to follow in his footsteps, but Flavius has other ideas. While Marcus has been busy earning cash from the slaughtered slaves in the arena, Flavius has secretly hidden some runaways in a cave, far from his father's prying eyes.

Later, as Marcus dines with Pontius Pilate, a messenger brings news to the Roman excellency, who snarls sarcastically at Marcus, "This may be interesting news to you, too." A runaway slave was found and tortured to reveal the hideaway, from which Flavius and the slaves were rounded up and taken to the dungeons, to wait their fate in the arena. Marcus pleads for his son's release, but Pontius Pilate says no deal, and Flavius and the slaves are sent into the arena. When Mount Vesuvius erupts, Marcus leaps in to save Flavius. During the deluge, a gigantic statue towering over the arena crashing down, crushing the panic-stricken crowds.

This is a spectacular sequence, with buildings collapsing, massive crowds fleeing and volcanic lava raining down, and compares well with the disaster scenes from *San Francisco* (1936) and *The Rains Came* (1939) and recent films, such as *Clash of the Titans* (1981). During this mass exodus, Flavius goes to free his girlfriend Cloida (Dorothy Wilson) from the dungeons, while a jailer pleads with Marcus to save his son, buried under rubble. At first Marcus refuses, thinking of his own boy's earlier predicament, and then agrees to help.

Fiery fissures open cracks in the earth and lava starts to cascade from the volcano, forcing people to jump from the now-collapsing ground into the boiling, steaming sea. Marcus instructs Cloida to go with Flavius

Willis O'Brien giving instructions via megaphone during the filming of the Temple of Jupiter miniature for *The Last Days of Pompeii* (1935, RKO).

to his boat, while he delays the Romans from getting to it by keeping the gates closed. After seeing them safely away, Marcus is suddenly speared to death by a Roman. The gates open, but the soldiers are crushed to death by falling rubble. Dying from his wound, Marcus sees the vision of the healer. They hold out their hands to one another. "Master . . . so many years ago . . ." gasps Marcus, and then dies.

The theme of *The Last Days of Pompeii* is similar to that of *Ben Hur* (1926), *The Robe* (1953) and its sequel *Demetrius and the Gladiators* (1954)—and many other films set during the biblical period: Christ unselfishly helps others, while the hero selfishly helps himself to fame and fortune, but pays the price in the end, after recognizing his mistakes

A publicity pasteup showing the effects of the volcanic eruption on the citizens of Pompeii.

through the suffering and unselfish sacrifices of Christ and the lives of others.

The theme is universal: the haves and the have-nots, the poor versus the rich, the greedy versus the nongreedy, and the good guys versus the bad guys, and is seen in every film, in various degrees. The film was remade in 1960, starring Steve Reeves, but the first version remains the most thrilling and effective of the two, containing excellent production values, sincere performances—particularly from Basil Rathbone and Preston Foster—and an exciting music score (which contained a few musical cues from *King Kong, Son of Kong* and *The Most Dangerous Game*) by Roy Webb, who later scored *Mighty Joe Young* (1949). However, the main attraction was Willis O'Brien's special effects, and the reviews recognized this fact, saying:

> The eruption scenes are the high spot of the production . . . the destruction of Pompeii by the volcanic eruption of Vesuvius is an unprecedented spectacular thrill.[27]

The *Motion Picture Herald* agreed:

> The earth shattering destruction, which climax all the previous spectacles, seldom if ever have been duplicated on the screen.[28]

Film Daily said:

> And for the climatic smash . . . with thousands of people fleeing from the arena has never been equalled for sheer magnitude and spectacular smash and perfect detail.[29]

Film Weekly noticed that

> in the reconstruction of an ancient city, in recapturing the cruelty and wild enthusiasm of the Roman arena, and in the scenes of volcanic eruption, this film provides some spectacle worthy of comparison with the best.[30]

But added:

> The rest does not match up to the standards set by the ingenuity of the model makers, art directors and trick cameramen.[31]

On one occasion, Darlyne O'Brien went to the studio to see her husband film the destruction sequence:

> Oh, once or twice I went, when there was something special being shot, like *The Last Days of Pompeii*. I visited once, when they were doing the shot of the little temple. For *The Last Days of Pompeii*, I know that Obie made some wonderful sketches. He was going to have a water arena and use the swordfish — you know — the rubber animated swordfish, but of course, that was all dropped — I mean they decided it would be too expensive, I guess or something — I don't know why, but they didn't have that in *The Last Days of Pompeii*. This temple that they built — miniature temple — Obie figured out a way to build it on this platform and have motors under it, so that it would shake just like a natural earthquake, and it was marvelous the way it fell, just perfect — and it was a very tense moment until they got it down. He had rods in the pillars, and they would drop these rods a little way, then they would shake it then they would drop them a little further, and a little further, so that in the end, the miniature was left standing, just as the real one is today. It was a beautiful shot. It took months of preparation, and every little detail was just perfect.[32]

After the success of *The Last Days of Pompeii*, Obie was hired to create the photographic effects for the second three-strip Technicolor feature film, *The Dancing Pirate* (1936), produced by Cooper's company, Pioneer

Pictures. Cooper had left RKO in 1935 to become executive vice-president of Pioneer—a company formed by John Hay Whitney and his cousin, Cornelius Vanderbuilt Whitney. The success of the award-winning Technicolor short, *La Cucaracha* (1934) encouraged Pioneer to make *Becky Sharp* (1935)—the first three-strip Technicolor feature film—which they had planned since 1933.[33]

In the early days of filmmaking, color had to be added to the film itself by hand tinting. By 1905, the Pathé company created the stencil process, which involved making "several positive copies of the film, from which, frame by frame, were cut those areas which were to be tinted in a particular colour,"[34] using six stencil films, one for each color. Various companies used this time-consuming system well into the 1930s. Others tried to improve on this method to create a more lifelike color process, such as Kinemacolor, Dufaycolor (a negative-positive process) and the British Raycol process, but the first really successful color process was used by Technicolor, a company formed by Herbert Kalmus in 1915.

The Technicolor method used two strips of film in one camera; both pieces of film were then cemented together and dyed red-orange and green. Called the "two-tone Technicolor process"—also known as the "two-strip" or "two-color" process—it was used at first mainly for big sequences on large-scale pictures, such as *The Ten Commandments* (1923), *Ben Hur* (1924) and *Phantom of the Opera* (1925), although Douglas Fairbanks' *The Black Pirate* (1925) was shot completely in the two-color process. Unfortunately, this system had a few problems. Sometimes, the two red-green images that were cemented together did not fit exactly—which resulted in an image that looked as if it had been shot in 3D, but projected without the special lens—showing the images out of registration. To overcome this problem, Technicolor invented "inhibition printing" (also known as "dye transfer printing"), which enabled it to transfer the two separate color images onto one piece of film without cementing. This process eventually evolved into the "three-strip" system, which used a camera that took separate cyan, magenta and yellow images to form a truer color picture. It was this new three-strip camera that was used in 1932 on Disney's first color cartoon, *Flowers and Trees*, followed by the first live-action color short, *La Cucaracha*, and by *Becky Sharp* and *The Dancing Pirate*.

The Dancing Pirate begins in 1820. Jonathan Pride (Charles Collins) is a young dancing master in New York who is shanghaied on a pirate ship bound for southern California. He goes ashore with the ship's gang for water, but is captured (when mistaken for a real pirate) and about to be hung by the neck when Alcalda's (Frank Morgan) daughter, Serafina (Steffi Duna), who just happens to want a few dancing lessons, saves him. The usual happens — they fall in love, and the jealous villain Don Baltazar (Victor Varconi) arrives with his loyal renegade soldiers, and take Jonathan prisoner. Meanwhile, Alcalda gets drunk and agrees to hand over Serafina to Don Baltazar but on the wedding day Jonathan enlists the help of the local Indian tribe who capture the soldiers. Alcalda decides to banish Baltazar. A great fiesta is held, and Jonathan marries Serafina. Naturally, they live happily ever after.

Most reviews zeroed in on the film's technical area. "You are not asked to be convinced by the story which is brightly farcical," said *Picturegoer Weekly,* "but you are asked to be amused by the cleverness of presentation and the characterizations and you will be hard to please if you are not." The review admitted that the film contained "crudities of color at times," although "their blending of blues, yellows and reds" was "particularly noteworthy."[35]

Film Weekly thought that since "this unusual and quite attractive little picture" had been made in color, it was "one of the most successful pictures yet shown."[36]

Monthly Film Bulletin was more businesslike: "The color shows no startling differences from Technicolor as we have come to know it. There is still a good deal of variability from shot to shot," and the "definition remains at its best in detail-shots."[37] *Kine Weekly* also zeroed in on the color, noting that there was "a certain artificiality in the close-ups" but recognized that the color photography was "remarkably free from eyestrain, and multiplication during movement."[38]

Despite some good reaction to the color photography, the critics did not like the film treatment of the flimsy story, and *The Dancing Pirate* became the second and last Pioneer Technicolor feature film to be distributed by RKO.[39]

O'Brien's involvement in *The Dancing Pirate* was brief, containing one glass shot for the film, but none of his animation work.[40] Although it is noteworthy because it was his first color film, it also marked the end of his successful seven-year period of feature film work.

Chapter 2

One Out of Four
(1938–1950)

This story gives an entirely new and modern imagi-
native picture. I think it has greater box-office appeal than *King Kong*, and will make more money.
—Merian C. Cooper's introduction to the "War
Eagles" script, September 20, 1938.

In 1938, Cooper began preparations to make another fantasy-adven-
ture film in the style of *King Kong*. "War Eagles" was the title, and it
promised to make *King Kong* look like small meat, indeed, in comparison.
Cooper saw the new project as "a super western of the air in which, instead of riders of the plains on horseback, we will have wild riders of the
air on giant prehistoric eagles," that would climax in "one great showmanship spectacle scene which will be unforgettable"—an elaborate aerial
battle over New York and the Statue of Liberty. Naturally, Cooper con-
sidered only one man suitable to help create the complex special effects
needed for "War Eagles." Paging Willis O'Brien!

"War Eagles" is about history professor Hiram P. Cobb, who has a
problem: He needs cash to finance his wacky idea of an expedition to the
Arctic to search for Vikings whom he thinks migrated there. The Museum
of Natural History is interested—slightly. "Have you got any equipment
of your own?" its representative asks him. "Well, I brought my heaviest
underwear," Cobb replies. The museum rejects his project, so Cobb
organizes a plane to make the journey, with Jimmy Mathews as the pilot.
On their way to the Arctic, they land on a beach and meet a Chuckchee
northern Siberian shaman—a witch doctor of the reindeer people—who
slashes at Jimmy with a giant claw. "It's proof at last!" exclaims Cobb, who
grabs the claw and takes off with Jimmy toward the Arctic Ocean. Flying

Preproduction illustration for "War Eagles" (1938–39).

through a violent gust of wind, their little single-motor plane is suddenly hit by a "great white shape" as large as the plane. The plane goes into a spin, crashes into the water below and sinks.

Jimmy and Cobb manage to save themselves and the radio and make their way through the mist to a ridge below the summit of a cliff. Here, they meet Naru, a girl wearing a down cloak, who takes them to her Viking people, where they meet Atok and four giant eagles tethered to posts beside their perches. "The prehistoric eagles! Snow eagles!" Cobb shouts. Dropping from the sky comes a white eagle. "Ay, the White One. He hunts alone, untamed," says Atok. Cobb goes to touch a giant black eagle, but Atok pulls him back. "Care little man!—I touch him, others not."

Meanwhile, Jimmy decides to try a little roping and fashions a lariat to capture the white eagle. "Ai, strong is the White One. Far will he go, fighting to throw his rider," says Naru, but Jimmy hauls himself up onto the eagle and rides him into submission. "He rode the White One!" exclaims the excited Naru. "Rode—my eye," says a dazed Jimmy, "I just hung on!" To get some food, Jimmy, Cobb and the Vikings travel to the vast, fertile Valley of the Ancients, where the dinosaurs occasionally visit. Atok warns Cobb: "Stay by the eagles, outlanders. Yonder lies danger." It is here that Cobb discovers the imprint of three giant claws on the ground. An allosaurus enters the valley and decides to liven things up by attacking a brontosaurus. The fight attracts other allosauri that kill Naru's eagle. One of them chases after Naru, but Jimmy kills the beast with a landslide, caused by one of his bombs—which closes off the lair of the allosauri. "This life you have saved. Take it. Guard it," says Naru's grand-father, Skal.

Sometime later, Naru touches Jimmy's radio. A voice comes on. "Air Intelligence is making every effort to verify reports that the enemy may attempt to use a neutralizing ray of great power." "Air Intelligence—why that means war," Jimmy says. "The end of our world, lad," Cobb remarks. Skal agrees to go with Jimmy to New York and fight the enemy. Leading hundreds of eagle-bearing warriors, Jimmy yells "Come on—you war birds!" To the music of the Valkyrie, they head for New York.

As searchlights crisscross the night sky, the huge multimotor black generator plane of the enemy—a flying fortress—becomes visible, approaching the city. Above it, hundreds of planes are aligned in formation. With their electrical neutralizing ray, the enemy have grounded all the American air force. It seems that nothing can stop the bad guys. But wait! As the bombers assume bombing formation, the commandant suddenly sees the white eagle shooting down out of the clouds, followed by other eagles, screaming over the drone of the motors. The planes break formation, as bombs rain down on them from the eagle warriors. A gunner fires at one bird, as its slain rider hits the top of the Empire State Building. Another eagle smashes into a plane. Skal's eagle is shot as Skal jumps into the open cockpit and fights the pilot. One eagle lands on the enemy's huge plane and slashes at the wing with its beak. Machine guns, wide open, rattle at the swooping birds, led by Jimmy on the white eagle, as they bomb the black generator plane. Smoking, the flying fortress drops through the clouds and strikes the water near the skyscrapers, exploding. Having won the battle, Jimmy, Naru and Skal on their eagles sit perched on the arms and shoulders of the Statue of Liberty, triumphant. Saluted by the boats, fluttering flags and whistles and cheering from the bay, Jimmy crys, "Ahoi, hoi!" and waves good-bye to New York. He leads the warriors with Naru on the eagles, and they fly over the city.

The script for "War Eagles" was written by Cyril Hume, who wrote another airborne picture, *Flying Down to Rio* (1933, RKO) and later did some of the excellent Johnny Weissmuller Tarzan films—*Tarzan Escapes*

Above and opposite: Duncan Gleason's preproduction sketches for "War Eagles."

(MGM, 1936) and *Tarzan Finds a Son* (MGM, 1939) and the science fiction film *Forbidden Planet* (MGM, 1956) and its sequel, *The Invisible Boy* (MGM, 1957).

It is interesting to note that "War Eagles," *Tarzan Finds a Son* and *Forbidden Planet* each contain a similar theme: Characters living in a natural unspoiled setting (Vikings in the Arctic, Tarzan in the escarpment and Altaira on Altair 5) are visited by outsiders who want to take one of the characters (Naru, Tarzan's son and Altaira, who all show moments of affinity with nature's animals) and bring them back to "civilization"—with various degrees of success.

Hume obviously was concerned about the pollution of a natural environmental state—be it the ruining of the mind, body or land by civilization—because this theme came through in the three films without being overbearing and was presented with a sharp sense of humor. Intelligently written, "War Eagles" unfortunately never went beyond the script and preproduction stages and was shelved in 1939. A considerable amount of planning went into the project. Artist Duncan Gleason drew many sketches, as did O'Brien. Animation models were created, and a test reel was shot showing an encounter with an eagle and an allosaurus.[41] According to the book, *The Unquiet Man*,[42] Cooper decided to walk out on his $100,000-a-year vice-presidency to help Claire Chennault organize the Flying Tigers—a "Quasi-mercenary band of pilots" who flew for Chiang Kai-shek in March 1940.

"War Eagles" was known by two earlier names: "The Cooper-Shoedsack Show" (obviously an early working title) and "White Eagle." All that appears to survive from this project is some 35mm color film frames that show a jungle-type setting in miniature; a series of Duncan Gleason's drawings illustrating the Valley of the Ancients scenes; various versions of the script, dated September 20, 1938, with additional script changes dated April 20, 1939;[43] photographs of the animation test reel sequence that was shot (this reel has not been found); and a "War Eagle" animation armature in the possession of Jim Danforth.

With its elaborate action sequences—a step beyond *Kong*, I think—the cancellation of "War Eagles" must have been an enormous disappointment to O'Brien. The film could have paved the way for future fantasy films from O'Brien and Cooper, made on the same scale. One can only speculate the effect it might have had on O'Brien's career and the technique of model animation, given the progress he had made in his work on *Lost World* and *Kong*.

Marcel Delgado said about Cooper and "War Eagles":

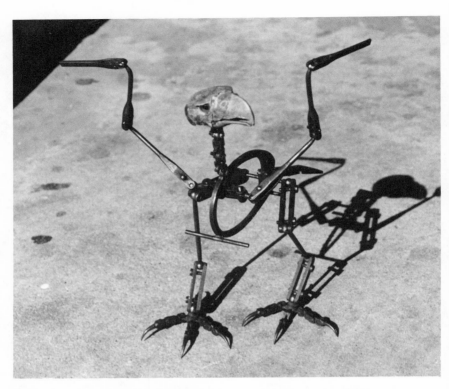

Above and opposite: The "War Eagle" armature as it looked in 1991. In animation, the term *armature* refers to the skeleton on which the model is built. The armature can be built of wire, wood or metal. In feature films, steel ball and socket armatures are normally used. Variations of the design used for the "War Eagle" armature were used by O'Brien for all his animation figures and remain the basis for most designs of animation armatures since his death in 1962 (photos courtesy of Jim Danforth).

Cooper was a funny guy. When we were working on "War Eagles," we made a sequence on it. I never saw it. . . . I don't know whatever happened to it, but Cooper wanted the Chief of the tribe in a costume especially designed for this fellow. He had a room full of sketches from different artists for this particular costume. Well, I found out that he was trying to find a costume for this tribesman, so one day I didn't have anything to do — and out of what I had on my table — scraps of chamois and rubber, I started making a costume for the little man — I had a little dummy. So I left the doll sitting on my table. Well, one day, Cooper comes looking around and sees the little doll sitting on the table and he picks it up and looks at it and says, "That's just the thing I've been looking for — who did this?" He asked everybody. "Well Marcel did it I guess. I've been spending a lot of money and this is just what I want." Too bad we didn't make the picture. I made some little natives and a couple of eagles about the size of a crow, and we made a short sequence with about four or five giant eagles with native warriors fully

dressed in their native costumes, riding on the eagles' backs, fully equipped with spears, clubs, stone-hewn instruments, etc., soaring at high altitudes and diving toward the gigantic dinosaurs and spearing them, using a 1-inch scale. The animation of the eagles was on very fine, invisible wires, and some stills were made of these settings. It would have been a tremendous spectacle.[44]

During the preproduction stage of "War Eagles," O'Brien was visited at MGM by Ray Harryhausen (who worked as O'Brien's assistant on *Mighty Joe Young* in 1949 and *The Animal World* in 1956. Harryhausen said this about the film:

I first met Willis O'Brien at MGM, when he invited me over to see early drawings of "War Eagles." I called him by phone at MGM and told him of my interest in prehistoric animals and animation. He said, "Bring some over." Of course I was awed by all of the 200 drawings and oil paintings for "War Eagles." I remember there was an enormous painting of the Statue of Liberty with eagles perched on the spikes of her helmet, and another painting of the eagles flying around a dirigible. Darlyne had a few watercolor drawings left that were not of a fantasy nature. I have one oil painting done by the artist who went on the expedition with Edmington to the North Pole.

It was about the same time as the Scott expedition. Obie had hired him to do backgrounds for the many glass shots to be used in the film. One painting is still hanging in my dining room in Los Angeles.

Obie told me later that MGM was against the picture. They gave O'Brien a place outside in a makeshift tent for his experiments. There was an antagonism by the staff at MGM — against somebody coming in from the outside and trying to do a picture there. This was before the independent companies became popular. Merian C. Cooper got MGM to put up the money for the development of the story. He had three to four writers on it. There was about a year's work on the film. Cooper was finally called into the armed services and so the picture was called off. O'Brien hired Marcel Delgado to make the dinosaurs. This is where Obie first met George Lofgen. George was a very talented taxidermist and prop maker who made the models of the eagles. I have one of the models of the Viking men used in the animation test reel. It is a small armature which we later used for Jill playing the piano in *Mighty Joe Young*. There was an actual War Eagles armature kicking around during the making of *Joe Young* but is now among the missing. I have seen stills from the test reel, but I've never seen the reel itself. Obie was in the process of making the test at the time of my visit. I do not know what stage they were shooting in but I never got to see the actual area. Miklos Rozsa, composer of *Ben Hur* (1959) and others told me that MGM took all of his scores, when the original MGM closed down, and threw them into the furnace. That may have been the fate of the "War Eagles" paintings and drawings as well.[45]

Hard on the heels of "War Eagles" came another disappointment for O'Brien, the cancellation of his "Gwangi" (1941) project at RKO, about cowboys who capture a prehistoric animal in a hidden valley.[46] Like "War Eagles," "Gwangi" was shelved after the script and preproduction stages, leaving O'Brien's storyboards, a few photographs of the animation model, a script and some other recently discovered material. Ray Harryhausen said:

A fellow called me up frantically on the phone saying he'd discovered some "Gwangi" material in the old RKO Culver City lot where we made *Mighty Joe Young*. He had found it in the attic. He wanted me to come to the studio to identify it. He had found a number of cardboard cutouts that were made for temporary "Gwangi" dioramas. They were originally used to show where the rear-screen projector was to be and where the live action took place. Unfortunately a lot of them were missing.

I do not know if any footage was photographed. O'Brien had many glass paintings made during preproduction. I saw six of them in his office. Marcel Delgado had made a beautifully articulated allosaurus for the film. I remember it had a wonderful skin texture, but it had not been painted. Obie had it in his apartment for several years. Unfortunately he sold it to Eddie Nassour who promptly dismembered it.

It was a great pity when we heard Jack Shaw, an artist, committed suicide right after working with us on *The Animal World*. He was a very fine painter and had a marvelous sense of depth in all his work. He worked with us for a

Willis O'Brien's artwork for Joe's first appearance in *Mighty Joe Young*.

short time on *Mighty Joe*. He did many background landscapes for the many table-top miniatures we used in *The Animal World*. Obie used to have three large oil paintings from "Gwangi" hanging in his office. Jack and he had worked together on the paintings. O'Brien drew the dinosaurs and the cowboys, and Jack did the final painting. Unfortunately Jack suffered from many extreme bouts of depression.[27]

After two disappointments in a row, O'Brien finally hit it lucky with *Mighty Joe Young* (1949). For the project, Cooper joined forces with director John Ford, and the two filed incorporation papers and formed their own company, Argosy Productions, with Cooper as president and financial head. Ford coproduced *Mighty Joe Young* with Cooper for Arko, Inc.,—a company formed by Argosy pictures and RKO for the purpose of making this one film.[48]

Mighty Joe Young is about a baby gorilla who is transported by natives in Africa. The natives are stopped on their way by a little girl named Jill Young (Lora Lee Michel), who decides to swap her father's flashlight for the infant ape. "That's Joe. Isn't he sweet?" she asks her father, who is now minus the flashlight. The story then fast-forwards 12 years to New York.

Max O'Hara (Robert Armstrong) is looking for a "new angle" for his African-style nightclub, The Golden Safari. Out-of-work cowboy Greg Johnson (Ben Johnson) goes to O'Hara, hoping for a job. Idly playing with his rope, he gives O'Hara an idea: "I'll take cowboys to lasso lions!" O'Hara exclaims. He hires Greg and other cowboys and goes to Africa to capture some lions for his act. Here, they encounter Joe — now more than fully grown and 10 feet tall! Inspired, O'Hara screams at his men: "Catch it! Rope it!"

This is the first appearance of Joe in the film — in his animated form — and he is given a superb introduction. Drumming his paws on his chest, à la *King Kong*, Joe hits a lion cage, shakes it and pushes it over, freeing the animal. He exhibits power, curiosity then rage in a more expressive manner than Kong, Jr., did in the earlier film. Realistically animated in this sequence by O'Brien's assistant Ray Harryhausen, Joe shows a range of expressions that are believable and impressively created. The scene progresses as Greg and his cowboys try to capture Joe in a lively sequence. Almost caught, the ape succeeds in freeing himself from their ropes and goes to Jill (now grown up and played by Terry Moore), who orders O'Hara's men to "Leave Joe alone, you big bullies!" Seeing the girl and gorilla together, O'Hara gets ideas and tries to talk Jill into coming with Joe to perform at his nightclub.

"Don't you see what a great chance this is?" pleads O'Hara. "Hollywood! You must have heard of Hollywood?" With the deal signed, Jill and Joe are now under contract and packaged as an act in O'Hara's nightclub. In their opening performance, she plays "Beautiful Dreamer" on the piano as Joe is revealed underneath, holding the platform that she's on to a stunned audience. A wow with the paying customers, Jill and Joe perform in many acts, including a tug-of-war and an organ-grinder act, but as the weeks go by, Joe becomes more and more morose. Working in a nightclub is not his idea of a great time. He wants out. Jill and Greg confront O'Hara about it, but he sweet-talks them into staying. Finally, the situation comes to a head during the organ-grinder act. Three bored drunks in the audience go to Joe's cage and get him totally sloshed with booze. "Poor old monkey! Bet old O'Hara never bought him a drink!" says one of the inebriated trio. The alcoholic ape breaks free from his underground cage and goes on a rampage in the club, smashing it to pieces.

Because of the damage he caused, Joe is sentenced to death by the court. Blaming himself for Joe's predicament, O'Hara decides to smuggle Joe away in a truck with the aid of Greg and Jill, but the police go after

Left to right: Lora Lee Michel, O'Brien and J. Roy Hunt.

them. During the pursuit, the truck is stranded in the sand. Joe gets out and pushes it free, and the police arrive and become briefly trapped themselves. In an amusing bit of "business," Joe spits at them and then drums his fingers idly as the truck pulls away. En route, Greg stops the truck at a burning orphanage, to help the children escape. With most of them saved, Joe climbs a tree opposite the building to save the last remaining child. But as he descends with the girl, flames engulf the tree, which crashes to the ground, taking them with it. Joe protectively covers the girl as a crumbling wall of the orphanage collapses on top of them. The police arrive. "Don't worry, kid," comforts O'Hara. "There's nobody in the world to shoot Joe now." Having redeemed himself, Joe is taken back to Africa by Jill and Greg, who wave to O'Hara in a home movie of themselves. "They're back home where they belong," says a pleased O'Hara.

Mighty Joe Young was a successful return to *King Kong* country, switching dinosaurs for lions and using a humorous approach that was an improvement over the seriocomic phantasy of *Son of Kong*. All the animation sequences are equally impressive and lively, but the three scenes that stand out are the roping sequence, the nightclub rampage — with Joe swinging about Tarzan-style, wrecking the place and fighting lions — and the fiery finale — showing Joe braving the flames to save the children as the building collapses. The excitement in these scenes is enhanced considerably by Roy Webb's driving, fast-paced music.

To-day's Cinema recognized that the film's story was

> expertly cast in the mould of *King Kong*, previous winner which [the] present film closely resembles on its clever trick photography, jungle thrill and night-club sensation . . . sure-fire hokum which should clean-up at popular box-offices.[49]

Paul Dehn (who ironically would later write the scripts for several *Planet of the Apes* sequels) said:

> This is epic stuff. What care I if some tattle-tale has put it about that "Mr. Joseph Young," who plays the title role, is no more than a specially constructed, ingeniously animated studio dummy? I scorn the notion. "Mr. Young" is as real as "Slavering Sam." He even spits!"[50]

Leonard Mosley, of the *Daily Express*, wrote:

> The gorilla is, of course, a Hollywood cheat. He is an edifice of steel and hide . . . [but] was much more human and had much more sympathy than any flesh and blood actor in the film.[51]

The *London Times* said:

> Mighty Joe Young, a mechanical gorilla, is, in effect, the King Kong of 1949, but Joe is a gentler and more pleasant animal than Kong, and ends up the hero.[52]

Technicians were not often recognized for their contribution to films in critics' reviews unless their work was outstanding enough to warrant it. In fact, studios were usually publicity shy about a film's "trick work" and preferred secrecy. However, two reviews recognized and acknowledged O'Brien's genius.

The critic in the *Daily Mail* (London) stated:

> The star of this film is a Mr. Willis O'Brien, who is described as its technical Creator, and is therefore, I take it, the man responsible for the ingenious

trick photography and the manipulation of this huge puppet. He has done his work well.[53]

Motion Picture Herald came to the same conclusion: ". . . the gorilla, by the way, is a model — the ingenious creation of Mr. Willis O'Brien."[54]

However, the ultimate, but belated recognition of O'Brien's genius came when he won the award for the best special effects of 1949 for his work on *Mighty Joe Young*. Without doubt, the fine special effects exhibited in the film were greatly helped by the talent of two new animators who assisted O'Brien: Ray Harryhausen and Peter Peterson. Harryhausen — who had long been an enthusiast of O'Brien and his animation work — began his first professional job as animator for George Pal's *Puppetoons* and finally realized his ambition in *Mighty Joe Young*, his first feature film. He said:

> I had been in contact with O'Brien all through the war, when he was making "Gwangi" and "War Eagles." Then *Mighty Joe Young* came about. It was touch and go for a year or so whether the picture was ever going into production. Finally we got offices in the old Selznick studio in Culver City. It was almost a year before we got the final go-ahead. At one time the film was to be made in Technicolor. We made some tests in color to see if the rear projection system would be satisfactory. After rebudgeting the complete film once again, it was decided to be shot in black and white, mainly because of costs. *Mighty Joe Young* went into production in late 1947 and finished in 1949. It won the Academy Award for best special effects for the year 1949. I went with Obie to the Academy Awards ceremony when he received the award. It was all very lavish.[25]

Ray Harryhausen said about Peter Peterson in 1990:

> I never saw Pete after the film *Mighty Joe Young*. I believe his profession was that of a studio grip. He had worked most of the time on pictures at RKO. He had a problem with his legs which made it difficult for him to get around easily. He was transferred to our animation stage. After a few weeks with us, he became very intrigued with animation and used to sit, in his spare time, and watch me work out my animation. His interest was so great that he started making experiments at his home, photographing people with tape pasted on their arms and legs in order to study their movements. He finally felt confident enough to ask Obie to give him a chance to animate. Obie set up a small situation for him in the corner of our stage. He surprised everyone by adapting himself to a new medium. He did much better than some of the other people Cooper and O'Brien had hired earlier to try and speed up the process of animation. At one time, Buzz Gibson and his brother did some animation. Scott Witicker and Marcel Delgado tried a few scenes, but their experiments were never used, nor were the scenes of Buzz and his brother.

The first appearance of Joe in *Mighty Joe Young* as he is about to hit the lion's cage, animated by Ray Harryhausen.

Scott Witicker was basically a cartoonist who was hired to make animated drawings of the . . . coins that were being thrown at Mighty Joe. He spent weeks rotoscoping *Joe* after I animated him. The coins had to be timed to match the movements of the gorilla's actions. Scott hired a lady assistant to help him with the inking and painting of the cells. Pete and Scott's assistant became interested in each other and after a period of time got married. Sometime after the picture was over, I heard that Pete's wife had passed away due to her delicate health.[56]

Cooper found Ray Harryhausen to be the smoothest animator he had ever worked with — a fine man and a likable fellow who had done some great animation for *Mighty Joe Young*.[57]

As Darlyne O'Brien said about Harryhausen:

Ray Harryhausen came to see Obie at the studio when he was about 16, and then every so often he would visit Obie and show him what he was doing. So finally, on *Mighty Joe Young*, Obie said to me, "Do you think I should give this young Harry a chance?" — he never could remember his name and say Harryhausen. He wasn't good at pronouncing names anyway, so he always

Joe holds Terry Moore in the nightclub sequence, animated by Peter Peterson for
Mighty Joe Young.

called him "Young Harry!" [laughs], and I said, "Well yes, because he seems
such a sincere young boy and working hard at it, to learn how to do these
things." So he put him on to help him on *Mighty Joe Young,* and, of course,
he . . . generously gave him screen credit. And from there on, of course, Ray
just went out and went on his own and [did] wonderfully.[58]

Although O'Brien was technical creator of the special effects for
Mighty Joe Young, he did little actual animation on the film—his work
mainly involving the planning and preparation. Most of the animation
was done by Harryhausen, with Peterson doing a few scenes and O'Brien
and Delgado doing just a few shots. As Delgado said about the models:

Mighty Joe was a better monkey than Kong because he had a better kind
of hair—unborn calf. I animated a shot of Joe climbing down the tree—that
was only a four inch gorilla; they used him in the close-ups. I made an inch
and a half scale for the close-ups. Obie never used it; he used the little one
for the close-ups. When the picture was finished, the model disappeared,
and I never saw it again. The little four-inch armature worked like a charm
and hardly ever needed adjustment; [It] cost $1,200 to make and took me
about three quarters of an hour to design. It really worked beautifully.

My job was to keep the models repaired because they received tremendous abuse and were worn out by the end of the day, so I had to get them
ready for the next day. On both *Mighty Joe Young* and *King Kong*, I stripped
the models down about three or four times and started from scratch, working many times on Sundays and very late at night to get them ready for the
next morning. I put in a lot of work doing this, but didn't get compensated
for it. They did not pay me any extra; I did it because I loved what I was
doing. I never asked for a raise, but they did not appreciate what you did
for them.[59]

However, the work on the completed film *was* appreciated, and
O'Brien and his team were rewarded for their efforts. With an award and
good reaction to his latest work, it would seem that O'Brien had a successful future ahead of him. Darlyne O'Brien recalled:

After *Mighty Joe Young*, several people said to Obie, "Well, from now on,
people will come to you with stories," so Obie just sat around. He was never
a good promoter anyway. It was sheer luck that anything ever did come
about. It just happened that Cooper and Schoedsack needed someone when
Cooper thought up *Mighty Joe Young*, and the same when Obie promoted
The Lost World and *Ghost of Slumber Mountain* and showed it to Mr.
Rothacker. But Obie just could not bring himself to go out and ask people
for anything—he said if he tried to be a salesman, he would say, "You don't
want this, do you?" [laughs].
    And so nothing happened right after *Mighty Joe* for about six months, and
Ray kept coming over and saying to Obie, "What are we going to do next?"
and Obie said, "Well, I don't have anything right now. I don't have anything
in mind."
    Ray kept wanting him to do something because naturally he wanted to get
going on his career and keep going. And so he said, "Well, if you're not going
to do anything, I am. I am going to do something." Well Obie thought,
"What can he do, if he doesn't have a story?" But he told Ray, "If I were going
to make another picture right now, I would make an undersea picture." So
Ray got this story of Ray Bradbury about the dinosaur falling in love with
a lighthouse and somehow or other, he got someone interested and they
made this first cheap picture. And when Ray told him what he was doing,
Obie said, "Well, I would prefer to make better pictures. I don't want to
make the smaller, cheaper pictures." Ray said, "But Obie, they make
money." And it's true, they do.
    Obie should really have gone into that field. But, he wasn't a good pro-
moter anyway for himself, and he just sat back and waited, thinking that
someone would come along with a story that they would want him to do.
But nothing happened. So, Ray branched out on his own and has gone great
guns ever since.[60]

Before Ray branched out, he joined O'Brien on another project, entitled
Valley of the Mist. Ray Harryhausen said:

Obie had prepared a rough outline of a script called "Emilio and Guloso," which was later retitled *Valley of the Mist*. Merian Cooper wanted to make "Food of the Gods," but finally abandoned it. Sol Lessor, producer of the RKO *Tarzan* films had an idea to make a film "Tarzan Meets Mighty Joe Young." Unfortunately, nothing more was heard about the project. In the meantime, producer Jesse Lasky became interested in "Emilio and Guloso," which seemed to upset Mr. Cooper. Cooper did not want to do "Emilio," but had no other immediate project for O'Brien. Jesse Lasky took an option on O'Brien's story and hired his [Lasky's] son Jesse, Junior, to write the script in conjunction with O'Brien. In the meantime Jesse Lasky, Senior, was trying to raise money at Paramount Pictures. He of course had other projects on the board as well. Obie and I were on a small retainer for about six months, after which the project seemed to fall apart.[61]

Valley of the Mist was based on the story idea "Emilio and Guloso," written by Willis and Darlyne O'Brien some years earlier. In 1956, a film entitled *The Brave One* was released, based on a story credited to Robert Rich—pseudonym used by writer Dalton Trumbo, who had been blacklisted by the film industry in 1947 because of his alleged membership in the Communist party.[62] To get work, Trumbo wrote screenplays, including *The Brave One*, under various pseudonyms. But *The Brave One* had a storyline that was similar to O'Brien's "Emilio and Guloso," and to the embarrassment of the industry, Trumbo's story—on which the film was based—won an Academy Award, credited to the blacklisted Trumbo. To add more intrigue to the situation, that *The Brave One*'s storyline was reminiscent of Robert J. Flaherty's "The Story of Bonito, the Bull" segment," which was intended for Orson Welles's aborted RKO project of 1942, "It's All True." The 1956 press handout for *The Brave One* said that the film's story was inspired by an actual incident that occurred at the Plaza del Toros in Barcelona on April 12, 1936. O'Brien was supposed to have written his story in 1944. Could it be that O'Brien, Flaherty and Trumbo got the idea from the same real-life event? One can only speculate.

Chapter 3

Color, CinemaScope, Cinerama and Low Budgets (1952–1962)

> Hollywood is a status quo town; anything with a revolutionary concept can't be sound. The studios are archaic; they're making and selling pictures the way they did thirty years ago. The public is so far ahead of them they can't even see 'em. The dam will break one of these days, faster than anyone thinks, and the industry will be done for. But the Big Numbers won't care. They created a one-generation business, and they don't care what happens to it after they're gone. They've lived selfishly and they'll die selfishly. Forget Hollywood. Let's talk Cinerama. — Mike Todd.[64]

For Willis O'Brien, the period from the 1950s until his death in 1962 offered small jobs on big pictures (*This Is Cinerama* and *It's a Mad, Mad, Mad, Mad World*) and slightly bigger jobs on small films (*The Animal World, The Black Scorpion* and *The Giant Behemoth*). The time he spent working on these assignments was brief, ranging from a few weeks to a few months. But O'Brien was not the only one affected by a drop in work. Many actors, directors and producers during this time found that their contracts were not renewed. The film business had changed. Movie audiences began to dwindle as television — a much cheaper form of entertainment — began to gain favor with the public.

The only way to try to draw the public back it seemed, was to offer something television didn't have: a big screen and spectacular production made in a lavish manner. Each studio did so in a different way. Twentieth Century–Fox used the CinemaScope process for its production of *The*

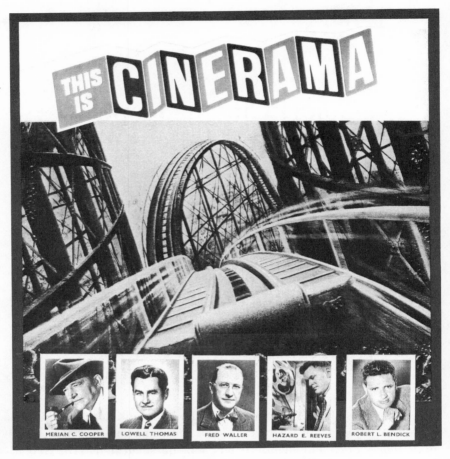

Poster art for *This Is Cinerama* (1952).

Robe (1953) — a system utilizing an anamorphic lens that compressed the photographic image, then stretched it out into a wide "letterbox" shape. Warner Brothers went for a third-dimensional effect for *House of Wax* that used two cameras and two projectors to create "3D." Paramount Pictures used the Vistavision process for *White Christmas*, which used the 35mm film horizontally (as opposed to running the film in the standard vertical way) that resulted in a picture that used twice the negative area and had a sharper, clearer image.

And then there was Cinerama. Cinerama, literally the biggest system of them all, used a camera that was, in fact, three cameras in one. Each camera was set at a 48 degree angle to the next; the center camera shot straight ahead, the right camera shot toward the left side and the left camera shot to the right side. Each lens photographed a third of the total width of the final picture, as shown on the movie screen, using a film frame that was six perforations high, instead of the standard four perforations. The inventor of this process — Fred Waller — wanted to use Cinerama to reproduce the peripheral vision of the human eye, thereby creating films that would completely cover the eye's whole field of vision and height the film's realism, so the movie audience would feel they were really there.

Robert Flaherty, the "father" of documentary films, was chosen to shoot this first film in Cinerama. But on the eve of production, he died, leaving the producer Mike Todd to shoot footage of Niagara Falls and the Shriner's annual parade, while his son filmed the roller coaster ride at Rockaway's Playland. But by mid–1952, lawyers were applying pressure on Todd to pay his debts, and by May 1952, Merian C. Cooper left Argosy and replaced Todd as head of production at Cinerama to coproduce the film with Robert L. Bendick. In December 1952, Cooper signed a contract to produce for five years, announcing that he would make a musical, a large-scale western with Tay Garnett, a Civil War picture with John Ford and "a spectacle along the lines of *King Kong*" with Willis O'Brien.

Cooper's idea was to bring back his King Kong character to the screen in a new film, using the Cinerama process and based on his story treatment, "The New Adventures of King Kong." To do so, he needed Willis O'Brien on the payroll.

Cooper wanted to use animation in a Cinerama film and told everyone that he was going to remake *King Kong*. His intention was mentioned in various trade papers of the day, but in reality, he wasn't going to do any such thing. What he planned to do was film the section of the *Kong* story that he skipped in the original screenplay. He was going to have the ship's crew wrecked on a desert island, where there were all kinds of animals. The crew would take Kong out of his chains, and the giant ape would rescue the girl and save the whole party. What stopped the Kong/Cinerama project was the death of the man who was to build the special stop-frame projectors.[65]

With the Kong/Cinerama project aborted, O'Brien was hired to work on *This Is Cinerama* — a travelog-style film — and the first film using the new process, to create artwork for the film's prologue. The film reunited six collaborators from *King Kong*: Cooper, Mario Larrinaga (both were credited on the film), Ernest B. Schoedsack, Ruth Rose, Max Steiner and O'Brien (who were not credited on the film). They never worked together again, and the film marked the end of an era.

This Is Cinerama opens with its title spelled out in Morse code, followed by Lowell Thomas's narration explaining how man has worked since the caveman days to reproduce in art the illusion of depth and dimension in nature, to convey the sense of motion. Thomas covers the early cave painting (which was the area that O'Brien was involved in)[66]; magic lanterns, and nickleodeons; and does a bit of name-dropping by mentioning Muybridge, Edison and Eastman; shows extracts from the silent black-and-white films on a small screen, when suddenly the screen opens to six times its normal size, as Thomas announces modestly that "Ladies and Gentleman — This is Cinerama!"

The film includes 12 unrelated shorts, starting with the roller coaster ride in the "Atom Smasher" (filmed at Rockaways' Playland, Long Island, New York), and including Venice and Saint Marks Square Venetian regatta; Scotland ("with its ancient capital of Edinburgh . . . the rally of the clans — kilts and tartans and bagpipes and drums!"); Vienna ("with its famous tradition of music — surely a natural for Cinerama!"); the Schonbrunn Palace, where "in the garden, we'll hear the Vienna Boys Choir . . . ."

Then on to Spain: (". . . and the crowd is as colorful as any you will find in the world!"); a demonstration of Cinerama's Stereophonic sound ("please note the enormous power, without distortion, when the full orchestra plays!"); the finale of Verdi's *Aida* at La Scala in Milan ("now for the great scoop!"); Cypress Gardens, Florida ("there's a spirit of youth and good nature about the place!"); the Florida Everglades ("weird . . . sinister!"); Washington, D.C. ("the sweeping panorama in motion is dominated by the Pentagon — that building famous for its size!"); Pittsburgh; Indiana; Chicago; Mount Rushmore; Salt Lake City ("where the world-famous Salt Lake City Tabernacle Choir is"); Mount Rainier; San Francisco and the Golden Gate Bridge; Hoover Dam; Imperial Valley; Yosemite National Park; the Bridal Veil Falls; the Sierra Nevada; Grand Canyon; and Zion National Park ("a breathless thriller for our finale!"). The film ends with a chorus singing "America, the Beautiful."

London's *Evening News* review said about the film: "I am shaken . . . and I will frankly say that I have never experienced anything in the field of entertainment quite so horribly real."[67] Unfortunately, like 3D and Vistavision, Cinerama eventually disappeared from the public view. *This Is Cinerama* was last reissued in 1973 and has not been seen since. (A new Cinerama cinema is opening on June 16, 1993, in Bradford, England — the only one in the world.)

After O'Brien's brief involvement with *This Is Cinerama*, he wrote a story in 1955 that became the basis for *The Beast of Hollow Mountain* (1956).

The Beast of Hollow Mountain starts with the main titles announcing "the new Nassour 'Regiscope' process animation in depth" system, backed by dramatic music. After the titles, we see Jimmy Ryan (Guy Madison) and Felipe Sanchez (Carlos Rivas) traveling on horseback across the Mexican landscape as the narrator speaks:

> Deep in the back country of Mexico, there rises a grim and mysterious mountain, which is said to be hollow. Its interior has never been explored because at its base lies an impassable swamp. The superstitious link the hollow mountain and the swamp and their folk legends as places of evil. Great evil. They tell of a strange animal from the dawn of creation that inhabits the area, coming forth to prowl and pillage only in time of draught. They tell of men and cattle disappearing without trace. But perhaps these are only tales. Tales told by simple people.[68]

The eerie sounds of birds screaming echo around the area. Jimmy and Sanchez find a dead steer stuck in the quicksand near the mountain. Jimmy seeks the advice of Don Pedro (Julio Villareal).

"I don't buy those superstitions, Don Pedro. I'm looking for a factual answer. Steers don't jump in the swamp," says Jimmy. He suspects Enrique Rios (Eduardo Noriega), a wealthy neighbor who dislikes Jimmy as a rival in the cattle business. When Jimmy encounters Enrique in the village, he says, "I'm gonna find out what kind of hombre you really are" and orders him to unbuckle his gun belt. They fight in the square, surrounded by a packed, screaming crowd. Jimmy wins and later finds a good price for his cattle. But Enrique wants to buy Jimmy's ranch before he sells his cattle. "Well, if it was up to me," Felipe says, "you'd know what I'd say." It's no deal. Meanwhile, Pancho (Pascual Garcia Pena), a hard-drinking Mexican, sets out alone for the swamp, leaving his son Panchito (Mario Navarro) at home.

Jimmy receives a message to meet his girlfriend Sarita (Patricia Medina) in the village graveyard, where she urges him not to defy Enrique. Meanwhile, Pancho arrives at the swamp, where a huge shadow appears over him. Jimmy decides to quit the ranch, but Panchito tells him that his father has not returned from the swamp. When they go to the swamp, they find only Pancho's hat. Panchito is taken into care by Jimmy and Felipe. During a colorful festival in the village, Enrique orders his men to organize a cattle stampede. Distraught over his father, Panchito goes to search the swamp with Sarita. Suddenly, the beast appears, kills two of

The monster rips the roof off the shack where Panchito and Sarito are hiding.

Enrique's men and causes the cattle to stampede toward the village. Jimmy and Felipe see the cattle, as the people in the village run for safety.

At the swamp, the beast appears, sees the boy and Sarita and follows them back to Panchito's home. The monster rips the roof off the shack where Panchito and Sarita are hiding. When Jimmy arrives, he tries to distract the beast by firing at it. The monster turns and chases after Jimmy and then gives Enrique a shock encounter at the swamp: It slides down the slope and traps the two of them in a small hole and then grabs Enrique, throwing him to the ground. Don Pedro arrives at the swamp with his men to help. Felipe takes Jimmy and leads the monster there. Jimmy wades into the swamp, attracting the beast's attention, ropes a tree in the middle of the swamp and then throws a knife at the beast, hitting it in the nose (similar to a scene in *The Lost World*). Jimmy then swings back and forth on the rope like a pendulum in front of the monster, tempting it closer and closer into the quicksand. Finally, it slips and sinks in, disappearing from sight, as a red patch of blood appears on the surface.

The Beast of Hollow Mountain was the first CinemaScope film that

O'Brien was connected with. I say "connected with" because unfortunately O'Brien supplied only the story for the film and did not create the special effects (for which Henry Sharpe was credited). Some of the animation shots of the beast used a cycle of animation models, similar to the Puppetoon method, and appear to have been shot on "twos." To get smoother movement, animation is normally shot on "ones." For a low-budget indpendent feature film, *The Beast of Hollow Mountain* was well directed, with good camera work (tracking shots) that shows the Mexican locations, village festival and cattle stampede to good dramatic effect. Guy Madison acted in a no-nonsense manner, similar to a young William Holden or Sterling Hayden. Both *Variety* and *Motion Picture Herald* noted O'Brien's involvement with the film, which was the first Cinema-Scope and color film to combine model animation with live action photography. The one big regret is that O'Brien wasn't given the opportunity to showcase his expertise in animation.

The next year, Irwin Allen hired O'Brien to work on *The Animal World* with Ray Harryhausen. Director-producer-screenwriter Allen began his career as a magazine editor, director and producer of a Hollywood radio show before going into film production in the 1950s. In 1953, his documentary *The Sea Around Us* won the Academy Award. *The Animal World* was planned as the second part of a trilogy, the third being *The Story of Mankind* (1957), based on Henrik Van Loon's book chronicling the highlights of human history. For *The Animal World*, O'Brien was hired as supervisor of the dinosaur sequence, with the actual animation created by Ray Harryhausen.

The Animal World is a documentary film that follows the evolution of the animal kingdom: from the one-celled animals called protozoa, which developed over a period of millions of years into vertebrate amphibians that left the sea, multiplied and gradually changed into terrible lizards known as dinosaurs. From there on, the film shows both the Earth and the animals evolving: the planet's climate cooling, the dinosaurs disappearing, the emergence of insect life and mammals, and the appearance of human beings.

Both O'Brien and Harryhausen were praised for their work on the film:

> . . . and animators Ray Harryhausen and Willis O'Brien, all deserve a commendation for the teamwork that has produced a masterpiece of its kind.[69]

> . . . animated with surprising realism by Willis O'Brien and Ray Harryhausen.[70]

Willis O'Brien and an armature during the making of *The Animal World* (1956).

The press information from the film's releasing company acknowledged that

> Irwin Allen's technical crew [was] headed by Willis O'Brien, the pioneer of animators. It was O'Brien who peopled *The Lost World* and created the cataclysm of *King Kong*, to name only a couple of his more spectacular accomplishments.[71]

Ray Harryhausen said about the film in 1985:

> I started working with Curt Siodmak on the script for *Earth vs. The Flying Saucers* in 1956. For some reason there was a delay. Irwin Allen, the producer of *The Animal World* wanted to buy some of my 16mm test footage from my defunked project, "Evolution." It was blown up into a 35mm color print. The quality was quite good, but unfortunately there was not enough of it. Irwin Allen did not want to spend much money on *The Animal World* and had hoped to use mostly stock footage. Obie became involved with the project, and Mr. Allen decided it was worthwhile to try to shoot some fresh scenes. He also had the idea of using still shots of miniature sets with prehistoric animals. He hired O'Brien and myself on a six-week contract. It was finally decided to go for full animation.

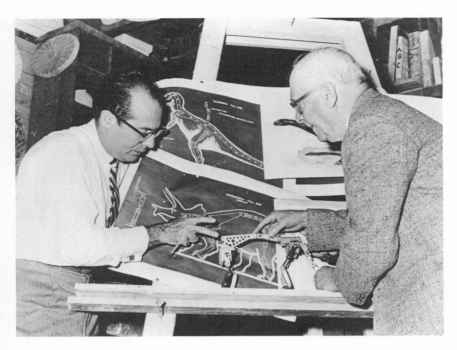

Irwin Allen (left) with Willis O'Brien holding the animation armature of the triceratops for *The Animal World* (1956). This was the first of two feature films that Obie worked on for Allen, the second being the remake of *The Lost World* (1960). Behind the armature are the drawing blueprints of the animation armatures.

> Willis O'Brien designed the models and backgrounds, and I was to do the animation. It was stressed that we were not to do anything really complicated. Basically it was all table-top photography with painted backgrounds. There would be two cameras on each setup, so we could get twice as much footage. The prop department at Warner Brothers built the animation models from Obie's basic design. Mechanical models, operated by wires, were to be used for close-ups. The necks would go up and down and the mouths open. Unfortunately the close-ups looked exactly what they were — mechanical models. Neither Obie nor I really approved but we realized it was out of our hands. The dinosaur sequence was the most talked about part of the picture.[72]

Footage from the dinosaur sequence was later used in *Trog* (1970). The next film assignment for O'Brien was *The Black Scorpion* (1957). Jack Dietz, coproducer of the film and *The Beast from 20,000 Fathoms* (1953, Ray Harryhausen's first film since *Mighty Joe Young*), originally went to Eugene Lourie to direct *Scorpion*,[73] but the film was eventually directed by Edward Ludwig. Born in Russia in 1899 and educated in Canada,

The King Scorpion animation model from *The Black Scorpion* (1957) (photo: Harry Walton; courtesy of David Allen).

Ludwig began in silent films as an actor and became a director in the early 1930s. Among the films he directed are *Fighting Seabees* (1944), *Wake of the Red Witch* (1948) and *Big Jim McLain* (1952). After *Scorpion*, he made one other film, *The Gun Hawk* (1963).[74]

The Black Scorpion is about how a peaceful day in Mexico is suddenly disrupted by a violent volcanic eruption.[75] The next day, Arturo Ramos (Carlos Rivas, also in *Beast of Hollow Mountain*), a Mexican, and Henry "Hank" Scott (Richard Denning) — both geologists — decide to check out the now-quiet area surrounding the volcano. They discover a pulverized police car at the back of a house and an abandoned baby. Then they go to San Lorenzo and meet Father Delgado (Pedro Galvan), a priest.

Dead cattle are found at a nearby ranch, their deaths blamed on some "demon bull." The army arrive on the scene while Hank and Arturo go to the volcano and meet Teresa Alvarez (Mara Corday) — a local rancher — and find a piece of "obsidian" (a yellow-black object that looks like glass, formed from molten lava that has cooled). Ramos breaks it open to reveal a scorpion trapped inside, still alive. Later, a giant scorpion

A 1961 photograph showing two scorpion animation models from *The Black Scorpion* with the giant behemoth animation model.

creeps out at night from beneath a bridge and strikes a truck with its tail and overturns it and then yanks a man from a telephone pole with its pincers and stings him to death.

The next day, Hank, Arturo and the army go to the volcano to investigate. One of the men falls into the crater. Hank and Arturo go down into the darkness to try and find him. They find him all right, but dead. They also have the bad luck to find a huge spider that tries to seize Hank, who shoots it. Then a giant worm gets into a fight with a giant scorpion. The scorpion wins and is about to eat its prize, when it is rudely interrupted by another scorpion—five times the size of the first. The smaller one tries to escape, but the giant one seizes it and rips its throat. "That's how they kill each other—that weak spot in the throat!" Hank says. Not wanting to end up as extras on the scorpion's menu, Hank and Arturo make for the cage that they descended in, but too late. The scorpion got there before them and has the cage in his pincers, swinging it back and forth, trying to drag the crane down with it. With the cables now cut, the cage lands in the molten lava, as more scorpions arrive on the scene.

This sequence is effectively staged in the cavernlike subterranean depths of the volcano, evoking images of what the unseen "spider pit" scene in *King Kong* might have looked like. Hank and Arturo narrowly escape an oncoming scorpion and are hauled up, holding the cable. Safely out of the volcano, they dynamite the chasm, apparently leaving the scorpions entrance/exit blocked for good. But the scorpions find a way out and decide to do a bit of midnight train wrecking, while Hank wines and dines Teresa. Like the earlier encounter in the volcano, the train attack is a lively, atmospheric sequence that brings back memories of the train scene in *King Kong*. Scorpions swarm over the now-overturned train killing the fleeing people. Then, the leader — the gigantic black scorpion — appears and kills all the other scorpions in a frenzied fight.

News spreads of the attack as the army prepares to confront the last scorpion in the bull ring. Not wanting to be left out, Hank joins them with a generator truck and a harpoonlike weapon. "The projectile enters the throat," explains Dr. Velasco (Carlos Muzquiz) ". . . attached is the copper wire . . . then the insulated wire . . . which leads to the cable and the generators. It should give six hundred thousand volts!" Lured by slaughtered carcasses taken from the local butcher, the scorpion enters the arena. Tanks fire at the monster. Helicopters attack it. The projectile is fired, but the scorpion's claw wards it off, pulls the attached cable and jerks the truck like a yo-yo. Hank cuts the cable, winds it back in and fires again. This time the projectile hits the mark as the operator throws the switch. Bolts of electricity shoot into the creature as it thrashes about in its death throes. Finally, it is still. The humans have won again.

Co-written by David Duncan, who wrote *The Monster That Challenged the World* (1957 with Pat Fielder) and *The Time Machine* (1960) and adapted the screenplay of *Fantastic Voyage* (1966), the script for *The Black Scorpion* (1954) is similar to the giant ant film, *Them!* (1954).[76] Despite being hamstrung by a tiny budget and the poor working conditions that they had to contend with, O'Brien and Peterson's work in the film is excellent. It is their work that makes the film worth seeing, with its dynamic action and active camera moves in the animation sequences, enhanced by screaming sound effects and low-key lighting. The reviews said:

> With its sprightly special effects by Willis O'Brien . . . this is considerably more lively than most of the recent examples of eccentric zoology.[77]

> It has some good special effects by Willis O'Brien and Peter Peterson . . .[78]

...and the special effects created by Willis O'Brien and Peterson compare well with the most convincing yet seen.[79]

Extravagant hocus pocus, unfolded in Mexico, covering ding-dong battle between geologists and giant scorpions. Yarn full-blooded, players eager, camera work clever, and highlights eerie.[80]

As Darlyne O'Brien recalled:

Obie and Pete Peterson made *The Black Scorpion* here in the valley when we lived here once before, about ten years ago, but, of course, Obie didn't get much money off of it, and we were in Mexico City for quite a while ... we just lived it up on the money we made there because if you live American style down there, it costs just as much as it does here, which we did, of course. We lived at the hotel, rather than have an apartment, and we didn't come home with any money at all. But it was fun; it was worth going. I loved it there.[81]

This was Peterson's first film with O'Brien since *Mighty Joe Young*. What he did between the two films is anyone's guess because there is little information about him. One of the few people who actually had contact with him was Jim Danforth (who later worked as an animator on O'Brien's last film, *It's a Mad, Mad, Mad, Mad World*). As Danforth recounted:

I spoke to him [Peterson] on the phone, but I never met him. He was very nice, but maybe embittered is the word. He just seemed to be very saddened and unhappy about the way things were going. Cynical, I suppose. And I guess also the fact that they [O'Brien and Peterson] had to do all these things on very low budgets. He said "It costs so much"—I was asking about armatures—"...to get these things made. I wonder if you can appreciate how expensive it is to have these made, why ... the last thing we had made cost $600, you know, and we had another little thing even more recently—just one part—it was $200." Of course now that seems like nothing, but this was in the late 50s. $600 then was about $1,500 today [1985].
    I don't remember how I found him. I think I found his number in the phone book ... or maybe Obie suggested I call him. ... And he wasn't doing much. I was encouraged to contact him because a friend of mine in junior high school had a father who worked as a lighting person, or *gaffer*, in the film industry, and he told a story about a fellow ... he knew that was doing a scene in animation. I was interested in animation, and he said, "Oh, yes, I know this guy who has been working for months and months doing scenes of strange creatures coming out of a space ship or something, and he has a disease where his legs go bad on him; he can't work for long periods of time, so when he can't work in the studios, he works on the animation at home.... And then I figured he was Pete Peterson and learned that he had multiple sclerosis. ... I got to see that test film after Peterson died—we found that reel—they weren't coming out of a space ship, they were coming over a hill. Beetle men. Ten beetle men, marching relentlessly. That was obviously what Pete was shooting.[82]

Peter Peterson's "Beetle Man" animation figure.

Peterson shot the Beetle Men animation in color. Another animation test that he shot which used the miniature sets made for *The Black Scorpion* was shot in black and white. It was an apelike figure picking a man out of a cabin, then later yanking a helicopter out of the sky and grappling on the ground with it. The armature of this apelike figure, called The Las

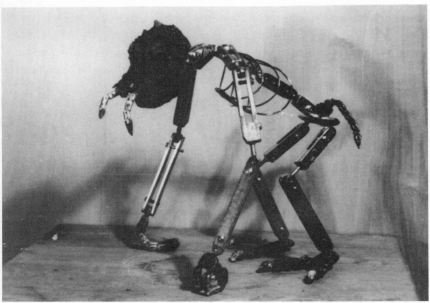

Top: The "Beetle Man" puppet. Most of them had simple ball bearings for eyes and didn't have hair between the joints—this is a "deluxe" model (photo: Harry V. Walton; courtesy of David Allen). *Bottom:* The "Las Vegas Monster" armature, circa 1960. The lower leg plates are not original—these are longer. The originals were used for David Allen's King Kong puppet in the famous TV commercial (photo: Harry V. Walton; courtesy of David Allen).

Vegas Monster, was later used for The Great God Porno in the low-budget science fiction sex spoof *Flesh Gordon* (1975). Another animation sequence in the film used one of the Beetle Men figures animated by Jim Danforth.

In 1959, Peterson worked with O'Brien for the last time on *The Giant Behemoth* (known in England as *Behemoth, The Sea Monster*).

Behemoth begins with American marine biologist Steve Karnes (Gene Evans) showing a film of atomic tests to scientists in London. In his speech to them, Karnes warns them: "Since the beginning of the atomic age, we have had 143 explosions such as these you have seen here on the screen. Now one millionth part such as these can poison a plant. What about the dumping in our oceans of our atomic waste? Granted, we are sealing them in lead containers, but lead disintegrates and corrodes at the bottom of the sea. There is no such thing as even statistical dispersion of radioactive materials. Now we checked samples of seawater in this area, and the radiation was insignificant. But it was two thousand times greater. And in the fish that ate this plankton, forty thousand times greater. And in the seabirds that fed upon these fish, the radioactivity was five hundred thousand times greater. Gentleman, we are witnessing a biological chain reaction. A geometrical progression of deadly menace!" In the audience is Professor Bickford (Andre Morell), who receives the remarks with skepticism.

Meanwhile, it's all happening in Cornwall. A local fisherman is found by his daughter on the beach dying of terrible radiation burns and gasping, "From the sea . . . burning like fire . . . Behemoth!" After his funeral, the daughter, Jeanie MacDougal (played by Leigh Madison), returns to the beach with her boyfriend John (John Turner) to discover thousands of dead fish washed ashore. While nosing around, John touches some white substance that burns his hand.

Back in London, Karnes sees a news report that blames the fisherman's death on a sea monster. Karnes persuades Bickford to accompany him to Cornwall to question Jeanie about the behemoth. "It's a prophecy from the Bible. It means some monstrous great beast," she says. Convinced that radioactivity has caused a tremendous upheaval in the depths, Karnes goes out in a boat at night and sights the beast, gives chase, but is ordered back. The next day, news comes in that the steamship *Valkyria* has been found beached with no survivors and its steel hull ripped apart.

While Karnes and Bickford organize a search, the monster appears in Cornwall and kills a doctor and his son with its radiation. A photograph

The Giant Behemoth goes on the rampage.

of the monster's footprint is shown to palaeontologist Dr. Sampson (Jack MacGrowran). "The old *Paleosaurus* family . . . he can stay underneath the surface for an age. Oh! but it's dreadfully dangerous. It's electric like an eel," Dr. Sampson says. "Electric? It's intensely radioactive!" Karnes replies. "Then the creature must be killed," adds Dr. Sampson sadly. From a helicopter, Sampson sees the monster, but is killed, along with the pilot, by the beast's deadly radiation. The navy and air force launch a search.

Meanwhile, the behemoth wrecks and capsizes the Woolwich ferry boat, killing everyone on it. The police order the streets cleared, and the Thames embankment is closed to all traffic. The army prepares to confront the behemoth in the streets, constructing barricades. Families are evacuated from their homes. A high-level conference takes place, during which Karnes and Bickford discuss how to destroy this pest.

The Behemoth attacks again, this time appearing at the dockyard near London Bridge, and comes ashore, destroying cranes, rampaging in the streets and crushing cars. People flee in terror. The army fires at it,

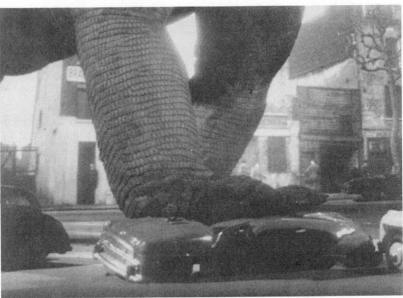

Top: The behemoth unleashes a lethal dose of radiation onto the soldiers in the streets. *Bottom:* This unfortunate animation shot appears in the film three times because of the lack of animation footage and was used to pad out the rampage sequence.

but to no effect; the behemoth's radiation burns them to death. Bickford gets an idea. A radium-tipped torpedo fired from a midget submarine! That'll kill the beast! By this time, it is now night. The behemoth relentlessly marches through electrical power cables, causing buildings to ignite into flaming infernos. Near Big Ben, the monster is sighted with searchlights; it destroys a car in its jaws and it jumps into the river.

Karnes and the captain follow it underwater in the minisubmarine while a helicopter above sights the target from the air. Finally, they track the monster and fire the torpedo at it. Surrounded by bubbling, boiling water, the behemoth dies. Karnes returns to the shore and is greeted by Bickford. "Well done!" he tells him, as the two get into a car and suddenly hear a radio announcement: "We interrupt this program for a special news bulletin. We have just received a report from America that mountains of dead fish are washing along the coast from Maine to Florida. We now return you to our normal program!" Karnes and Bickford—without a word—just drive away.

Reviews for the film recognized that "*The Giant Behemoth* has been around before, terrorizing citizens and generally tearing urban and rural life to shreds"[83] and that it was "a modestly made, routine science-fiction yarn which cannot be regarded as more than a useful dualer for average audiences."[84]

Variety added:

> Unfortunately, variable photography and uneven matching rather takes the gloss off some good artwork and special effects.[85]

The Daily Cinema recognized the intelligently written script, saying:

> All the talk about biological chain reaction at the beginning only helps to make the possibilities of a sea monster convincing.[86]

And *Monthly Film Bulletin* stated:

> This is considerably better than many recent essays in monster science-fiction, both in its suspense and staging.[87]

Both *Film Daily* and *Variety* gave special mention to the effects team for the film, which included Jack Rabin, Irving Block, Louis DeWitt, Willis O'Brien and Peter Peterson.[88] Free-lance effects cameraman Phil Kellison, who created the miniature of the dockside cranes, ferryboat and barges, said of O'Brien:

A small van publicizing the British release of *Behemoth, the Sea Monster*.

Obie wasn't animating anymore. Out in Encino he and Peterson had a concrete block building which, after having gotten into this project [*The Giant Behemoth*], I suddenly discovered was about two blocks away from where I lived! Obie needed some miniatures made, which is how I got on *Behemoth*. I volunteered to do them free lance. I was impressed by O'Brien, of course, and I put my heart and soul into the miniatures I made. They were working cranes, yet they were set up so they could be animated and collapsed. I took them over to Obie and asked him if they were good enough. He looked at them and said, "They're too goddamned good." I wasn't sure if that was a compliment or not, but I suppose it was![89]

About Peterson, Kellison said in the same article:

I don't know how badly crippled he was at that time. I thought he had to animate sitting down only because the [miniature] sets were built so low. As far as I know, he didn't have an assistant. It must have been enormously difficult for him. I was there for the first animation shot of the Behemoth walking onto the dock. It was such a long walk from the end of the set-up to the camera lens. They couldn't follow focus on the Behemoth because the background would go out of focus. Obie was using a 20mm lens. When I asked what F-stop they were using, Obie said, "Well, I don't know!" What they had done was pull the pin on the leaf of the aperture in order to stop down further than the lens was intended to go! Essentially they were working with a pinhole aperture. Obie said, "We don't know what the aperture is. We just make a test until it's right, and that's what we'll light to!"

On the night scene that showed the behemoth in front of the Houses of Parliament, Kellison noted:

> Anyone can look at that scene today and see the animated spotlight travelling over the convolutions of the buildings. You think you're seeing in dimension. Not so! They were absolutely flat photo cutouts! The strange thing is, they weren't even well cut out. Some grip went around them with a cutout and dissected them rather crudely. But the way things were set up and lit, it really looked quite good.

About the ferryboat scene, he recalled:

> The ferryboat was about 30 inches long. I built the boat from existing photographs. There were no blueprints. They were many vehicles on top of the deck, and some were very distinctive. We had a lumber lorry. We were extremely fortunate to have been able to find English Dinky Toys which precisely matched the vehicles on the real boat filmed in London. Because we could get those vehicles, and because of the size of the tank, the size of the ferryboat was dictated by the size of the toys!

Kellison also created, together with O'Brien, the mechanical prop head of the behemoth:

> We were delighted when Obie returned it [the head] to us covered with those beautiful skins [cast from a real iguana]. It was gorgeous! Even the eyes worked. One of the actions demanded was that the creature arch its head under the boat, turning it over. That was the intention. However, there was a very impetuous technician on the set. He got so excited working the levers that he broke them all! During the rehearsal it was working just fine. But by the time we got to shoot, the neck would no longer arch and the mouth remained open. We had rented lights, a high-speed camera, a pump for the tank—it was "shoot it today," or that's it. There wasn't any more money for another day. We finally had to use the Behemoth's head as a battering ram, and that's the way it appears in the picture.

The Giant Behemoth brought O'Brien's career full circle, with its story dealing with a monster terrorizing the citizens of London — similar to the climax of *The Lost World*. It also was his last work in which a monster is brought to life by animation. An interesting piece of trivia is that the camera operator on this film, Desmond Davis, later directed Ray Harryhausen's last film, *Clash of the Titans*, in 1981. Irving Block, who did effects work on *Behemoth*, said about O'Brien:

> We [Block and Jay Rabin] worked for a while with Willis O'Brien. Jack worked with him on *The Giant Behemoth*. He [O'Brien] was a wonderful man. Here's a guy who got screwed — he didn't get his due. A wonderful artist and so imaginative. He sure understood animals.[90]

The following year, 1960, O'Brien was hired as effects technician on Irwin Allen's remake of *The Lost World*. Using the same storyline as the 1925 version, but setting it in 1960, the remake used live lizards, rather than animation for its "prehistoric animals."

The Lost World begins with zoology professor George Edward Challenger (Claude Rains) returning home to London from South America to announce that he has discovered a "lost world" where Jurassic monsters from 150,000,000 B.C. still exist. Naturally, his claim is doubted by the Zoological Institute, so he offers to lead an expedition to the area to prove it. Joining him is playboy and big-game hunter Lord Roxton (Michael Rennie); Jennifer Holmes (Jill St. John), daughter of an American newspaper executive who finances the venture; David Holmes (John Graham), her brother; Ed Malone (David Hedison), an American newsman and photographer; and Professor Walter Summerlee (Richard Haydn), a scientist.

The troupe fly to the Amazon and arrive at the usual remote trading post, where they are joined by two others: Gomez (Fernando Lamas), a helicopter pilot, and Costa (Jay Novello), a jungle travel agent and guide. Gomez takes them in his helicopter to the "lost world" and leads them on a trek through the jungle. A brontosaurus knocks the helicopter over the cliff, where it's smashed to pieces below. The next day, Summerlee almost gets eaten alive by a large tuliplike vegetable.

After an attack by a pterodactyl, they discover and capture a 17-year-old native girl — "an invaluable female specimen" — observes Challenger, whom Malone saves from a giant spider's web. However, Indians decide to attack and capture them and take them off to their Cave City, where the girl helps them escape and leads them to an isolated cave containing

Willis O'Brien, aged 74, with his storyboards for the remake of *The Lost World* in 1960.

an aged and blind Burton White (Ian Wolfe), sole survivor of an earlier expedition.

They leave White and encounter the "Fire monster," which eats Costa alive. Ed Malone and Gomez push against a tree that breaks a dam holding molten lava, which engulfs the monster. Gomez, laughing like a maniac, falls into the boiling hell. The remaining group stagger out of the "lost world" to the base of the plateau, amid earthquakes and volcanic explosions. Safely away from the chaos, Jennifer clings to Ed as Challenger and Summerlee are consoled by the fact that a baby *Tyrannosaurus Rex* which they plan to take back to London, has popped out of the dinosaur egg.

Three things came to the attention of most reviewers of *The Lost World*. The updating of Conan Doyle's story, the special effects and the unintentional humor. As *Variety* observed:

> The production is something to behold. The dinosaurs are exceptionally lifelike—although they resemble horned toads and alligators more than dinosaurs.[91]

Motion Picture Herald thought the film was "...thrilling and realistically presented..." and that

> special credit is due to Winton Hoch as director of photography, Willis O'Brien as effects technician, and Howard Jackson and Sid Cutner for the orchestration.[92]

The Daily Cinema recognized that

> the special effects, despite some shots that we have surely seen before, are not unconvincing.[93]

London's *Daily Telegraph* amusingly noted:

> The dialogue is often a delight. I liked "After her, Malone, she's invaluable!" referring to a nubile native girl with a cleverly-cut sarong and a very pleasing pair of legs. "How horrid, eaten alive!" also makes its mark, thanks to the delivery which was very "method" and matter of fact.[94]

But *Kinematograph Weekly* found that

> The picture brings Conan Doyle's book up to date, but the modifications and modernization broaden its scope at the expense of conviction....
> It is, nevertheless, good fun, as well as suspenseful and spectacular "pocket serial." Jill St. John looks a treat, though incongruously attired in skin-tight pink pants, as Jennifer.[95]

The 1960 remake of *The Lost World* was a follow-up to the previous 20th Century–Fox release of 1959, *Journey to the Center of the Earth*, which had live reptiles to represent prehistoric animals. Producer-director

Irwin Allen decided to use the same method to create the dinosaurs in *The Lost World* by having iguanas and alligators with rubber stuck-on fins. Unfortunately, this method naturally runs the risk of harming the animals and is rarely used in films today, for the obvious reason that lizards simply do not look like dinosaurs.

In a 1961 book, Obie voiced his opinion of the film:

> The story is completely changed. You wouldn't recognize it. They claim that the live technique looks smoother, that animation is jerky. I don't think so. I'd like to see them use a copy of real dinosaurs with animation. But I guess it's all a matter of taste. They felt it would take too long to animate. I don't agree with them. It takes quite a crew with these reptiles. With the big screens, you can't carry focus with CinemaScope and you have to be farther than five feet away." He added sadly: "It makes for complications."[96]

At this time, Willis O'Brien was contacted by Jim Danforth, who later became an exceptionally talented special effects craftsman and film-maker. Danforth said about O'Brien:

> I had several phone conversations with him when they were remaking *The Lost World*. There was an article in *Variety* or *Hollywood Reporter* that Willis O'Brien was going to be hired to do the remake. So I called him up. I had spoken to him—previously in 1957—and he told me he wasn't doing anything at the moment, and if I wanted to see how animation was done, I should call Ray Harryhausen because he had just started on a picture which turned out to be *The 7th Voyage of Sinbad*—and that's how I eventually got in contact with Ray Harryhausen—through Willis O'Brien's suggestion. Well, he was very quiet, very soft spoken. Just a very quiet, mild, very nice pleasant person. I always got the feeling that he was a little bit embarrassed, when I talked to him—particularly the first time—that he wasn't doing anything. It was almost as if he wished he could say, "Yes, come out; I'd like to show you what I'm doing," but he had nothing going on at that moment. I also learned later from Darlyne that . . . he was never comfortable around young people because, I guess, of the fact that he lost his own sons.
>
> When I talked with O'Brien about *The Lost World*, we had a nice conversation on the phone, and he said there would be a very good possibility that he would need somebody—an assistant or something on the film—and to please keep in touch and call him back, but it was still premature. Well, of course, what ended up happening was that O'Brien got relegated to doing nothing on the picture, except to make a lot of storyboard sketches—they didn't let him do any animation.[97]

During the lean periods of unemployment in the 1950s, O'Brien created many story ideas and illustrations in the hopes of interesting a prospective producer to hire him and his talents. Although he sold a few,

The 13 faces of the Frankenstein monster, with an X next to the chosen version. Obie made several designs of a creature before deciding which one to use.

none of them, except for *The Beast of Hollow Mountain*, actually made it to the screen. He continued working on these ideas right up until his death. From 1960 to 1962, O'Brien worked on what would be his final story idea, "King Kong vs. Frankenstein," for which he created many watercolor illustrations. Sadly, although the basic idea was used for a film entitled *King Kong vs. Godzilla*, his animation technique was not. As Darlyne O'Brien recalled:

> This picture ["King Kong vs. Frankenstein"] ended in San Francisco, and he [Obie] was gonna have King Kong riding a cable car, but he didn't get the illustration finished, and he had marvelous action in it. That was about 10 years ago [1960], when he had the idea of "King Kong vs. Frankenstein." He did [have a story], but it ended up as *King Kong vs. Godzilla*. He didn't have anything to do with it, but it was supposed to be what they were promoting, but it didn't turn out that way. They were supposed to meet on this island, and have this big battle. People would come all over the world to see this big fight. And he drew these pictures . . . [showing illustration of the 13 Frankenstein designs], and drew about half a dozen others, but they were taken to Japan and they were never returned to us. So this is where he was testing out different characters to see what he would like best, and this is

FRANKENSTEIN'S CREATION.

A large watercolor sketch by Obie of the Frankenstein monster, which shows size comparison and details of the character.

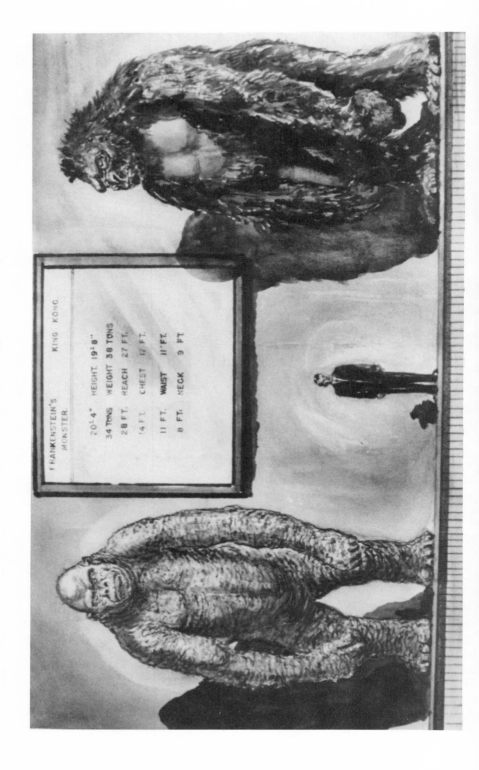

the way he would find his characters, by drawing all different types and sometimes perhaps selecting part of one and part of another to make the character. That first [version of the Frankenstein monster] he decided against that one, and used this one instead [the final design of the Frankenstein monster is shown fighting Kong]. [Bronlow: "There was no thought to make it like Boris Karloff?"] No, not intentionally, I don't believe. And this other one shows that he was having the girl walk the rope, and of course, King Kong didn't like that, so he is gonna get angry....[98]

Sadly, all O'Brien's efforts were wasted. A Japanese film company used his idea for its cheaply made *King Kong vs Godzilla*, but neither O'Brien nor his animation talents were used. "King Kong vs. Frankenstein," as O'Brien planned it, was never made. Darlyne O'Brien's nephew, Donald E. Hughes, commented on this sad situation:

> I think there was a lawsuit pending, and I think it was dropped, because financially, the lawyers will eat you out of house and home, and basically that's what happened, so it was dropped and nothing came of it. I don't recall how he [Obie] found out, but he did, and that's when they instigated the lawsuit.[99]

The last feature film O'Brien worked on was *It's a Mad, Mad, Mad, Mad World*. This film told the story of people in a quartet of vehicles traveling on a desert highway who witness a car swerving off the bend of the road and crashing, leaving the driver, Smiler Grogan (Jimmy Durante) sprawled on the ground, dying. The occupants of the four vehicles—J. Russel Finch (Milton Berle), president of the Pacific Edible Seaweed Company; Ding Bell (Mickey Rooney) and Benjy Benjamin (Buddy Hackett), two gag writers; Melville Crump (Sid Caesar), a dentist; and Lennie Pike (Jonathan Winters), a massive-shouldered, thickset, peanut-brained truck driver—go down the rocky slope and try to help Smiler. Breathing his last gasp, Smiler reveals to the group: "There's this dough, see. All this dough. Three hundred fifty gees buried under a big double yah" in Santa Rosita State Park. Shortly after Smiler literally "kicks the bucket," the group, unable to agree how to split the money, race off to the park to get the loot. On their way, they each pick up a fellow treasure hunter: Englishman J. Algernon Hawthorne (Terry Thomas); the bespectacled Otto Meyer (Phil Silvers); and Finch's fast-acting, slow thinking, frenetically mother-fixated beach bum brother-in-law, Sylvester Marcus (Dick Shawn), among others.

During the frenzied struggle to reach the park first, the greedy group are unaware that the hen-pecked Captain Culpepper (Spencer Tracy), of

Opposite: **The two titans weigh in for "King Kong vs. Frankenstein."**

the Santa Rosita police, is having their every move watched. With picks and shovels, the money-crazed troupe arrive at the park and begin to hunt feverishly for the hidden loot. Finally, Pike finds the spot where the money is buried, under four palm trees that grow to form the letter W. The group unearth a case filled with cash, when Culpepper steps in and suggests that they all give themselves up. They agree to do so, when they realize that Culpepper has taken off with the money for himself! They chase him into an old building and find themselves fighting over the money on a fire escape, which begins to collapse beneath them. In their struggle, the case splits open, raining the entire $350,000 down onto the crowd below. A fire engine arrives and extends its ladder to save them, but their combined weight on the ladder causes it to sway dangerously in all directions, throwing the characters off the ladder one by one. Miraculously, they all survive and end up in the hospital, where Mrs. Marcus (Ethel Merman) strides into the ward, slips on a banana skin and lands flat on her back, causing howls of laughter from the bandaged patients.

The film was photographed in the then new single-lens Cinerama process, which replaced the old three-camera format used on *This Is Cinerama*. O'Brien was hired by Linwood Dunn's effects studio, Film Effects of Hollywood, to work as a consultant and director of animation on the climactic "ladder" sequence. To achieve the effect of the character being flung off the ladder, it was decided to use three different scales of miniatures: a quarter-inch scale for extreme long shots of the swaying ladder photographed at 24 FPS, a 2-inch scale for high-speed photography at 72 FPS, and a 1-inch scale to be used for the stop-frame animation work of the characters clinging to the ladder and then being thrown off.[100]

Together with wire-work specialist Howard Lydecker, matte painter Howard Fisher, effects photographer James Gordon, model maker Marcel Delgado, among others, O'Brien worked for several months on the film, planning the effects. Joining the team as animator was Jim Danforth, who had just finished working at Projects Unlimited.[101] He said in 1985:

> I went over to Film Effects of Hollywood to see what they had going on, and I somehow found out they were going to do *It's a Mad, Mad, Mad, Mad World*. I knew that Willis O'Brien was going to do it, so that really appealed to me, because I wanted to work withObie. I got to say hello to him — I had met him before, when he came through Projects Unlimited when they were doing *Dinosaurus!* I first met Obie about 1959. He died after I met him the

third time. Between the time I first interviewed for the *Mad World* job and the time that the job eventually materialized, Obie died. That's one of the reasons Film Effects of Hollywood needed me, although I don't know whether Obie had ever intended to do the animation himself anyway.[102]

Willis O'Brien never lived to see his work completed on *It's a Mad, Mad, Mad, Mad World*. He died during its production on November 8, 1962, at age 76. Darlyne O'Brien said to Kevin Brownlow:

Well, he was a kid right up to the day he died. He was 76 when he died, but he was still just a boy and a dreamer. He never seemed to grow up. He really didn't. Everyone thought he was much younger than he was. And he was a Pisces, and if you believe in astrology—well, he was a true Pisces, because they're unpredictable and they're dreamers. He was very lovable, but not very dependable. I mean not the type to make what you would call "a good husband." He always said that he was the world's worst husband! He had a very artistic disposition—you know how artists are—he didn't care about or worry about how he looked with his clothes. He loved to go pub crawling [laughs], around the different pubs and meet the characters and talk to them. He really preferred that to formal entertainment. And, of course, he loved horses. That was our main recreation, you might say. He was Irish. His grandparents, I believe, were from County Cork. But he was born here in Oakland, so there wasn't any Irish accent in the family. But he had a lot of the characteristics of the Irish and, of course, he loved his bourbon! He always had his bourbon every night before dinner. He was a lot of fun. He really was.[103]

Part II. Story Ideas

Chapter 4

Ideas for Films

She would help him create ideas to write the stories,
and she worked on them with him. She typed most
of the work and he would do sketches and that's
how those ideas became an entity. And then they
would rush them over to Cooper, and he would say
. . . no! — . . . or . . . ah ha! — Donald E. Hughes.

The story ideas presented here, together with illustrations — all by
Willis O'Brien — were left to me by the late Darlyne O'Brien in 1985.
O'Brien wrote many others that he succeeded in selling. Of the ones that
he sold, only *The Beast of Hollow Mountain* actually made it to the screen
and was credited to him. The others — which I don't have in the collection — have never, to my knowledge, been made into films and remain,
along with the unsold story ideas that I have, unfilmed.

Many of the ideas for these stories appear to have been drawn from
either O'Brien's own life experiences or other real-life events (as in the
case of "The Elephant Rustlers" and "The Story of Emilio and Guloso").
Most of these ideas were written during the 1950s and show how O'Brien
actually went about preparing a story with illustrations that he would present to a film producer. This approach to selling a possible idea for a film
can still work today. The success depends largely on the way the idea is
presented and the foresight and imagination of the prospective producer.

Naturally, the main technique to be used to bring the monster or
beast to life in nearly all these stories was stop-motion animation —
O'Brien's specialty. Although some 30 years have passed since his death,
the model animation methods which he pioneered are still in use today
by the current leading masters of the art, which include Randy Cook,
David Allen, Phil Tippet, Jim Danforth and Ray Harryhausen — despite
the increasing use of animatronics and computer animation.

Above and opposite: **Watercolor illustrations, undated, possibly intended for "The Story of Emilio and Guloso," by Willis O'Brien.**

"The Story of Emilio and Guloso" was the basis of the 1950 Jesse Lasky project, "Valley of the Mist." No date appears on this nine-page story idea. Page 7 has faded handwritten notes that are unreadable. Two watercolor illustrations of a bull are presented here, although it is unknown whether they were intended for this project. Ray Harryhausen drew three black-and-white drawings for "Valley of the Mist" that were published in his *Film Fantasy Scrapbook.*

The Story of Emilio and Guloso[104]

In the hills of Mexico lived a woodcutter, Juan Fernando, with Rosa, his wife and Emilio, their only son. When Emilio was approaching 12 years of age, some *vaqueros,* driving a herd of cattle through a nearby mountain pass, gave him a newborn calf. Emilio laboriously carried it home in his arms, shouting gleefully to his mother to come and see his wonderful prize. The little calf ate so fast and so much that Emilio named him "Guloso," or Greedy.

Guloso grew into a truly magnificent bull, and Emilio would climb onto his back and off they would go into the back country, where Emilio had made friends with the Indians, sometimes not returning until long after dark. Late one evening, while Juan and Rosa were enjoying a little

wine and music in the patio with Emilio's uncle and his friends who had arrived that day, Emilio came in wide eyed and excited and, after hurriedly greeting his uncle and the rest of the company, told of having seen a lizard animal larger than a house with scales on its flesh and a tail as large as the big trees of the forest. Emilio stopped breathlessly, at a loss for further words.

The company looked at Juan and burst into laughter. Emilio's uncle said to him with a smile, "What tale is this? You tell me he is riding in the hills on the *toro* and now he says he has seen an animal so big . . . will your *vino* do this also?" Seeing their disbelief, Emilio flushed with embarrassment and turned and ran into the house. Not knowing quite what to think, Juan said to Rosa, "I think our son is sick with the fever." Then turning to his brother, he told him about the wonderful Guloso and invited him to walk out to see the animal. Rosa went into the house, and the rest of the company continued the merrymaking, forgetting the incident.

After a time, one Señor Garzan, having heard of the magnificent Guloso from the natives bringing their wares to the markets, came to see Juan about purchasing the animal for the bullring. Señor Garzan offered a generous price, and Juan, feeling secretly that the boy would be better off without the animal and badly needing money so Rosa could receive medical attention, agreed. Emilio could not bear the thought of parting with Guloso, and when he heard his father agree to sell him, he protested. But upon being reminded that the money could pay the *médico* to make his mother well again, he said no more, but ran out to where Guloso was.

Señor Garzan paid Juan the money and went out to get Guloso. He found Emilio with his head against Guloso's neck, stroking his face and looking so downcast that Señor Garzan, thinking to say something to cheer him up, began to talk of what a wonderful show he would give and how the people would flock to see Guloso—when the boy suddenly brightened. An idea had come to him, and he told Señor Garzan that he knew of a *"lagarto grande,"* a huge lizard, that the people would marvel to see; he would take the señor there to see it if the señor would like him to. With a look as though he had just begun to understand something, Señor Garzan slyly winked at his vaquero, believing the boy to be *loco*, and agreed that the people would surely marvel to see such an animal, but that he didn't have time to see it then because the fiesta and bullfight were to be held soon. Emilio, thinking fast and not realizing that Señor Garzan did not believe him, asked if Señor Garzan would pay as many pesos for the animal as he did for Guloso if Emilio brought it to him. Señor Garzan smilingly agreed that if Emilio brought an animal like that, he could have Guloso back and a thousand pesos besides, but in the meantime he would take Guloso. Excited, Emilio gave Guloso a loving pat and ran toward the house.

Emilio found only his mother in the house. He excitedly told her that the kind señor had promised that if he brought the lizard, the señor would give Emilio's beloved Guloso back and a thousand pesos besides. His friends, the Indians, would help him get the animal. So, could he go right away? Rosa, knowing with a mother's heart how fond the boy was of Guloso and thinking that the lizard, if it did exist, and surely her Emilio would not tell an untruth, only seemed large to his boyish mind, agreed to let him go. She said he could go while she and Juan were at the médico.

Emilio raced down the trail that he and Guloso had traveled so many times. When Emilio reached his Indian friends, they understood his great loss and agreed to help him, working almost night and day to get the animal in time for the fiesta. After making many preparations, they went down into a tropical valley, where they could barely distinguish one another through the mist, and the vegetation was lush and green and everything grew in huge proportions. Large hawklike birds attacked them and carried off one of the cows they had driven into the valley to use as bait for the animal. However, they drove the birds off with torches and, by many clever and dangerous ruses, attracted the animal out of the valley into a portable trap they had built for it.

The trap was a huge, strong *carreta*, pulled by many oxen. After they started on their way, laboriously guiding the carreta, Emilio, anxious lest they be too late, took a burro and rode ahead into town to find Señor Garzan. Everything went well with the trusty Indians and their charge until they reached a bridge spanning a gap of some hundred feet with a sharp turn at the end. The narrow road caused the long team of oxen to pull the carreta too near the edge of the embankment, allowing the wheels on one side to slip over. The carreta tipped, spilling the animal out and cutting the oxen loose. The helpless, frightened Indians saw the animal tumble down the sides of the canyon and their oxen dashing away in all directions. Meanwhile, Emilio reached the town, and as he rode through the streets on the burro, he saw many signs and pictures telling of his wonderful Guloso and that the bullfights were to be held that day.

The animal, with one of the posts of the carreta dangling from a rope around its neck, made its way to the road. As it ambled along, it came upon a truck loaded with pigs, that was stopped by the roadside while the driver, Pedro, took a siesta. The animal sniffed at the pigs, but decided to go on to something more interesting. The rope around its neck became entangled in the rear wheels of the truck, so as it walked away, the truck came after it with a terrific jerk.

Pedro awoke with a start to find himself and the truck facing the other way but still going toward the town. At first he laughed, exclaiming, "The truck she is loco, she looks the wrong way but is going the right way." Then suddenly realizing that the motor was not going and he was driving it, he began to pray fervently to the saints to preserve him. Beads of perspiration broke out on his face. After bumping and careening along for a few hundred yards, the truck overturned, spilling pigs and Pedro into the dusty road. Pedro, getting his first sight of the animal, knelt in the dust with pigs all around him, too frightened to move.

When Emilio reached the bullring, he could hear the music of the bands and the applause of the people as they viewed the parade before the bullfight. However, poor, ragged Emilio could not convince the gateman that he had had business with Señor Garzan at such a time, and

Emilio had to find another way to reach the señor. With so much at stake, he would not be turned back, so he went around the outside of the ring to the stalls where the bulls were kept.

Emilio could see his Guloso in the stall nearest the entrance of the arena, and watching for his chance, slipped quietly to the back of it and climbed in. He petted Guloso and talked quietly to him until he saw an opportunity to slip over the gate and into the stands. He made his way cautiously along the aisle until he found the señor's box. Waiting until the *policía* were away, he slipped over to the back of the box, and hissed to the señor. The señor gave a quick look, turned away and then looked again, recognizing something familiar about the boy. He leaned over toward Emilio, and Emilio quickly told him that he had the animal. His Indian friends were bringing it into town and he asked if the señor wanted it brought to the ring. The señor looked startled for a moment, but then a slow smile spread over his face and he patted Emilio on the shoulder. Motioning toward the seats higher up, he said, "That is good, *bueno*, but just sit down for a while and see the bullfights; then we will talk."

Emilio began to understand that the señor did not believe him. He looked around bewildered, not knowing what he could do to convince the señor, when the policía came over and asked Señor Garzan if the ragged boy was annoying him. Señor Garzan graciously said, "No, no, give him a seat up there." So Emilio allowed himself to be gently pushed along to the seats higher up.

Emilio sat quietly for a moment, trying to find a way to tell the señor, when there was a great commotion in the street — much screaming and crashing, as though houses were being crushed under a great weight. The animal, getting the scent of the bulls, forced its way into the ring, breaking down two of the stalls in passing. The two bulls it had freed ran into the arena before it. The animal thrashed around, killing one of them with a lash of its tail and grasping the other one in its mouth, threw it high into the stands. It stood for a moment, bewildered by the confusion, then started toward the panic-stricken people in the stands. The men in charge of the ring saw that swords or guns would be useless against such an animal and that unless something was done, many would be killed. Emilio saw the danger, too, and jumped down from Señor Garzan's box into the ring and raced around to the stall where Guloso was penned. With a word of encouragement to his pet and a loving pat, he opened the gate.

When Guloso saw the animal, all his fighting instincts came to the fore, and he attacked it with such savagery as had never before been seen. Guloso was mortally wounded in the fight, but he went on until the monster lay dying; then Guloso died in Emilio's arms, with Emilio stroking and soothing him until the last. Emilio was broken-hearted, but he knew that Guloso would understand everything now and would know that he, Emilio, had done all for love of him, so Emilio returned sadly to his home in the hills.

Bounty

Author's Note: "Bounty" is a two-page unfinished typed story idea with no name and no date on it. Many of the ideas in this story seem to have been taken from O'Brien's own life.

It was early in the morning when Tom Ellery, a boy about 12, entered the street from a cheap rooming house. It was on the San Francisco waterfront, and a cold wind was pushing in a heavy fog. He turned his coat collar up around his neck and pulled his hat down to keep the fog from dipping in his face, while he tried to make up his mind which way to go. This was all new to him. He had been raised by his widowed father, who had arranged for Tom to work on a farm near Stocton, where he got 10 dollars a month and his board for 14 hours a day, seven days a week. After two months of this work, his father came to visit and borrowed his 20 dollars and left for parts unknown. After working another month, he drew his 10 dollars and walked to Stocton and took passage on a stern-wheeler to San Francisco, where he landed around midnight. As he looked to his right, he could see through the fog the outline of the cable and horse cars making their way to the ferry building, and he could see by the clock on its tower that it was not yet five o'clock. Yet, the city was waking up; the delivery wagons, pulled by four big drays, were rattling over the cobblestone streets toward the docks, where four large masted ships were tied up.

Across the bay, Tom could hear the foghorns, the dock bells and the tooting of the tugs. As he looked toward Market Street, he could see the lights, and felt that he was too shabby. Across the street on the docks, he could see some activity—men were loading and unloading the ships, and the big drays were starting to back up to the warehouse. Tom thought that he might like to work on one of the ships and travel to far-off lands, but his stomach told him he was hungry. He put his hand in his pocket and clutched his silver dollars and walked toward Fishermen's Wharf.

The Westernettes

Author's Note: "The Westernettes" is a two-page description of an amusement ride that O'Brien devised during the early 1950s, together with a similar idea for a "Trip to the Moon."
    Obie prepared a series of short stories for television called "The Westernettes," which would have children playing the principal parts and using small-scale buildings and Shetland ponies. A watercolor illustration for one of the episodes (which dealt with a kidnapped girl who is rescued by a giant lizard from an underground cavern) appeared in Forrest J Ackerman's "The Shape of Things That Never Came," published in an issue of *Filmfax.* Obie created a series of detailed watercolor sketches for this project that are still in existence today. They have never — to my knowledge — been published. Unfortunately, Obie was unable to sell this idea. The version of the story presented here had no author's name or date with it when I received it.

The following is a description of a new kind of show for amusement parks, beach resorts, state and county fairs, carnivals, etc. The idea is to have the children appear with their favorite motion picture cowboy. At the time their tickets are purchased, they are presented with metal deputy's badges. They enter the tent and are seated on mechanical horses. The lights dim and the sound and film come on. The villain rides into the scene, shooting, and rides out again. Our hero cowboy follows. He stops, faces the children and swears them in as deputies. He turns his horse and gallops after the villain, the mechanical horses starting up simultaneously. The hero catches up to the villain and ropes him. He then turns to the children and thanks them for their assistance in catching the villain and tells them they can get a closer look at the man they have caught as they leave by a side door.

Outside the door will be a dummy sitting in a jail cell. Nearby, there could be a concession where the children could have their picture taken with a large photo of their hero, for a slight extra charge. Also, there could be concessions selling cowboy accessories. We will seat 20 for each ride, and the picture will run about five minutes, which will allow about 10 shows per hour. The admission charged will be 25 cents per child. On this basis, a five-hour day, four days per week, would bring in $1,000 per week. Allowing five cents per horse for rental of same, we would deduct $200, leaving $800. Concession charges would cost approximately $250, which would leave $550. Labor costs would be (approximately) $150, leaving $400 per week. The housing would be designed for easy assembly and breakdown and, including electrical work, projector and screen, should cost (approximately) $350. The film would cost (approximately)

$1,000. Therefore, for an investment of, say, $5,000, one should get a return of at least $200 per week. Naturally, the more concessions distributed throughout the country, the more return there would be.

Wetback Material: The Littlest Torero or The Littlest Wetback or The Littlest Bracero

Author's Note: The material for "The Littlest Torero," "The Littlest Wetback" and "The Littlest Bracero" seems to be three unfinished versions of a story about a Mexican boy that appears to have been inspired by a newspaper article entitled "Little Wetback Has a Different Story," written by Paul V. Coates, dated November 30, 1959. Obie's ideas for this story were registered with the Writer's Guild. No. 75610. "The Little Wetback," the second version, was handwritten and has no date. The third, "The Littlest Wetback," which has no date or author's name, is taken from the handwritten notes—some of which are faded and are hard to decipher. No illustrations appear to have survived with this material.

Version 1

This is the story of a poor little Mexican boy who assists some American tourists when their car gets mired in the mud in one of Mexico's torrential rains in the back country. He is so pathetic in his poverty and pleads so earnestly for them to take him to the United States so he may learn to speak English better and get more education that he reaches their hearts, and they agree to bring him back home with them. They do so, and he repays them a thousandfold by a wonderful act of bravery that saves the life of their daughter.

He finds their home and ranch to be beyond his wildest dreams of luxury. It is well staffed with servants and farm helpers, some of them Mexican. As in all situations, there are sometimes disagreements among the workers. The little daughter, a year or two younger than the little *bracero*, accidentally witnesses the murder of one of the workers by two others. The murderers know that she has seen and can tell. They devise a plan to get her killed by a vicious bull. But they reckon without little bracero, whose secret ambition had been to be a torero in Mexico and who had learned a substantial amount of the art. When he sees the little girl running through the pasture where the bull is kept, trying to retrieve her doll that the men have tossed there, he knows that the bull will be attracted by the little flying skirts. He quickly grabs a saddle blanket from the tack room and goes into the pasture waving the blanket and calling

"Ahjo, Ahjo" to the bull. The bull is undecided at first which target to go for. But the little bracero skillfully maneuvers the bull around, so his back is to the little girl. He then yells at her to get out and calls loudly for help in between his maneuvers with the bull.

The mother, riding by on horseback, hears the cries for help and is horrified to see her little girl in the pasture. She dismounts and goes in after her. She gets the girl out just as the bull rushes at them and watches in wonder at the bravery and dexterity of the little bracero as he continues to wear the bull down until it stands in confusion, allowing him to escape over the pasture fence. The little bracero is praised and promised that in the future he shall return to Mexico to fight bulls if he wants to.

Version 2: Little Wetback

"Ahjo, ahjo" Pepe taunted the oxen, his brown eyes sparkling and eager, his ears hearing the strains of the *paso doble* all around him. (Describe countryside.)

So engrossed was he that he did not see Lopez emerge from the trees and come toward him menacingly, carrying a strong switch. "So," Lopez shouted angrily, "you do not work for me. I give you this (hitting him) and this (hit) and this (hit). Pepe shielded his face from the blow and giggled. "But, Señor Lopez the ox would not go." "The ox would not go!" Lopez smiled. "You would not go! You think I will give you *inijoles* and tortillas for this — now go — with this" — (hitting him once more). Pepe's eyes became large and doleful for just an instant, then he pushed his hat down on his head. "OK Señor Lopez, I go." He picked up the reins and whipped up the oxen. Lopez, grumbling to himself, walked toward the distant house, often glancing back.

Version 3: The Littlest Wetback

Father Lopez says: "He has the strength of four because his heart is pure." The villain accused him of stealing money, but this could not touch him. He prayed. Little Pepe's heart was pure, and when he assured his companions that he would one day go to the United States and become a great man, they jeered, but they knew he would. Things did seem to work out miraculously for Pepe. They had seen it happen, and when they would ask him how he brought these things about, he would put his hands together, as if in prayer, and say, "I'm a good boy" and laugh and dance away to some adventure. He was so fond of practicing fighting los torritos (the little bulls) and was so alert and adept at it that when the family from California agreed to sponsor him, his friends were sure he would change his mind and become a matador.

Perez, Antonio Pepe loved life-goodness. Sonchez, Richardo Louis had a happy disposition. Lopez, Jore Carlos was adopted.

Foster father to him (he is not resentful)—plays bullfighting with oxen. Beaten, he begs the tourists to take him along. They agree and bring him back to the United States. Or goes back? Little daughter knows who did it. Villain plans to kill him—throws her into bull pasture. Boy fights bull and saves her life. She adopts him and sends him to the home of the priest's parish house in Mexico. Old man (or old priest)—or let the story unfold— narrates the life story of Pepe who has returned to Mexico from the United States and becomes a great matador? (Great statesman or official?)

"Ahjo! Ahjo!" Eleven-year-old Pepe (Sonchez taunted the cows?) flung the ragged blanket about, his eyes shining and eager, then suddenly, he lost interest. A mood of pessimism came over him. This was not for him. Hurling the blanket over the head of the cow, he turned to leave the small arena where the novices practiced bullfighting.

"Oh Pepe—come back, come back, you do good passes." A chorus of voices called out to him to "come back," but he shook his head and waved "mañana," but he knew he wouldn't be seeing them mañana. He ran up onto the busy avenue and darted between the cars to the other side, watching hopefully for someone who would give him a ride into the city, always making a special effort to catch the attention of cars with American passengers, calling out to them "Pepe will show you" when the traffic would slow down enough for him to run alongside a car. After several tries, he goodnaturedly ran back to a battered old truck riding along. The driver was a Mexican farmer.

Pepe: Señor, a ride with you? Por favor?
Lopez: Si, si, OK. Where you go?
Pepe: I go to Father Christs', sometimes, sometimes to Juanitos'.
Lopez: You got no home?
Pepe: (*shrugging his shoulders*) Sure, I dorn no, that much.
Lopez: Not that much? How you say that? (*laughing*)
Pepe: (*laughing, always glad to be laughing*) Juanito say I ain't enough old yet to pay.
Joe Lopez: (*looking at him shrewdly*) You work for me, you don't pay.
Pepe: (*agreeably*) Sure, Pepe work for you.
Lopez: You wait. I get a drink and we talk.
Pepe: OK. I wait.

Huddled in the back of the truck, Pepe slept. Lopez staggered to the truck, got in and they started out. After what seemed like hours to the sleepy and hungry Pepe, they drove up to a little adobe hut. Lopez clambered out and stumbled into the house and threw himself onto the crude bunk bed in the corner. Pepe followed him in, and hopeful of getting something to eat for himself, tried to rouse him.

Pepe: Señor, you don't want something to eat?

Lopez: (*motioning him away*) No, no, no.

Pepe looked around the room, lighted only by the moonlight shining through the door and the window. He helped himself to a spoonful or two of beans from the pot on the crude stove and curled up in a corner to sleep. He had seen the effect that too much pulque had on people before and mañana everything would be all right. When Pepe awoke the next morning, Lopez was sitting on the bunk regarding him with a calculating look. Pepe rubbed his eyes sleepily and sat up. Lopez took a long pull at a bottle of tequila.

Pepe: (*laughing*) You gonna get drunk again, Señor.

Lopez: (*shrugging*) So—OK—you gonna do the work?

Pepe: Sure. OK. (*getting to his feet*)

Lopez: (*waving the bottle toward the stove*) Eat some *frijoles* and *tortillas* and call me Joe.

Pepe: (*agreeably*) Si, Joe. You don't want some?

Lopez: Nah—*asta* (later). *Asta.*

Pepe, not relishing the cold beans, ate only a few mouthfuls.

Pepe: OK, Joe, now I work.

Lopez: (*shuffling over to the table and setting the tequila on it*) Come, I show you.

Pepe followed him out to a dirty, crudely built corral in which were two oxen and a dirty goat and burro. Lopez tossed a small bale of millet to the oxen, and while they munched contentedly, he showed Pepe how to harness them to a crude plough. When they were ready, he slapped the rear one on the rump and gave it a shove.

Lopez: Hi! Hi! Go now!

Pepe held the reins and struggled long and arduously, keeping the furrows straight as possible, returning late in the afternoon, hands blistered and exhausted. Lopez was stretched out asleep, the empty tequila bottle on the floor beside him. For a moment, Pepe felt dismayed, but his persistent optimism soon returned. He took a spoonful or two of the cold frijoles and sat down, resting his head on his arms. Soon he was sleeping soundly, forgetting that the oxen were unhitched. . . .

The Bubbles

Author's Note: "The Bubbles" is a five-page unfinished story idea, typed with handwritten corrections and additions and with no date or author's name on it. No illustrations survived with it.

The door of the reception room at Angel's Hospital opened, and a nurse announced to three reporters that they could now interview young Tommy Tycoon, who had been brought in, unconscious, three days before, from his yacht, which had been found drifting helplessly at sea. It was a mystery that the authorities could not explain. When the reporters entered, they found Tommy sitting up, his head still bandaged. Rather apologetically, they explained that they were anxious to report anything of so exciting a nature, and Tommy, placing his hand to his head as though slightly dizzy, assured them that he realized their ambitions and would get to the story at once. He seemed hesitant, however, as though he was running over in his mind the events that had taken place, which, in fact, is just what he was doing. Upon realizing just how fantastic the events would sound, he momentarily decided he just couldn't go through with it. Still he knew that he was going to have to have help solving the mystery in the future, which he intended to do, so he slowly began to recall what had happened, fact by fact.

He said that when he was about 500 miles off Midway Island, he had set course and left Tony, his helper, at the helm and gone below. It was calm, with a fair breeze, and he fell asleep almost at once. He didn't know how long he had slept when he was thrown from his bunk with such force that he was knocked out. When he came to, the boat was listing. He managed to pull himself up and and stagger to the deck. Up there he found everything a shambles. The main mast had been sheered off. Tony was nowhere to be found.

At this point, Tommy hesitated and looked around the room, almost as though seeking something or someone to corroborate his story, and it was several minutes before he continued. The boys waited patiently, wondering if they should venture a remark or question that would help, but Tommy, almost as though he doubted himself, said that as he had stood, reeling dizzily on the deck, he saw several balloonlike objects off to the side. One was floating on the water, and several others were drifting lazily down to it. Suddenly, about 200 yards away, another object shot out of the water to a height of about 500 feet.

There was silence in the room for several minutes, as the enormity of Tommy's statement spun around in their minds. Finally, one of the reporters dared to mention that the balloons could only have come from below. It was obvious that they had, but hearing it put into words made the facts even more startling. Tommy reached for a glass of water, gulped it down and looked at them with almost a challenge in his eyes. He said that the balloons were semitransparent and those that were floating on the surface seemed to pulsate as though they were made of some soft, silken gossamer and there was a suction of air inside them. Feeling ill and dizzy, he didn't remember how long he had watched them, certain at times that he could see movement inside them and just as certain at others that he had imagined it. Suddenly, the one nearest the boat seemed to split open and a very large manlike creature emerged and splashed into the water, the balloon sealing itself up with no sign of where the opening had been. In panic, Tommy had started the auxiliary motor, getting away before the creature could reach the boat. He went as far as the fuel lasted and then drifted. He ran out of food and water and, from sheer exhaustion, lay in a stupor for days. He remembered nothing of being brought to the hospital. The reporters thanked him and with exasperating politeness, said good-bye.

Tommy knew they had found his story incredible. Sometime later, at the inquest into Tony's death, he repeated the story just as he had told it at the hospital. At the intimation of one of the interrogators that the apparitions might have been hallucinations from shock, Tommy was relieved when someone reported that the Coast Guard recently received a radio message from a yacht that it was surrounded by queer, balloonlike objects floating on the water. But the sender had failed to give the location or name of the craft, and nothing had been heard from him since that time. Of course, this did not prove Tommy's story was true, but at least it seemed more feasible than before. After the inquest, Tommy hurried to the Coast Guard to get more data on the report, but was disheartened that nothing more was available. Determined not to allow the opportunity to explore something unearthly to pass, Tommy charted a seafaring yacht, with a crew of five, provisioned it and obtained permission to equip it with a three-inch gun. The yacht then went to the approximate location where Tommy had encountered the strange objects.

At the time they dropped anchor, Tommy had sighted what appeared to be a pleasure yacht in the distance. After several hours, he noticed that it had not come any nearer. Through the binoculars he could see that no one appeared to be aboard and some of the top structure was broken. He decided to investigate. As they drew near, Tommy called out.

No one answered. The boat was much larger than the one Tommy had charted. Tommy's boat came alongside, and Tommy took two of the crew aboard with him. Leaving them above, Tommy went below, but finding no one, was about to ascend when he heard a low moan. Listening for a few moments, he heard it again. Calling out to whomever it was, he was answered by a weak rap on the door, somewhere along the corridor. Retracing his steps and listening, he located what appeared to be a closet door with no ventilation. He tried it, but it was locked. He heard a cough inside and looked about to find something with which to force the lock. The two crewmen were examining everything for a clue to what had happened, when they came across a strange, sticky, rubbery mass of whitish substance draped across the lifeboat. It was sticky and sprung back with a rubbery response when opened out. In spots there were holes with irregular edges, as though it had been nibbled on or picked at by gulls. It was grayish white and semitransparent. It wasn't alive, and there seemed to be no living creature about.

As the crewmen started below to find Tommy, they were astounded to meet him coming up carrying a comely, blond woman in his arms. She was alive but barely conscious from near-suffocation, hunger and thirst. After they made her comfortable on deck in the fresh air and helped her to sip some water, Tommy went with the men to see their find. As they approached the lifeboat, Tommy gasped as he recognized the substance as being one of the balloons he had seen. This one had evidently landed on the boat by mistake, and the creature it had contained had left it. Here was some proof of his story.

Author's Note: The Story ends here with a handwritten note that says: "Don't know where we would have gone from here. D."

The Eagle

Author's Note: "The Eagle" is a 16-page story idea. There is a registered number on the manuscript, but it is unreadable because it is badly faded. There is no date with this story idea, and no illustrations appear to have been created for it. The story seems to be a variation of Obie's "The Beast of Hollow Mountain."

About the time of the first stage runs, Andy Daley and Clyde Russel, friends since boyhood, came west and settled near the Grand Canyon. They became good-natured rivals in the cattle business, although Andy, a nature lover at heart, found himself much more interested in the wildlife around his ranch. In the craggy mountains in back of Andy's ranch lived a giant eagle. Andy watched it soar gracefully many times and admired its majestic stature when it landed on some lonely point. He desired greatly to become friends with it, never dreaming that he would, very soon. The eagle had lived in the mountains for many years and had become a legend with the Indians thereabout. It had evidently found food to be plentiful, for there had been few complaints of missing stock until some time after Andy and Clyde arrived. Then stock began to be found, terribly mangled and torn and only half eaten. The eagle seemed the logical suspect. One day the big bird was within range of an irate rancher's gun and the rancher wounded it in the right wing. Andy was standing among the trees along the boundary of his back pasture when he saw the eagle start to soar and then lose altitude rapidly and come toward his barn.

Andy could see that it was hurt. It landed with a plop, its wings spread out on the ground. As Andy came nearer, it flopped a few feet and looked helplessly toward him. Andy knew he should finish killing it, but his heart was filled with pity for a thing so helpless, with all its great size and strength. He stood watching it for a long time. He knew the danger in the sharp beak and huge claws too well, but for some reason he didn't really fear it. It lay watching him, too, the naturally sharp eyes focused with frightening intensity. Andy walked around the corner of the barn, trying to decide what to do. He then filled a shallow pan with water, placed it on the ground and pushed it within reach of the eagle's beak, using a long stick and making no effort to come nearer. He made sure the gates leading into the corral were closed and fastened securely and then went into the house. Andy tended the eagle faithfully, seeing to it that it always had fresh water and chunks of fresh meat, placed before it on a thin board so the food and water were clean. Andy was sure that he could detect an attitude of gratefulness in the kingly bird.

There weren't many things that Andy kept from his friend Clyde, but it was some weeks before Clyde found out what Andy had been busying himself with. By that time, Andy had contrived to get a splint on the eagle's damaged wing, and the eagle had regained its strength enough to stand and move about the corral. Clyde didn't scold Andy, for he understood perfectly Andy's great kindness of heart and his extreme interest in all nature's creatures, but he did remind Andy that someone else would probably kill the eagle when it took flight again. Andy agreed that that probably was true and expressed the wish that he could keep it with him. During their conversation, Andy expressed doubt that the stock killings had been done by the eagle, reminding Clyde that it had always been his opinion that eagles usually carried off whatever they chose as food to their nest and didn't leave it mangled and torn. There had also been a report of a new killing since the eagle had been wounded. Clyde said that he supposed there always would be some killings since there were other wild animals about, and they would just have to wait and see what developed from then on.

It was some time before the news that Andy was nursing the eagle back to health reached the rancher who had shot it, but when it did, he became angry and talked it around that he intended to shoot the eagle again the first time it came near his ranch. In fact, he tried to convince the sheriff to demand that Andy kill the eagle at once. But the sheriff, preoccupied with other matters, did not feel that one eagle, more or less, was going to do away with the rancher's stock, so nothing was done.

Every now and then there would be talk around town of some rancher losing stock. The incriminating thing was that they were all ranchers from a certain vicinity, farther north and nearer the mountains than Andy's, and in the general direction that the eagle had always come from. Upon the instigation of the man who had shot the eagle, several ranchers got together and decided to ride over to Andy's and have a talk with him. They found Andy engaged in braiding a *riata*, and he welcomed them in a friendly way, but sensed that there was an undercurrent of threat in their manner. They came right to the point. They told him that they had been losing stock and had heard that he was keeping the eagle on his ranch and asked what he intended to do about it. Andy, who had a peace-loving disposition, quietly assured them that he had heard of their losses and admitted that he had lost some himself. He explained his doubts that the eagle had been to blame and reminded them that there had been some losses since the eagle had been laid up. They had to agree that was true. He told them that he knew he probably should have killed the eagle. Andy attempted to explain that it was of such an unusual size and such a grand, beautiful creature, but found himself at a loss for words before their incredulous stares. He ended by nervously inviting them to come with him to the corral and see for themselves how grand it was. There were some murmurs of dissension, but they stumped behind him obediently.

They found the eagle amusing itself with a boulder, the size of which it could barely get its claw around. It was walking about carrying the boulder, which caused it to hobble as though one leg was shorter than

the other. This sent Andy into a gale of laughter. The eagle paid no attention to them, but walked over to a stump, smaller in circumference than
the boulder, and attempted to place the boulder on top of the stump. The
boulder would fall off, and the eagle would try to place it on top again.
This was extremely amusing to Andy, but the others took no interest in
the antics of the big bird. Andy, seeing their disinterest and impatience
with his amusement, quickly became serious again. They stood for a few
moments, and if any of them had been interested in watching longer, they
didn't dare show it before the disgruntled ones, so they soon turned away
and walked toward the house.

There wasn't much Andy could say except that he didn't know just
what he did expect to do with the bird, if anything, and they probably
were right that he should destroy it. He told them that he was glad they
had come out and that he hoped they wouldn't have hard feelings toward
him. Some said friendly good-byes, some said faintly amused ones,
some said gruff ones, but they all waved a hand as they rode off. Andy
stood for some time rubbing his chin and thinking it over. It seemed like
a man ought to be able to do about what he wanted, away off in the country, but he guessed people made everybody's business their own in this
day and age. He walked thoughtfully into the house. He knew, and
had known for some time, that it wouldn't be long until the eagle would
take off, maybe never to return or maybe to return with someone else's
cow or calf. Andy dreaded that. He didn't want trouble with his neighbors.

It wasn't many days later that Andy went out to the corral and found
the eagle gone. Well, Andy mused, he had expected it every day lately,
and with a prayer in his heart that the bird would stay out of gun range,
he got on his horse and turned toward Clyde's ranch. He found Clyde
finishing up some minor tasks and felt him out as to what he had to do
in the next few days. Clyde admitted that just then he found time hanging
heavily on his hands and inquired what Andy had in mind. Andy confided
that he just had a hankering to pack into the mountains and cook their
coffee and bacon over an open fire, like they had done back home. Clyde
looked at Andy rather searchingly, but, since Andy didn't volunteer any
further reason for the trip, Clyde didn't press him.

They left the next morning, and as they jogged slowly along, humming tunes and conversing now and then, it occurred to Clyde to ask
Andy about the eagle. Andy confessed that it had been gone since the
morning of the day before. Clyde asked him if this trip was to find it, and
Andy said no, but he just thought they might run onto the trail of some

kind of killer that had been attacking the stock. Clyde didn't think so, but it didn't matter much. He thought the trip would do them both good anyway. He noticed Andy scanning the skies a great deal of the time and, though he said nothing, it amused him that Andy tried to hide his concern for the eagle.

They camped for the night among cottonwoods, near a stream that flowed down a canyon. The canyon seemed to curve away toward the heart of the mountains. At dawn, they were disturbed by the nervous stamping of the horses. Andy was the first to awaken. He lay listening for several minutes. He got up, dressed and walked to the edge of the trees. At first he saw nothing, but when he started back his eye caught a movement of something across the creek. He could discern the movement, but the outline of the thing moving was so huge that he thought he must be dreaming. He ran a few steps toward camp, called softly to Clyde to get up and dress quickly. He ran back to the creek, and in a few seconds Clyde was beside him. They watched a creature some eight or nine feet high, which seemed to be thrashing about in the bushes, not sure which way it wanted to go. The horses were becoming increasingly nervous. The thing came down to the water's edge and, in the increasing light, they could see that it had a long tail that thrashed about menacingly. Andy regained his presence of mind to tell Clyde that here was the stock killer.

The beast began to wade into the creek when Andy, loath to kill but, knowing a killer when he saw one, fired a volley of shots at it. The shots didn't kill it by any means and it took off in the direction of the canyon in great leaps and bounds. Andy and Clyde, ever on the alert, got their breakfast and broke camp, heading into the canyon, hoping to get a glimpse of the beast in daylight. They rode all that day into the canyon, which seemed to end in a sheer wall of rock farther on, but they saw no sign of the beast. They took turns watching that night and the next morning decided, reluctantly, that they had better start back. Andy secretly wished for a faster way to travel. He was sure now that the eagle had not been to blame for the killings of the stock and confided to Clyde that he wanted to go farther into those mountains, stating that if they only knew what kind of beast it was or where it stayed most of the time, they could fix some kind of trap for it. Clyde agreed that it probably would be best to trap it in its own lair, but didn't know how they could do it. Andy wasn't satisfied with the brief sighting they had of it and vowed to think of something. When Andy arrived home, he heard a familiar shrill whistle. He dashed to the corral, and there was the eagle. Andy felt such joy at its return that he wished desperately that there was some way he could keep it there. He wondered if it would be possible to rope it, or would it become frightened and fly away. Well, he thought it would be a new experience to try it. He went to the house, got some fresh meat for the bird, took his new riata and went back to the corral and worked his way outside the fence, toward his back pasture. He held the meat up, and as he walked on, the eagle watched him intently. At last, when he didn't look back but went steadily on, he heard the whir of the great wings and a rustling as the bird settled itself in some trees to his right. He tossed the meat to it and stood back while the bird ate. Then when it sat up and raised its head, looking right and left, he swung the riata. The bird didn't move until the rope was over its head, but when the loop slipped down around its great neck, it took off with a great swoop and, Andy, trying to save his new riata, was carried along. It was fortunate that he had made a loop in both ends.

Andy hung on with one hand while he slipped his foot into the loop, then used both hands to grip the rope as they skimmed over the treetops. The bird, evidently puzzled by the extra weight, decided to circle back and settle in the pasture again, much to Andy's relief. His landing was rather rough, but the grass in the pasture helped some. It was a thrilling experience, and he stood and thought about it for a few minutes. As he started toward the bird, it fluttered its wings as though to take off again. Andy didn't want that, so he talked softly to it as he approached, a step at a time, finally slipping the loop over its head just as it raised its wings to take off. Andy hated to see it go and refused to think that perhaps this time it really wouldn't come back.

But he needn't have worried, for a day or two later, there it was in the corral again, contentedly playing with the boulder, as a child would that had been away from a favorite toy. Andy watched it delightedly, but he was ready for it this time. After his experience in the pasture, Andy had gone to Clyde's and told him that he believed he had found a way to get a look into the deep recesses of the mountains. He told Clyde about the short flight he had taken, quite by accident, and said that he believed that the bird would carry him the next time because it would understand that he was the extra weight and would not be frightened.

At least it was worth a try, and Andy told Clyde that if the bird came back, he intended to rope it and keep it there for a day or two and then would try to go away with it. That is, he would do this if he could rely on Clyde to ride in the general direction it took and bring along Andy's horse just in case he should drop off in the rough country. Clyde thought it a crazy scheme, but agreed to come whenever Andy gave him the word. Andy then set about making himself a sort of harness to fit under his arms and around his chest with straps and loops attached for his feet. This harness was to be hooked to a double-strength riata. So, now that the eagle had returned, Andy carried out his plan and tied it to the corral post. The eagle didn't dart away this time when the rope slipped over its head, but soon began to resent being tethered, so Andy hurried to Clyde's, not sure that it would be there when they returned. But it was.

Andy wore a small pack on his back and an extra rope, which added a little more weight, but the eagle was eager to get away and took to the air immediately, though not for long. It circled back, just as it had done before, and landed in the pasture. Andy wasn't sure just how things were going to work out then, but when he made no move to take the rope off its neck, it took to the air again, with almost an air of resignation, Andy thought. They flew away in the direction of the very canyon where Andy and Clyde had camped. Andy, glancing back, could see Clyde and the horses, like tiny specks below.

Up, up they went. This was a new experience for Andy, and he enjoyed every minute of it. The view from up there was magnificent as they passed over the first low range of mountains. Soon he could see what appeared to be a giant bowl of green, seemingly surrounded on all four sides by rocky, barren mountains. He was studying this sight when he realized that they were losing altitude. Down, down they came, closer and closer to the green treetops. He wondered if this could be where the eagle's nest was. Sure enough, he could see the huge nest resting on a ledge of the mountain, somewhat to the right of their direction of flight. Suddenly the big bird swerved in direction and came in toward the ledge. Andy watched carefully and contrived to land feet first, though he rolled over a couple of times after landing.

The sight that met his eyes was something Andy had never dreamed of. He looked down into a tropical valley below and could see a stream fed by a great waterfall at the north end. There were all kinds of lush vegetation, varieties Andy had never seen before. As he looked, there suddenly appeared a giant beast, the kind he and Clyde had seen. So this was where they came from. But where was the entrance to the valley? Andy couldn't discern one at either end. Now this was something to be looked into. Andy started to unhook his harness from the riata, then hesitated. Perhaps the eagle might leave him there, but, after all, this was the eagle's home. Everything generally returns to its home. He would have to risk it. He unhooked the harness from the riata but continued to wear it. He then fastened the extra rope around a point of rock at one end of the ledge and lowered himself into the top of a tall tree, where he sat, for some time, studying his surroundings.

The eagle watched Andy a little while and then suddenly took off for the far end of the valley. Andy saw him go and for a second felt lonely and afraid, but his love of adventure was too strong to allow him to stop now. Andy left the rope dangling down the cliff, where he could reach it to ascend, and climbed down from the tree. He could hear the great beast thrashing about in the brush some distance away and kept himself hidden by shrubbery wherever possible. He made his way toward the heart of the valley, where he had noted a grassy plain with fewer trees. Suddenly he heard another beast crashing through the brush. He quickly hid himself in a thick bush and watched. This beast was smaller than the other one.

After the beast had passed, Andy quietly went on through the giant ferns and other tropical plants. He had heard of such places as jungles and tropical valleys, but had not known that such places existed here, in his own country. This was the answer to the stock killers, but where did these beasts enter and leave the valley? Andy carefully went toward the stream, thinking his progress was unobserved, but as he knelt to drink, there was a sudden rush behind him, and he turned to see a beast, obviously a young one, coming toward him. He waved his arms and shouted at it, but it came on. He waded into the stream and crossed to the other side. The water deterred the little one, but the watchful older one, attracted by the slight ruckkus, came over and waded into the stream after him.

Andy ran toward the south end of the valley, though all he could see ahead were sheer cliffs. He ran into the brush and out again, but the beasts bounded after him and he became exhausted. He glanced up and there, high in the sky, was the eagle. He waved his arms sideways and then put his fingers to his teeth and gave a shrill whistle. Maybe the eagle would recognize it, having heard him whistle at the ranch. Sure enough, it began circling. He couldn't stop running, but had to stay out in the open so the eagle could see him. The eagle came lower, and he could see that it was carrying something in its talons. He couldn't watch it. He had to keep running. Suddenly he fell. The largest beast was almost upon him. As he scrambled to his feet, he looked back. The eagle had dropped a baby antelope and was attacking the largest beast furiously, flying into its eyes with talons extended. The beast was being successfully deterred from the chase, and the smaller one had stopped and was gorging itself on the antelope. Andy slowed down, wiped his brow, but continued to make some progress.

When he looked back again, the larger beast had gone back to look at the feast the young one was having. Then the eagle, as though to make sure that Andy was all right, swooped down ahead of him and rested on a boulder. Andy ran up to it and, taking no further chances of being left behind, hooked the riata, which was still around its neck, to his harness. The eagle looked around nervously and suddenly took off. The great beast, finding the morsel of antelope too small to hold its interest, had taken up the pursuit again and missed Andy's dangling body by inches as the eagle climbed in flight. As they passed over the south end of the valley, headed in the direction of Andy's ranch, Andy watched the landscape below and saw the answer to the valley entrance. It was as though erosion had left a wall of rock standing apart from a narrow opening but extending beyond the sides of the opening, which to anyone approaching on the ground, would give the appearance of a solid wall of rock and which probably accounted for its having remained undiscovered. Andy could see the beast running along on the ground and heading for the opening on the right. It probably expected Andy to fall into its clutches as the baby antelope had fallen into the smaller beast's.

As they sailed along, Andy mulled over ways to close the valley. From the great height, Andy could survey the landscape for miles, and he suddenly spotted Clyde below, on his horse and leading Andy's. He could also see the beast following their flight from behind. If he could only have warned Clyde or have talked to the eagle. Then he saw that Clyde had seen them and was waving his arms. He began to jump and tug on the riata with all his strength. At first the eagle paid no heed and they passed over Clyde and the horses, but then the eagle began to swing downward. Clyde whistled and released Andy's horse. The horse ran on ahead. Then Andy whistled and as the eagle came down, Andy got into the saddle on his horse and quickly unhooked the riata and turned to wait for Clyde. Clyde had seen the beast and was racing toward Andy. The eagle circled back and flew into the face of the beast, which beat the air with its short arms in fury, but continued in their direction. When Andy realized that they were nearing the town, he thought to distract the beast by changing directions, but it had already got the scent of the horses and stock and headed straight for the main street.

The eagle circled, almost as though ready to give up the fight, but, at Andy's whistle, it returned and followed the beast into town. The appearance of the beast sent horses running away, wagons and contents spilling along behind. People screamed and ran for cover, and a state of general confusion reigned. The eagle made a few low passes at the beast as it stood for a few seconds, looking around, bewildered by the buildings.

Andy climbed up on a balcony and threw a rope over its head, while Clyde roped it from his horse. This distracted it for a time, and in response to Andy's whistle, the eagle came back at it with a vengeance. The beast's arms became tangled in the ropes. Suddenly it dropped to the ground, writhed in pain a second and was still. The great talon of the eagle had pierced its brain, killing it almost instantly. People crowded around while Andy told the story of the valley and discussions began as to ways of closing it. Later, as Andy and Clyde jogged peacefully toward home, they saw the eagle become a tiny speck in the sky and watched until they could see it no longer.

Umbah

> *Author's Note:* The original material for "Umbah," written by Willis and Darlyne O'Brien, consists of three pages of scenes, giving characters, locations and figures for animation; two four-page versions of the story idea entitled "The Story of 'Umbah' in a Nutshell," one 14-page version (which is presented here, together with the "nutshell" version) and three storyboards painted in watercolor by Obie that show only the villain Tavotz. There is no date with this story.

NOTE: The names of Umbah and Tavotz were taken from the ancient Indian legend of the creation of the Grand Canyon. Umbah was a warrior and Tavotz was the storm god.

LOCATION: The Grand Canyon, natural masterpiece of awe-inspiring beauty.

PRINCIPLE CAST: Tom Hardage: just 21, born and brought up in New York, heir to a ranch in Arizona that had belonged to his uncle of the same name.

Sharon Oliver: a girl of 19, born and brought up on the cattle ranch adjoining that of Tom Hardage and recently orphaned.

Frank Oliver: Sharon's unscrupulous uncle and executor of the Oliver ranch.

The Old One: a very old Indian, father of Umbah, chief of the cliff dwellers.

Willis O'Brien's illustrations showing the villain Tavotz from his story idea, "Umbah."

FIGURES FOR ANIMATION (results of Dr. Hardage's experiment):
Umbah: a 15-foot Indian giant with a very large head, long arms and a good disposition; can talk some.

Tavotz the Bad One: a giant Indian, even larger than Umbah, but cruel, cunning and mentally regressed.

A horntoad, over 15 feet long.

A gila monster, at least 30 feet, keeping same characteristics except the legs, which are longer for better animation.

The Important Action Situations

NOTE: The scenes are best depicted by sketches and paintings.

1. The descent of Tom Hardage and Sharon Oliver into a deep bowl in the earth, by rope ladder.
2. Their experience with a 20-foot horned toad.

3. Battle of the Indian and giant horned toad.

4. The escape of Tom and Sharon from Tavotz the Bad One, to the caves of the cliff dwellers.

5. Battle between the cliff dwellers and the giant Tavotz.

6. Tavotz stealing Sharon from the cave.

7. Boy rescuing girl (good chase).

8. Tavotz being attacked by the giant Gila monster (exciting fight).

9. Tom and Sharon climbing a rope ladder, almost reaching the top.

10. Tavotz trying to throw them off by whipping the ladder.

11. Tavotz pulling on the rope ladder, dislodging a pinnacle rock, causing a landslide that opens up an exit from a bowllike valley.

12. Tavotz pursuing Tom and Sharon through the badlands.

13. Umbah, some of the Indians and a few of the giant animals leaving the valley through the new exit.

14. Tom and Sharon hiding in a ranch barn. Tavotz, searching for them, pushes over a windmill, tears the roof of the house off and causes the stock to stampede. Tom and Sharon escape in a ranch truck.

15. Tavotz, on the highway, wrecking cars and trucks, continuing the search.

16. Tom and Sharon are stranded on the edge of the Grand Canyon when the truck breaks down. Tavotz is about to reach them when Umbah enters the scene. Terrible fight ensues between the giants, ending in both falling into the Grand Canyon.

17. Tom and Sharon return to ranch, find everything in a turmoil, guns firing, stock running about, buildings flattened and a huge gila monster tearing a man apart.

18. Tom takes a long cow pole, mounts a horse and runs the cow pole through breast of the gila monster.

19. Death throes of the gila monster.

The Story of Umbah in a Nutshell

Registered, Writer's Guild of America–West, No. 66842

Dr. Tom Hardage had come to the remote regions of the Grand Canyon to carry out experiments on animals without interference from the curious and the restrictions of city life. The West was young, and the region sparsely inhabited. He lived there for many years and, when he died, willed his ranch to his nephew, of the same name. The nephew lost no time in coming west to claim his inheritance and found his nearest neighbor, Sharon Oliver, an interesting and sportsmanlike girl. They became great companions, and when Tom found his uncle's diary containing accounts of giant animals he had produced with his experiments, she became as obsessed as Tom with a desire to visit the remote valley and see the results.

Sharon's uncle, Frank Oliver, having been appointed executor of the Oliver estate after the death of Sharon's parents and harboring plans to usurp her rightful property, was only too happy to encourage her to accompany Tom and volunteered the assistance, on their trek, of one of his henchmen, planning to prevent her return. The morning following their first day's journey, they left the man at camp and, following the meticulously drawn map found in the diary, they came to the bowl in the earth, well marked by a pinnacle rock that the doctor had used as an anchor for a rope ladder, by which they descended into the valley. Their first encounter was with a huge horned toad from which they were unexpectedly saved by a giant Indian, Umbah, who killed the beast with his great bow and arrow. Their next encounter was with another Indian, not friendly. Tavotz the Bad One, a cruel, demented creature, caused them to flee for their lives to the sanctuary of the caves of cliff dwellers, high in the cliffs, where the ladders could be drawn up and there was no other ascent. There they met the Old One, Umbah's father. He told them that Tavotz had tried many times to kill Umbah, that Umbah was good and that Tavotz's father hated the white doctor because Umbah was smarter than Tavotz.

The Old One and his people well understood Tom and Sharon's plight and pelted the giant below with boulders and arrows, driving him away. But during the night, Tavotz returned and ingeniously contrived to get up the cliff far enough to reach into the cave where the girl was asleep and steal her. Tom could not prevent Tavotz from taking her, but followed them instead. When Tavotz was attacked by a giant gila monster and was forced to drop her, Tom succeeded in reaching her side, and together they raced to the rope ladder, almost reaching the top by the time Tavotz subdued the beast and found them. Tavotz tried to throw them off by whipping the ladder, but instead caused the pinnacle rock to dislodge, bringing down a landslide and opening up an exit from the valley.

Tom and Sharon threw themselves clear of the slide, but it caught Tavotz, and they were well away from him before he could extricate himself and take up the pursuit again. Umbah, a few of the Indians and

Willis O'Brien's illustration of Tavotz from "Umbah."

one or two giant animals also made their way out of the valley. Sharon and Tom hid in the barn on the first ranch they came to and, Tavotz, furiously searching for them, pushed over the windmill, tore off part of the roof on the house, and caused the stock to stampede. Sharon and Tom slipped out to a ranch truck and got away. Tavotz followed along the highway, tipping over cars and trucks coming his way, still searching for them.

Suddenly, on a high curve at the edge of a sheer drop into the canyon, the truck refused to go any farther. Tavotz was nearing them when Umbah burst out of the forest. Umbah and Tavotz became engaged in a terrible battle, ending with both falling into the canyon. Sharon and Tom went on until they came to another ranch and found everything in turmoil, buildings flattened, stock running wild, and a giant gila monster tearing at a man. Tom, seeing that bullets had no effect on the beast, grabbed a cow pole and mounted a horse. Running full speed at the beast, he drove the pole through its breast. The beast writhed and twisted in agony and died. Though they were exhausted, Tom and Sharon borrowed a truck and hurried to warn the ranchers in the area to beware of other giant creatures that might have gotten out of the valley but when they returned to the Oliver ranch, found that they were too late. Frank Oliver had been killed by a giant gila monster as it had passed through the vicinity, hell-bent on destruction.

Umbah

Author's Note: What follows is taken from the full 14-page version of the story that contains different character names and different situations.

Bob Stratam, owner of The Golden Sage, a new and fabulous hotel in Las Vegas, seeking publicity for it, hired a Hollywood stuntman, Harry Barbee, to navigate a small, jet-propelled craft of new design up the Colorado River. Maureen Gayle, a beautiful swimming star from the hotel, accompanied him. The stunt was well publicized, and the takeoff attracted many tourists and onlookers. The trip was televised from cameras set up along the river and was followed with interest by many people across the country. The little craft, streamlined, with wings, looked much like a small plane and could be refueled from helicopters en transit. It seemed barely to touch the water as it circled Lake Mead and skimmed over the rapids of the Colorado, much as a salmon would swim upstream, and seemingly the trip was going to be a great success.

Maureen and Harry safely negotiated the river to the clean, sandy banks below Phantom Ranch in the Grand Canyon, where the television cameras and crews and newspaper reporters were to interview them. After hot food and a rest, they set out to buck more rapids and to reach the next television setup at Lee's Ferry. The weather became threatening, and by the time they reached the end of Granite Gorge, it was raining very hard and the river was rising rapidly from heavy rains in the backcountry. Soon the full blast of the storm came sweeping down upon them, and they were forced to abandon the craft at a tiny, protected cove and climb to a shelf under overhanging rocks up the side of the canyon.

They sat for some time, huddled in their shelter, when they were startled by the roar of falling boulders and tons of earth washing down into the river. The slide continued for several minutes and opened up a vista of rocky, perpendicular canyon walls leading far, far back into country, obviously closed to the outside world until that time.

When the storm subsided, they carefully made their way across the slide into the canyon and along the higher ground, hoping to discover a way to the mesa above, where help could reach them more easily. They began to see many caves that showed evidence of once having been occupied but were now deserted. It was growing dark, and, to their joy, they saw the glow of a fire coming from a cave far above them with ladders leading up to it. They were puzzled by the fact that beside the normal-sized ladder was one with rungs some four feet apart and jocularly remarked that perhaps giants were expected. They climbed the ladder and reached what appeared to be an empty cave. As their eyes became accustomed to the semidarkness, they saw, huddled back against the rock wall, a wrinkled old Indian who was watching them silently. They made gestures and, to their surprise, were answered in broken English. He offered them food, such as it was, and bitter tea of some kind. Harry noticed bows some 20 feet long and arrows in proportion.

Harry went to them, picked one up and asked the old man if they were his, but the old man said that they were his son's. Harry thought surely the old Indian's mind must be gone and interpreted Maureen's glance to mean that she thought so, too. Harry put the weapon back and returned to the fire. Just then the top of the ladder began to move, and the old man said, "Umbah come now." Soon the giant, misshapen features appeared above the top of the ladder. Harry and Maureen were stupefied at his size. He was at least 20 feet tall. His body and arms were long and powerful, his legs short and bowed. He was attired in a long blouse of gila monster skins that they thought, at first glance, to be heavy. His hair was done after the manner of the Navajos, with a red band and knots of hair at the back. He carried two good-sized deer in one hand, as an ordinary person would carry rabbits. In the other hand he held a huge, dead gila monster, and one of his arms was bleeding from its bite. Harry remarked on the size of it, and the old man said, "More, more big one."

Umbah stared curiously at Maureen and Harry for a long moment and then dropped the gila monster and the deer, explaining to his father that the gila monster had tried to take his deer from him. The old man looked closely at the bleeding arm and said something like "Must cure now." Umbah sat down, crosslegged, studying Maureen and Harry intently. It was evident that he did not have the intelligence of his father but was good natured and slow. Although his features were horrifying to look upon, they felt that they had nothing to fear from him.

The old man busied himself back in the cave with extensive preparations for some time and then called Umbah to him. Umbah sat down, and the old man began a weird chant, making a design of colored sand on the floor as he sang. The scent of incense was in the air. Umbah sat, nodding drowsily and looking very ill for a time. When the chant was finished, he rolled up in a blanket and slept. Harry asked the old man if Umbah would be all right, and the old man said, "Him sleep now, all right tomorrow." He then said, "You sleep now; come, I show you. No gila come." He gave them blankets from pegs in the wall of the cave, and they followed him to an opening in the cliff wall not far from his cave. The space through which they entered was so narrow that it was necessary for them to turn sideways and enter one by one.

The moonlight was as bright as day, and from the reflection of it on the clean sand in front of the cave, they could see that the interior was very clean, though totally unfurnished. They rolled up in the blankets and prepared to sleep. After some time they heard a ladder being placed along the side of the cliff and soon it creaked under some tremendous weight. They looked out and saw another giant, more hideous looking than Umbah. He was deeply scarred, which added to his vicious appearance. Luckily, there was a ledge of boulders protruding from the rear wall of the cave where they took refuge, for this was no good-natured creature, and he growled menacingly as he tried to reach in for them. The small opening would not allow his great hulk to pass, and the cave, hollowed out of solid rock, made it impossible for him to break in. He succeeded in grasping Harry for a second, but Umbah, disturbed by the growling and commotion, came out and, with an angry roar, pulled him away. They were at each other's throats then and the cliff shook under the impact of their giant bodies when they fell to the ground. They struggled and fought furiously, Umbah coming out the victor and Tavotz, *the bad one*, crashing to the rocks below. The old man had come to watch and explained: "Tavotz bad. He try kill Umbah many times." Then he and Umbah went back to their cave, and the rest of the night was uneventful.

After the experience of the night before, Harry and Maureen, worried about their chances of reaching the mesa safely, asked the old man if there were other giant creatures about. He said, "Don't know how many; Umbah take you." They thanked him for that, and he, reliving the excitement of the night, talked on and on about Umbah and Tavotz, the bad one. He said, "Tavotz, he bad son. Umbah good, always good."

"White man, he make Tavotz and Umbah grow big. Other babies, too. Women of tribe afraid. Kill big babies and white man. Go 'way. Say white man make gods angry. Me chief. Me stay with sons." Harry asked who the white man was. He said, "Come, you see." He took them to a cave that was very large with two small windows high in the wall. There were rough furniture and bunks filled with dusty pine boughs and, in the far end, crude benches on which were scores of chemists' flasks and bottles containing the flakes of fluids long since dried up. Everything was covered with layers of dust, but, upon poking about, they found a pile of old books and papers. The old man, evidently willing for them to see them, dug them out. There was a very large book of yellowed parchment pages, written in a strange script they could not read. Then he brought a smaller one, leather covered. They blew the dust off it and opened it. The signature read Dr. Wm. Hardage, and the first entry was dated February 12, 1900.

Harry and Maureen became engrossed in reading the diary, and the old man slipped out and left them there. The entries, covering a 10-year period, told of experiments on various animals of the region and of the remarkable size and grotesque shapes they were attaining. Then, on May 10, 1910, there was an entry that told of the chief of a tribe of Indians living nearby having come to ask that he cause the men of the tribe to grow like the animals so they could vanquish their enemies, and brought his two small sons to live with him. Subsequent entries told of his refusals and of the persistence of the chief and the other men of the tribe and expressed trepidation as to the future if he did not comply and, finally, of his torture and being *forced* to treat the babies of the tribe. The entries skipped over some years, then one appeared expressing fear that the oldest son of the chief, Tavotz, although growing, was mentally regressing to a primitive state. There were no other entries. Harry and Maureen concluded that his death must have occurred at that time.

They closed the book and went back to the old chief's cave to bid him good-bye. Then they started on, what was for them, the long trek across the canyon.

Umbah, covering ground with his giant strides, found many opportunities to sit and rest while he waited for them to catch up. Once, when he had gotten out of their sight, he heard Maureen scream and call his name. He returned to find them crouching behind boulders, watching a giant gila monster and a giant snake locked in furious battle. The struggle continued for moments, then the gila monster, having had enough, crawled away. The snake, aroused to action, looked about for further prey and came toward Harry and Maureen. Umbah, watching from a little distance, came into the scene and attracted the attention of the snake. Umbah grappled with it, but his wit and strength were too much for it, and he soon killed it.

The pathway up the cliffs, on the other side of the canyon, was so narrow that Umbah's shoulders brushed boulders from the sides as he passed, but Harry and Maureen were far behind to escape the danger of being crushed. When they reached a small plateau near the top of the cliff, Umbah gestured that he would lead them up to the mesa from there and for them to wait while he went on. Maureen was frightened, but Umbah was so gentle in helping them that she regretted having misjudged his simple heart. The old man had given Umbah a basket of pine nuts for them to eat and the proper sticks to start a fire that Umbah showed them how to use. The fire helped the 'copter pilot (who was still searching for them) to locate them when he returned, and they were picked up and taken back to Vegas safely. Umbah watched them take off, with an expression of dumb wonderment and admiration.

When Stratam heard of their strange experience, he immediately saw the possibility of a great publicity stunt and became determined to bring Umbah and the giant gila monster to Vegas and put them in a show. He took the gamble that he could do so and made great preparations.

A large outdoor set was built, with a huge painted backdrop. A large hogan was built, to house Umbah and his father and an elaborate cage was constructed for the gila monster. The 'copter pilot knew the approximate location where he had picked Harry and Maureen up, and Stratam prepared to go there and stay a month if necessary. When everything was set, Harry and Maureen returned to the mesa with Stratam and several photographers and took them to the cave of the old chief. They had very little difficulty in persuading him to give his consent to their plan, after which they returned to the mesa. Stratam lost no time in starting operations. From the radio-phone in the 'copter, he called for several more 'copters, large steel nets and two large trucks. Then they set up camp and prepared to wait for the equipment to arrive. When the 'copters arrived with the nets, Umbah searched for the giant gila monster, but discovered that it had gone down the Grand Canyon through the new opening to the outside world.

Reports began to come in on the 'copter radio of the destruction the gila monster was causing as it meandered down the river. The 'copters sought it out and followed it, reporting back to Stratam. When it reached the flat country, Stratam and the trucks went to the location, Umbah, bouncing and jouncing along in the rear of the truck, thoroughly enjoying the ride.

They encountered no difficulty dropping the nets over the giant gila monster and, in thrashing about, it entangled itself so thoroughly that Umbah easily tied it securely. It was hoisted to the bed of the truck by crane and the trip back to Vegas was uneventful. Stratam really had something to exploit and went all out with advertising. The crowds that flocked to Vegas were unprecedented and the show was a colossal success. But keeping a giant, wild thing like the gila monster was a constant problem. Umbah, to provide extra thrills for the spectators, would enter its cage and tantalize it to action, side-stepping its onrushes with great agility, until one night, as he was leaving the cage, it slid past him and out into the street.

The gila monster roamed at will, turning this way and that, and creating panic and havoc as it became more and more frightened. Gangs of police could do nothing more than herd people away from the danger, and Umbah did the best he could do, hampered as he was by his great size and unable to enter some places. The chase led him far out into the desert where he was bitten by the gila monster and forced to kill it to escape being killed. Harry, Stratam, Maureen and the old chief had followed by car, of course, and Umbah, knowing what the bite meant, gathered his father up in his arms and headed into the desert. He did not know that he was going directly across the forbidden territory of an atom bomb proving grounds.

They all pleaded with him not to go, but he would not listen, crying urgently that he "must cure bite." He stepped easily over the high steel fence and, just as the dawn was breaking, was silhouetted for just one instant in the light of the exploding bomb. A sad end to another of man's futile attempts to improve on God's handiwork.

Matilda, or the Isle of Women

Author's Note: In a letter from Darlyne O'Brien to Mike Hankin, dated March 16, 1982, she mentions "The Giant Pelican"—an idea Obie had developed with writer Jerry Cady about the Marx brothers being shipwrecked on a prehistoric island. She said about the idea:

> The story about the Marx Brothers and a "Giant Pelican" was never really a story. Obie and I had written a comedy which we called "Isle of Women," which Obie had thought would be good for Lum and Abner, a popular radio team at that time, but he made some sketches using the Marx Brothers just to see how it would go and, unfortunately, he let a writer borrow those sketches and the writer committed suicide and we never got them back. And they were so wonderful, too!

> The "Matilda" story idea is one of two original 11-page versions that were both typed, but with no dates. A third incomplete five-page version was also written, which appears to have been torn up and then stuck back together again with tape.

Elmos Grubb, a shy, corpulent dreamer is sleeping soundly under a tree at the far corner of the little ranch where he lives with his mother. All around him, in various stages of dozing, are his pet mule, at least three dogs, a rooster and a couple of hens. His pleasant nap is interrupted by his mother's heartiest hog-call, which to Elmos means that something unusual is afoot. He stirs himself and with various sounds, urges his troupe of pets to follow as he walks toward the house, scanning the front yard for the cause of the interruption of his siesta.

As he draws near, his mother beckons anxiously, excited that his old pal Horace Pie has come back from the city to see him, having been gone for several years. Visitors are rare at their place, especially visitors from the city and especially someone who *might* inspire a spark of ambition in Elmos, so Ma Grubb hastens to make the visitor welcome. The greetings are hearty, and Elmos is visibly awed by Horace's city clothes and his manifest wealth, but is unresponsive to Horace's enthusiasm for his job as a salesman and his city girlfriend. Elmos had a girl once; Tildy was her name. Having been somewhat of a dreamer, too, she and Elmos could spend hours together without saying much. That was what Elmos had liked. He not only didn't want his dreaming disturbed by conversation, and feared most women, although he didn't fear Tildy.

But Tildy was persuaded by someone else and went away with her new love. After that, Elmos was less interested than ever in women. Horace, having a flair for fantastic ideas *gets one* as he watches the pigs devour the garbage Elmos pours into their pen. He thought that they were almost as good as the new electric garbage disposal units he had seen in the city and though somewhat crude, would still serve the same purpose for rural dwellers. He glibly talks Elmos into the idea of peddling his pigs for that purpose. Finally Elmos gets the spark and agrees to do so.

They first approach the Widow Watkins, who is more progressive than most of her neighbors, and Horace has little trouble convincing her of the advantage it would be to have their deluxe model with the three pigs, telling her that they will install it free and how nice it will be in bad weather, and how she will be keeping up with the city folk. She and Horace have tea in the parlor while Elmos makes the installation, with much hammering and sawing of wood. When he is finished, he invites her to try it. She puts some greens and other scraps down the hole and the pigs under the sink begin to grunt loudly and enthusiastically. When Horace sees the widow's consternation at the noise, he assures her that in a day or two the pigs will get used to the idea and will quiet down; talking constantly, he urges her back to the parlor. She is about to pay Horace for the job when the pigs break out with a crash and rush squealing into the room, knocking her down, upsetting the what-not, lamp tables, and tea table, making a terrible mess of everything. Elmos and Horace are helpless to stop them. Horace helps her up and she races for the broom, chasing Elmos, Horace, the pigs and all out of the house, denouncing them as frauds and assuring them in no uncertain terms that she will have the law on them for the damage they have done.

When Elmos and Horace return to the ranch, they see the constable on the porch talking to Ma Grubb. The constable is the *last* person they want to see just then, so Elmos turns the mule and wagon around and hustles up the road. Ma Grubb, thinking Elmos must be crazy, sends the constable after them. Elmos turns off onto a very bumpy side road leading to a creek and loses the crate of pigs en route. In the middle of the stream, the mule stops to drink, and nothing short of dynamite could move him. The constable, bouncing and jouncing along in his old car, is delayed somewhat by the pigs scrambling over the road but finally arrives at the edge of the creek. Horace and Elmos stay in midstream until the constable assures them impatiently that he only wants to give Elmos some important papers. Elmos thanks the constable nervously and passes the papers to Horace to read. Horace's face lights up as he reads them and informs Elmos excitedly that Elmos has *inherited a carnival*, troupe and all, from his deceased uncle, Josiah P. Grubb. Elmos, never having seen a carnival, wonders what he will do with it, but Horace, seeing a new field for his own talents as a salesman, promoter, inventor and what-not, assures him that he will help him run it and they'll make a million. Elmos agrees to go 50-50 and takes him in as a partner.

The carnival is located on the outskirts of San Francisco, and Elmos and Horace go there to make their claim as the new owners. Josiah Grubb's *former* right-hand man, a big burly fellow, sees his own plans for acquiring the carnival going astray. He resents the intrusion of these two, but cooly consents to take them on a quick inspection tour. They see the usual concessions of chance games, the Ferris wheel, the merry-go-round, the sideshow of freaks, the fortune teller, the tent for a few animal acts and the gas balloon and basket, which fascinates Elmos more than anything else. Seeing an opportunity to get rid of these new claimants, the big fellow winks slyly at a wily little fellow who has been lurking in the background and encourages them to get into the basket, promising to ascend with them. Once they are in, he quickly sends the balloon up and cuts the anchoring ropes. Carried by a stiff breeze, they are soon far out to sea.

Having passed a very uncomfortable night, Elmos grieves for the comfort of his quiet life at home, but Horace, ever the optimist, assures him that this is the greatest thing yet, that when they return they will have their names in all the papers and can write a book about their adventures. Elmos, feeling not at all reassured, gazes longingly down and sees an island ahead. Horace begins trying gadgets and stumbles onto a valve that released the gas from the bag. The balloon loses altitude fast and drifts toward the island, passing over a lake and finally catching in the top of a tall tree. Elmos and Horace are shaken up by the sudden stop and after surveying the situation decide to cut the ropes from the balloon to assist them in getting down from the tree.

They are busily engaged in cutting the ropes when they hear a crackling of branches nearby. Elmos looks over the side and frantically pulls Horace down to the floor of the basket. A huge brontosaurus has come out of the lake to investigate this strange thing in the trees. It nudges the basket and looks over the side; neither Horace or Elmos dare to move. It takes the basket in its jaws and lifts it free from the tree, carrying it to a small clearing where it sets it down with a bump. Before they have a chance to scramble out, the animal grabs Elmos by the pants and lifts him in the air. Horace makes a run for it, but the brontosaurus (whom they call "Bronty") sees him, drops Elmos and gives chase. Horace ducks in and out among the trees, giving Elmos a chance to get away also. They race through the jungle, calling to each other, and meet again at another clearing. Exhausted, they lie down under hanging vines and shrubbery. Elmos, chiding Horace about his *great* knowledge, asks for an explanation of the Bronty. Horace informs him that it is a "dinnysoorus," but that he is puzzled as to how it could be living in this day and age. Feeling that they are safe for the moment and being tired and hungry, they lie down and soon fall into a sound sleep.

The brontosaurus seeks them out and waits patiently until they awaken. Elmos tries to scramble away, but the animal gently pulls him back by the seat of his pants and proceeds to lick his face with its long tongue, almost bowling him over each time. Horace quickly gets under way, which again distracts the Bronty from Elmos, and again they play hide and seek among the trees. Coming to a deep ravine, they start across on what appears to be a good-sized log. Partway over they discover that they are not making any progress. They fall to their knees and hang on for dear life, riding the thing back. Bronty is waiting for them and seems overjoyed at having Elmos back, a fact that Horace calls to Elmos's attention. Elmos, with his penchant for making pets of animals, tries a little pat on its head and scratches its neck, and the animal purrs like a kitten. Feeling less afraid now, Elmos and Horace start to walk in the direction of the lake, Bronty following docilely along.

Across the lake they can see some kind of settlement and, being both tired and hungry, they seek some way over. Elmos climbs upon some rocks, scanning the countryside while Bronty still insists upon nuzzling him. This gives him a thought. He strokes its neck, working down toward its back, then gently slips one leg across. Bronty doesn't seem to mind, and Elmos says "pst! pst!" to Horace. Soon they are riding jauntily along as Bronty swims into the lake. The trip is pleasant until they attract the attention of some kind of water monster that insists on snapping at their legs. The water having made Bronty's back slippery, they have difficulty keeping out of reach of the monster's powerful jaws, but they arrive and slide off Bronty's back, searching eagerly for some sign of the inhabitants of the island. Not a sign of them can they see.

Some distance from the edge of the lake there is a huge wall, but they begin to search for fruit or berries, unaware that they are being observed by many pairs of eyes well concealed in the shrubbery. They wander along and when they converge at a small clearing, find themselves surrounded by a bevy of women dressed in skins and carrying spears. Fat ones, thin ones, short ones, homely ones, pretty ones, blonds, redheads and brunettes. Horace doesn't mind a bit, but Elmos is terrified. Not a word is spoken by the women. Horace, thinking they must speak some kind of native dialect, tries several, but they do not seem to understand. They close in on Horace and Elmos, tie their hands and feet, bind them to long spears and carry them inside the walled village, much as hunters do dead lions and tigers. There are more women and there is much oohing and ahing and chatter as they are carried to what seems to be a kind of throne. Soon a large, well-proportioned woman emerges from folds of draperies in back of the throne and, to their surprise, the women carrying them address her in fair English. The queen reprimands them for treating *men* like animals and orders Horace and Elmos to be bathed, fed and dressed in the finery of the island. Horace and Elmos are lowered gently to the ground, untied and helped to their feet by many *willing* hands. They are then escorted to the bathing pools. Horace begins to strip, but Elmos, thinking they will be left alone, delays as long as he can but the women give no sign of leaving.

When the women see Elmos hesitating, they think he wants them to help him, and they strip him down to his long underwear, with much resistance on his part. He then jumps into the water and removes his underwear under water. He refuses to allow them to soap him and shoves water at them with the palms of his hands whenever they come near the edge of the pool. Finally they get the idea and lay some clothing and drying towels nearby and draw back among the trees, peeking now and then, allowing Horace and Elmos to dress in peace. And dress in pieces is exactly what they do. The robes seem to be squares of material of various colors and textures. Horace wraps one around his legs like a diaper and one around his head like a turban and sticks the others into the diaper, allowing the points to hang down like a sash. The girls then bring him necklaces and bracelets and even large rings to hang over his ears. Elmos is too fat to make a diaper of his material, so he ties two together and makes a sarong and wraps his head like a gypsy. He, too, is supplied with a necklace and bracelets.

When they are thus arrayed, they are escorted to a feast, Horace seated on one side of Queenie and Elmos on the other. There is much giggling and tittering and the women who serve can't resist tweaking the men's ears or patting their heads or shoulders as they pass, which brings scowls and reprimands from Queenie. After the feast they are amazed at the music made by the women's orchestra on the strangest instruments: harps made from dinosaur ribs, horns from mammoth tusks, etc. Dancing begins, and Horace and Elmos are pulled this way and that, more than one fight ensuing among the women as to who shall dance with them next. Finally, exhausted, they refuse to dance again and are escorted to their sleeping quarters, Elmos carefully barring the door. The next morning it occurs to Horace to wonder if there are any men around. Intending to do a little investigating, they arise early and slip out quietly, thinking they will be unnoticed. They wander around at will for a time, but discover there are women guards around so Horace asks them about the men. A guard takes him to a grave covered with flowers and a headstone reading, "Here lies the former *fifth* husband to our queen, having entertained Her Grace faithfully for three years." Horace rubs his chin thoughtfully, thinking three years is a very short time.

After that, Horace understands Queenie's attitude toward him, and he and Elmos plot their escape. Horace, with his aptitude for showmanship, realizes what a hit the women, with their strange instruments, would be in the carnival and promises to take them where there are lots of men and persuades them to assist him and Elmos secretly to build a form of howdah to strap on Bronty's back. When the howdah is finished, the girls and Horace and Elmos take off in the early dawn and are well out to sea when their escape is discovered. But Queenie's best spear

Animation models as they looked during the 1960s. *Left to right*: **An unfinished Oso Si-Papu, a monkey for an unknown project, the worm and spider made for *King Kong*, but used for *The Black Scorpion*, and a Beetle Man model (courtesy of David Allen).**

throwers are unable to reach them with their most expert shots, and they go merrily on their way. They reach the shores of San Francisco late at night and, coming along the highway toward the carnival, cause a few pileups of late motorists who are overcome by the spectacle.

When they reach the carnival, the few workers who see Bronty take to their heels. After the rigging is removed, Bronty attempts to follow Elmos into the animal tent, ripping the whole top off and causing a stampede among the beasts. They get things under control and obtain a tent large enough for Bronty. Elmos, unable to determine Bronty's sex, if any, affectionately names her Tildy and succeeds in teaching her a number of tricks, such as balancing on a large ball while holding a seal on her head and allowing girl trapeze performers to swing from bars held in her mouth while a cannon on her back shoots a ball that the seal catches and balances on her head. Business flourishes, but Horace thinks a parade through the city would help it even more. "Tildy" is draped with gaudy velvet and gold and pulls a large float in which the women's band, with their odd instruments, ride. Behind them in a smaller float ride a few of the freaks. As they cross upper California Street, a fire truck with sirens wide open races down the street and frightens Tildy so much that she breaks loose from the float. The float rolls down California Street, the girls screaming frantically. Tildy tumbles and slides down after it, causing cars to pile up and creating general havoc. Horace and Elmos, seeing a cable car that has been abandoned by its motorman, board it and try to follow Tildy, but are unble to control it and zoom downhill, passing both Tildy and the float and land in the bay.

By this time the entire riot squad is out, but nothing can stop Tildy in her panic. She crashes through Fisherman's Wharf, and by the time Elmos and Horace are rescued from the bay and reach Golden Gate bridge in a squad car, Tildy is swimming madly out to sea.

The Last of the Oso Si-Papu

Author's Note: In a letter dated March 16, 1982, to Mike Hankin from Darlyne O'Brien, she said:

> "The Oso-Si-Papu" was based on a story of an Indian legend that I got out of *Arizona Highways* magazine. Of course, there was no description of the Si-Papu so Obie designed a sort of bearlike creature, and we added the word *oso*, which is bear in Indian. Obie was never successful in raising money to get either the "Oso Si-Papu" or "Elephant Rustlers" on the screen before he died. He just didn't seem to know how to push things, and it wasn't his disposition. He would rather be creating something new. He was very young for his age, and childlike, enjoyed playing and having fun, and I did, too. I can't find anyone else like him.

O'Brien made 90 small watercolor storyboards and seven large illustrations and wrote a 10-page technical supplement and an 18-page story idea for "The Last of the Oso Si-Papu." After the death of Peter Peterson, an animation model of the Si-Papu was found in a collection of other animation models from "The Black Scorpion," "The Giant Behemoth," "The Las Vegas Monster," "The Beetle Men" and a model ape dressed as a bellhop for a TV commercial.

(Note: Oso Si-Papu is Indian for "bear from the darkness of the underworld.)

Tom Mederson, a personable young man, free from college studies for the summer, is scanning the help-wanted ads. He is immediately interested in one with an Arizona address, requiring a young man with the ability to ride well and be an expert in the use of the bow. Tom excels at

A closer view of the Oso Si-Papu animation model and a monkey as a bellhop model for an unknown TV commercial (photo courtesy of Jim Danforth).

both, having won a championship in archery. His application accepted, he outfits himself with new jeans, a 10-gallon hat, and high-heeled boots and goes by train to a small town where he transfers to an ancient bus that bumps over unpaved, washboard roads to the one-street town of Haden, which bears the same name as the ranch where he is going. Haden consists of a small hotel with a combined restaurant and saloon, a general store, a garage, a few small shacks and corrals. Scores of Indians, their wagons loaded with their belongings, are passing through the town, and, Tom notes, a group of whites and Indians is waiting to take the bus back. Tom goes into the bar to inquire the way to the Haden ranch, which, he assumes, is a dude ranch. The bartender informs him that it is about 10 miles out, but that it is not a dude ranch. Tom, recalling the specification for bow and arrow, ponders this for a moment then asks why the migration?

The bartender says, rather derisively, that the Indians believe that some demon or demons from the badlands are coming and will destroy them, as they say happened years ago. At that moment, Jean Haden, a

The animation model for the Oso Si-Papu (photo courtesy of Jim Danforth).

beautiful, wholesome-looking girl, enters the bar and asks Tom if he is the new man her father is expecting and tells him she has come for him in the jeep. On the way to the ranch, Jean tells him of the Indian superstition and that her father, a retired professor, has made a lifelong study of the Indians and believes there may be some truth in what they say. Therefore, he and Dr. Thaddeus Brown, paleontologist at the university, have made plans to try and capture whatever it is the Indians fear. Tom is thrilled at the prospect of such excitement, but has no time to question her further because they have arrived at the ranch.

After introductions, Professor Haden takes Tom into the study to meet Dr. Brown and Ha-Ta-Lih, a very old Indian man. Ha-Ta-Lih has been a frequent visitor and has come this day to tell his friends that the signs are increasing that the Si-Papu are getting close. Ha-Ta-Lih assures them that the other Indians are leaving but that he intends to stay with

The last of the Oso Si-Papu try to tear each other apart in a violent battle to the death.

his friends, then stands quietly by as Tom and the professor begin to talk. He studies Tom closely for a few moments before slipping silently away. Indians never say good-bye. Professor Haden explains to Tom that the legend is that the beasts come to life only once in many moons, like locusts, and then kill everything in sight. The deer and other animals sense when they are coming and run far into the forests, and the buzzards follow the beasts, in huge flocks, to clean up the kill.

He shows Tom a crude drawing made on a piece of hide. Ha-Ta-Lih claims that this was made by his great-greatgrandfather. It is very, very old but the picture plainly shows a great bearlike creature, covered with scales like a gila monster. It stands at least 20 feet high, holding and eating a buffalo. Many Indians are depicted shooting at it, and a great flock of buzzards hover over it. Dr. Brown says he thinks its height to be somewhat exaggerated, but shows Tom a portion of a great skull, with teeth almost a foot long, which belonged to no animal ever known to have lived.

All this whets Tom's anticipation, and when Professor Haden explains

The Si-Papu awakens from its drugged sleep and attacks film producer Joe Kane and his camera crew.

that they plan to capture one of the beasts by shooting it full of arrows tipped with hypodermic needles filled with dope, he is keen for the adventure. The next morning finds Tom trying out horses, finally selecting one and putting it through its paces. He practices arrow shots at various and difficult targets. Jean watches with interest and encourages him. They find that they are very compatible. Responding to the dinner gong, they are surprised to find the professor talking rather heatedly to several strange men. The comings and goings of the Indians arouse little local interest, normally, but this migration, being unusually hurried and large, causes Jared Drake, the editor of the *County Seat News Weekly*, to inquire about what is causing the stir.

Always hoping to win himself some national recognition, Jared gives a short account of the legend and migration to the leading wire services. The item is read and noted by Joe Kane, a producer of cheap, monster movies. Deeming this an opportunity to get scenes of a beast without cost, to cut into a picture later, he hires a photographer and assistant, and they invite themselves out to the professor's ranch, arriving a day after

Tom. The professor is annoyed that the news has been given out and resents the intrusion of these strangers. He refuses to allow them to accompany him to the pueblo, stating that the Indians would not allow it and tells them they will have to wait until the beast is captured.

Joe and the boys leave, politely, though secretly undaunted in their determination to accomplish what they have come for. A day or two later, Ha-Ta-Lih's nephew, Sin-ha-lo, rides into the ranch, his pony on a dead run. He tells Professor Haden that the Si-Papu are not far away from the pueblo and there is not much time to get the old people and the children away. Everything has been well organized, and the professor sends Sin-ha-lo away with the promise that all shall be saved. Red, Max and Bill, three top hands, are summoned, and the big truck, tractor and trailer and a smaller truck are sent on ahead to the pueblo.

Dr. Brown, Professor Haden, Tom and Jean mount their horses and follow the trucks. The pueblo is situated on a high mesa at the edge of the badlands, a grim, forbidding expanse of huge boulders, sheer cliffs and deep canyons. The trip is a scenic one, taking them across bridges, the river a mere ribbon below, through deep canyons, warmed by the sun only at high noon, and under overhanging boulders of immense size. As they approach the mesa, they can see on the horizon a great, dark flock of buzzards, continually circling. They hear drums beating an insistent rhythm. From the tiny houses and along the narrow streets, the old and children are being helped into the waiting trucks. A few of the young, strong Indian men wait, tensely, on the terraced roof.

The professor's plan of action is deliberately to draw the beast toward the pueblo, into more open country. Jean and Tom, equipped with his bow and arrows, ensconce themselves on a rooftop. A steer is staked out, for bait, a little distance from the pueblo, and Dr. Brown and the professor ride toward the badlands. Tom carefully lays out the arrows, and everyone waits tensely. They can see nothing on the horizon for a time — then suddenly, a huge hulk of a beast is silhouetted against the sky. A shout goes up, and the drums stop. The beast stands for a moment, then, it ambles along behind boulders for a time, but its direction is unquestionably toward the pueblo. Those on the rooftops catch glimpses of Dr. Brown and the professor as they ride through the sagebrush and trees, directly in its path. They are not unaware that it is drawing near. The circling buzzards give them warning, and they stop now and again to listen for the crashing of brush and falling rocks.

Opposite: **A design of the Oso Si-Papu by O'Brien in watercolor.**

The Si-Papu chases one of the men into the desert valley...

The beast also moves with caution, making it difficult for them to judge their distance from it. At last, as they circle a huge rock, they come face to face with the monstrous creature. It rises from a crouch with an earthshaking roar, reaching a height of 20 feet or more, as it stands on its hind legs. Here before them — alive — is a monster that has never been recorded in the scientific annals of the ages. The beast lunges clumsily toward them, but misses. Professor Haden wheels his horse, perilously near it, swinging his hat in the air and yelling. The beast takes off after him.

The horses easily outrun the hulking beast as Dr. Brown and the professor maneuver carefully and dangerously, ducking in and out from behind boulders, drawing it on until it will be attracted to the steer and be within shooting distance for Tom. Both riders cleverly sidle away as the beast comes nearer the steer. Tom, bow and arrow poised, waits. Jean stands by with other arrows to pass on him. The beast comes in on all fours. Tom shoots, the arrow glancing off, unable to pierce the armor of the beast. The steer threshes madly about, straining to break its bonds. With one swipe of its huge paw, the beast knocks the steer over and, gathering it up, stands and sinks its foot-long fangs into the warm flesh.

At that instant, a shout is heard from the rooftop. Another of the

. . .and corners him and an associate near a mountain.

Si-Papu is arriving on the scene. Instantly, the first beast becomes a monstrous, bristlng mountain of anger and menace. The ground and walls of the pueblo shake as the two creatures roar at one another.

A series of quick cuts to Tom, Jean, the Indians, Dr. Brown and the professor on the rooftops.

As the beasts thrash about in mortal battle, walls are caved in, corners of buildings are broken off and everyone is forced to scramble for refuge on higher roofs. Tom is unable to get in a shot until the battle subsides and one beast is the victor. It stands, dazed for an instant, facing him. Then Tom hits the vital spot. The beast paws at the arrow, vainly trying to pull it out. The dope takes effect quickly and the beast staggers about, fighting to keep its senses. It drops on all fours, paws the dirt, and almost pitiful in its helplessness, sprawls full length and is still. Everyone gathers around the terrifying mounds of monsters, but keeps a safe distance. Professor Haden advises Tom to drive another arrow into the living creature, to forestall any possibility of the dope wearing off while they are loading it onto the trailer.

The professor and Dr. Brown supervise the loading and send Red on alone with the tractor pulling the trailer on which the beast is securely chained, telling him that Tom will follow and dope the beast again if necessary. After inspecting the dead animal at great length and instructing

Max and Bill in skinning it, Dr. Brown and the professor take a shortcut to the ranch and Tom and Jean take the road, intending to catch up with Red.

Red, humming and whistling by turns, jounces along on the tractor, proceeding slowly over the tortuous road. He is a likable cuss, always agreeably inclined, and reacts with pleasure when he comes upon Joe Kane and the boys in their station wagon, stopped along the roadside. They wave seemingly friendly greetings and offer him cigarettes and beer. He stops and they view the unconscious beast, discussing its capture and how long the dope will keep it out, garnering the information from Red that it may need another shot before reaching the ranch. Joe, having long ago decided that there would be little chance for action shots after the beast reaches the ranch, devises a quick plan to hijack the animal.

It is but the work of a moment for one of the boys to slip up behind Red and deliver a knockout blow with a tire iron while he is preoccupied with the conversation and beer. They quickly deposit Red behind a heavy growth of sagebrush, and Joe drives the tractor off into a dry wash in the desert, with the boys following in the station wagon. When they reach the foot of a rocky butte, Joe instructs the boys to drive the station wagon behind a clump of ironwood trees and take the camera up to a vantage point from which they can photograph the beast.

Joe then maneuvers the big trailer around so they will be able to see the beast when it awakens. He then climbs up to a higher point from where he can direct operations. They do not have long to wait. The beast fights its way free of the effects of the anesthetic with amazing speed, and they begin to realize, almost at once, that they had sadly misjudged the ferocity of the thing. It breaks its chains almost immediately and tears at the sides of the trailer with such fury that the trailer is reduced to splinters. Ravenous, the monster turns this way and that, trying to catch the scent of food. At last, catching a glimpse of slight movement on the butte, it madly claws at the side, but slides back as often as it progresses. Joe and the boys arm themselves with boulders and prepare to fight it off until they can reach the station wagon. The sun is lowering and the huge boulders cast long shadows as Tom and Jean approach the scene of the skirmish.

They pull up sharply as they come upon Red, holding his head and staggering to the edge of the road. Emerging from a groggy haze, he tells them that he has no idea which direction the hijackers went. A little reconnoitering on Tom's part shows them clearly which way to go.

The Si-Papu slowly advances toward the cable car lift.

Following the tracks of the cars, Tom and Jean quickly reach the scene, taking in the situation at a glance. The swift desert dark is sweeping down, and in the distance the twinkling lights of an oil field can be seen. Tom shoots an ordinary arrow at the beast, attracting its attention. They yell and wave their hats, and ride in the direction of the oil field, keeping just out of reach of the beast.

Many of the wells in the oil field are being pumped with the new mechanical pumps that resemble some prehistoric animals, but there are a few remaining derricks. Tom and Jean ride through the maze of machinery and turn their horses loose, spanking them on their way, and race to climb a derrick.

Cut to Red walking down the road. Dr. Brown and the professor riding toward him.

The beast runs in bewilderment first to one pump and then to another, plainly astonished when, upon swiping at one with its paw, it is roughly repulsed, and with no sign of submission by this new and mystifying opponent. Tom and Jean watch with amusement while the beast rattles around below and then settle down for the night, unable to better their situation in any way. At dawn the next morning, they are awakened by noises and shooting below. An oil worker, arriving in the semidark, goes into his shack. Feeling the shack move, as though in the grip of a huge hand, he rushes out and meets the beast coming around the corner. He screams and runs into the shack for his gun. The beast breaks the shack in splinters. The man extricates himself from the wreckage and fires at the beast. The volley of shots have no effect. The man runs for the derrick. Tom and Jean shout encouragement to him. The beast is one leap behind him as he begins the ascent.

Cut to Joe Kane and the boys driving up.

The beast tries to climb up the derrick, but the ancient timbers refuse to hold its weight, which frustrates it no end. Growling and roaring in fury, the beast tugs and pushes and pulls. The oil-soaked frame, creaking and groaning, begins to crack under the strain, toppling at last. Tom and Jean ride it down from the tower railing, jump clear, and tumble onto the ground. The beast, feeling that it has vanquished one enemy, turns on Joe and the boys in the station wagon. Joe starts the motor and races toward the open country, unaware that he is on a road that leads directly to the canyon edge. The beast follows.

Cut to Professor Haden and a posse arriving at the oil field, then following the beast.

Arriving at the apparent end of the road, Joe and the boys make for the cable car lift, which goes across the canyon to the bat guano mines. The walls of the canyon, at this point, are perpendicular. They climb aboard the empty car and start away, leaving the puzzled beast pacing madly back and forth, growling and roaring its anger. The buzzards, swooping fearfully close to the car, claim their attention for a time. When they look back, they are horrified to see that the beast has entered the cable car room and is grasping the cable in both its paws. Unable to understand the mechanics of pulling the cable back, it tugs and shakes the cable, causing the car to tip violently from side to side, making it impossible for them to keep a grip on anything. One by one, they fall to their death.

Tom and Jean and the posse arrive too late to save Joe and the boys. Occupied with the cable, the beast has not noticed their arrival, and Tom is able to take up an advantageous position, screened by some ironwood trees. As the beast turns full front toward him, Tom sends a doped arrow into its neck. The beast reels about, grasping at the arrow. The professor and Dr. Brown dare to come nearer, hoping to entice it away from the sheer drop to the river below. Tom sends another arrow into it. For a time it looks as though the beast will go into the brush, but in its last efforts to resist the maddening oblivion, it turns its eyes toward the canyon, and almost as though in defiance of its would-be captors, stumbles and reels to the canyon edge.

Nothing can save it. Dr. Brown and the professor look sorrowfully after it, realizing that never again will it be possible for them to capture one of the Si-Papu.

Alternate Suggestion for Introducing the Girl into the Story: Rather than establish her as the daughter of Professor Haden, bring her in as a young starlet hired by Joe Kane to accompany them and make scenes to be cut into a motion picture later. Tom falls for her, and realizing the danger she may encounter, makes it his specific duty to look out for her, incurring the wrath of Joe Kane, who proves himself to be a genuine heel when he refuses to wait for her when they board the car lift.

Baboon: A Tale about a Yeti

Author's Note: "Baboon: A Tale about a Yeti" is an idea that originally derived from one of the three stories entitled "Assignment Himalayas," mentioned in Don Shay's *Cinefex* article on O'Brien. Jim Danforth says that O'Brien wrote further variations on this yeti theme, including some comical. The material presented here consists of the foreward and "suggestions for action sequences," the six-page story idea, and 10 illustrations. No date appears on the manuscript.

Foreword

The following is an outline of an adventure story using the Himalayas for location. The locations are new and snowy, rocky scenes can be duplicated in miniature realistically. This is not a "horror" picture, and the baboon is not a *true* baboon, but an animal of that type, which I have used because of its great agility and flexibility for animation. Also,

Obie's charcoal drawing that shows two size comparisons: a 15-foot-tall scale with the man on the left and a 10-foot tall scale with the man on the right.

this figure resembles that of a man, so that a goodly portion can be shot without animation. Exciting action sequences were the keynote of the success of *King Kong, Son of Kong* and *Mighty Joe Young*. This idea, properly planned, for action, should make a fast-moving, thrilling picture and with a new twist. *King Kong* had 18 action sequences, and *Mighty Joe Young* had 12. Another important contribution to the realism of this type of picture is to have the animated beast *in contact with the humans at every* opportunity where the story makes it feasible. If my third-dimension animation requires a name, it could be "Origimation," since I was the first in this field.

The Cast

Dr. Edward Towne .... Anthropologist
Marian Towne .... his daughter
Kent Carr .... Business manager for Dr. Towne
Flemming Ward .... Showman
Taylor Smith .... Showman

Dr. Edward Towne and his daughter, Marian, a lovely, young woman scientist, went to the high Himalayas in search of the yeti (Abominable Snowman), but, upon the advice of their Sherpa friends, she returned home, planning to rejoin her father when the weather was less rigorous. Dr. Towne, finding that his faith in the yeti was not shared by his colleagues, was forced to finance his own expedition and, therefore, appointed a young man, Kent Carr, to manage his business affairs at home and keep an accounting of the expenses on the trip. When Dr. Towne failed to return from his last venture into yeti country, his personal effects were returned to Marian, among them a can of exposed film. The film was not of the best quality, some was scratchy, overexposed and static, but all were viewable. It showed rugged country—blowing snow and sleet, bridges suspended high above turbulent rivers, narrow mountain passes and briefly, at the last of the film, a vague image of a huge beast. Vague though it was, it was enough to convince Marian that her father had encountered the yeti. In the interest of preventing the professor's funds from becoming exhausted, Kent persuaded two showmen, Taylor Smith, procurer of rare animals for circuses and zoos, and Flemming Ward, producer of tent shows and any kind of unusual exhibits that can be highly publicized, to finance a trip to the Himalayas on which he and Marian could accompany them.

When they reach the yeti country, they come upon an ancient city, which, the natives tell them, was mysteriously plundered and destroyed and no trace of the inhabitants or the plunder was ever found. They search diligently and track the yeti through the rugged and interesting country (stock shots). Coming upon great caves in the mountainside, they enter and find enormous hoards of idols, jewels, gold objects, carved chests, etc.—plunder from the countryside. Suddenly, they are confronted by a giant cobra that has slithered out of one of the many crevices in the walls of the cave. It sways and hisses and approaches nearer. As they scramble toward the opposite side of the cave, the yeti enters. A terrific battle ensues between the yeti and the cobra, with the yeti coming out the victor.

Fearing that the yeti may attack them and being cut off from the entrance of the cave, they enter a narrow crevice through which light can be seen penetrating the roof of a cave beyond. Coming into the cave, they are amazed to see the implements of human habitation—a crude bed, table and chair. They hear the yeti grunting and growling and trying to force its way through the crevice and are startled to hear a booming voice call out a sharp command. The yeti turns back. Dr. Towne, hardly

Dr. Towne finds the yeti in a cave that contains "enormous hoards of idols, jewels, gold objects, carved chests . . . plunder from the countryside."

recognizable behind his huge beard and long hair, enters the cave and is stunned to find Marian and the others there. A joyous reunion is soon followed by a warning that they must leave the cave immediately. The doctor tells them that the whole area is deteriorating and that slides are becoming more and more frequent. Even as he speaks, the mountain creaks and groans.

They follow Dr. Towne out, obeying his warning to beware of the yeti, which is viciously snarling on the other side of the cave. He shouts a command at it as they pass. It bounds ahead of them and out of the cave, watching them from a distance. Now greed rears its ugly head, and Flemming Ward insists that his partner, Taylor Smith, help him take some of the treasure. Dr. Towne insists that there is no time. They hurry on, but discover that Ward has lagged behind, and after they are across a small valley, they look back. Ward appears at the entrance to the cave, loaded with everything he can carry. Then there is a roar of an avalanche that traps Ward and seals the cave forever.

As they proceed down the mountain, they are dismayed to find a new crevasse, thousands of feet deep. Dr. Towne, aware that the yeti has been following them and observing them from a safe distance, sees to it

In another version of the "Baboon" story, a character called Bruce Thomas sits on the back of the yeti as it leaps across the chasm.

that the rest of the party is ensconced behind a barricade of rocks and snow. He calls the yeti to him. Unwinding a strong rope, which he hastily snatched up in the cave, the doctor secures it to a giant boulder and climbs upon the yeti's back. At a command from him, the yeti bounds easily across the crevasse.

The doctor sends the yeti off, and the others follow across the crevasse, inching along on the rope. The continuing trip down the mountain is interspersed with exciting incidents, suspension bridges, slides, etc., the Yeti slinking along. But greed continues to be a constant companion. When they reach the lower country, Taylor Smith, upon learning that Dr. Towne plans to drive the yeti back to higher country, insists that he must capture it.

The doctor refuses to hear of it, and, unknown to Marian or Carr, Smith ruthlessly shoots the old man with a tranquilizer shot. With the aid of the natives and tranquilizer shots, they capture the yeti. Marian and Kent believe that Dr. Towne has become ill. The party embarks on a tramp steamer, securing the yeti in chains below. During a storm at sea, the yeti breaks its bonds and comes above, wreaking havoc and demolishing everything at hand, including the pilot room, tossing some of the crew

During the storm sequence, the yeti breaks free from its bonds and comes above, wreaking havoc.

overboard and forcing all to go below and secure the hatches, leaving it cold and lonely above. It is then discovered that Smith tossed all guns overboard, anticipating that a situation such as this would arise. The yeti could be killed. (Many other suspenseful situations on board ship can be contrived.)

Seeing that the ship is drifting helplessly toward a rocky island, Dr. Towne, in desperation, volunteers to put out in a small outboard motor boat and entice the yeti to jump into the water and follow him, to allow repairs to be made on the steering gear. The Yeti jumps into the water, but killer whales approach and cause the small boat to tip over. The yeti, fighting off the whales, lifts the doctor above the water and paddles toward the boat.

Smith attempts to keep the yeti in tow by throwing a rope over its head as it approaches to place the doctor on the boat. The yeti pulls on the rope, in which Smith becomes entangled and is pulled over the side. Marian and Kent and the doctor watch with pity as the yeti and Smith fight to the death with the killer whales.

The yeti is attacked by killer whales.

Suggestions for Action Sequences

1. Viewing the film returned from the Himalayas, with the thrilling realization that the yeti exists.
2. The discovery of the ruins of an ancient city (to be accomplished with miniature projection).
3. The thrilling discovery of giant tracks leading to the great caves.
4. The suspenseful entry into the caves and the exciting discovery of vast treasures.
5. The horrifying entry of a giant cobra.
6. The darkening of the cave as the huge hulk of the yeti fills the entrance, followed by the mortal battle between the yeti and the cobra.
7. The desperate escape of the party into a narrow crevice, to avoid the grasp of the yeti.
8. The amazement of finding the doctor's living quarters and the exciting reunion between the doctor and Marian.
9. The fearful roar of a falling avalanche seconds after all but one get out of the cave.
10. The rigors of the trek down the mountain, crossing suspension

The yeti lifts the doctor up to the ship and safety.

bridges at dizzying heights, small avalanches and other suspense-filled incidents.

11.   The discovery of the new, and very deep, crevasse with the doctor resolving the dilemma by anchoring a rope and leaping across on the back on the yeti, with the others following on the rope.

12.   The exciting action at the lower camp, with showman Smith arguing with the doctor over the capture of the yeti and Smith shooting both the doctor and the yeti with tranquilizer shots and capturing the yeti.

13.   The interesting transportation of the Yeti to the boat by elephant? or truck?

14.   A possible exciting sequence of the yeti amok in an oil field, tipping over derricks, etc.

15.   The suspenseful scenes of the yeti breaking its bonds on the tramp steamer and wreaking havoc on the top deck.

16.   The desperate doctor, putting out in the outboard motor boat, enticing the yeti to jump into the sea and follow him.

Giant lizards attack Cass Currier and Sandu.

17. The touching scene of the yeti saving the old doctor from the killer whales and placing him back on the boat.
18. The thrilling underwater shots of the yeti battling the killer whales.
19. The pathetic, final scene of the yeti sinking into the bloody sea as the steamer pulls away.

The Elephant Rustlers

Author's Note: In 1960, Obie and Darlyne created a three-page story idea with illustrations for "The Elephant Rustlers." Darlyne said to Kevin Brownlow about it:

> This was going to be in Burma, where they train the big work elephants, and they steal these work elephants and sell them in other parts of the country just like the western cowboys steal cattle here. And so we worked up the story, but nothing was ever done with it. . . . Another sketch which Obie had not completed showed that he was going to have a band of monkeys attack. In another sketch, the elephants were carrying poles through the village to knock the whole village down.

Giant lizards attack Cass Currier.

In a letter to Mike Hankin, dated March 16, 1982, Darlyne revealed where the idea for "The Elephant Rustlers" came from:

> "The Elephant Rustlers" I got from a very small item in the newspaper, which told about the work elephants in Burma being stolen and sold in another part of the country. As you know, the work elephants become very valuable after they are trained, so we worked the story idea up with cowboys from America going there to do the same thing.

By this time, Merian Cooper had retired to a small house in Coronado, California—a military retirement community across the bay from San Diego. He had left the film business in June 1956. Obie took "The Elephant Rustlers" project to Cooper, but it was never developed further. No author's name or date appears on the three-page typed manuscript for "The Elephant Rustlers."

Suggested Story Outline

The gloom in the atmosphere of the bunk house at the J. H. Ranch is due to more than the dull, rainy day. Everyone of the boys silently grieves over the fact that their buddy, "Mace," is going to be hanged in a month for murder and rustling that they know he did not commit, but

A man is saved from the jaws of death by an elephant.

the villain who did it has disappeared, and the situation looks hopeless. Smokey Charlie, a faithful Indian cowhand is looking through a pile of dog-eared magazines when he is suddenly stirred to action. The picture he has come upon is of a working elephant *Keddah*, or roundup, in India. There, standing in the sidelines, unmistakably, is Cass Currier, the very man they would each give their life to get and whose return would save Mace.

The room buzzes with guesses and speculations and suggestions as to how they can get him. Everyone offers to contribute his pay, and when that amount is supplemented with a generous contribution from J. H., the owner of the ranch, Brad Baxter and Charlie are elected to get Cass and bring him back. Very soon, Brad and Charlie find themselves being whisked, by the magic carpet of the jet plane, to the strange land of India.

In India, Cass has joined forces with a shady character, Sandu Gersha, and they have collected several good, working elephants and various others and secreted them in a remote part of the jungle, planning to dispose of them at some distant Keddah. Sandu, who knows the ways of elephants, tells Cass that it will be impossible to drive the assortment of elephants through strange country without the help of at least one *Kunki*, a trained elephant. Sandu knows of one, a giant tusker, old Akabar, which belongs to old Singh Suresh, for whom Sandu once worked as an elephant boy. Sandu knows that Singh will recognize him; therefore, Cass is obliged to do the job of stealing Akabar himself.

When Cass hears from an elephant boy that two white men have a picture of him and are looking for him, he knows he has no time to lose. Old Singh catches Cass in the act of stealing his best elephant, Akabar, and Cass beats him, but Singh gets a good look at Cass and recognizes him instantly when Brad shows him Cass's picture. Cass and Sandu get a slight head start, but when Singh learns they are after Cass, he furnishes Brad and Charlie with elephants, and the chase begins. Old Singh deliberately selects elephants for Brad and Charlie that he knows will recognize the trumpeting Akabar and will answer him. Therefore, Cass and Sandu soon become aware that they are being followed.

In their haste and eagerness to elude Brad and Charlie, they attempt to pass through a dangerous part of the jungle. Their elephants are attacked by tigers, and several of them are killed. They are forced to fight off droves of vicious monkeys and battle with giant lizards. Other elephants stray off. Sandu, seeing that there will be no money from the elephants for him, deserts Cass. Cass becomes ill and delirious, and Akabar is allowed to go his own way, which he does, and leads them directly back to old Singh. Cass, in moments of lucidity, realizes where he is and attempts to get away on foot, but too late. Brad and Charlie ride into camp and take him prisoner, elated that Mace will now go free.

The following sequences should furnish ample excitement during the chase:
Tiger sequence
Pit Sequence
Giant lizard sequence
Forest monkey sequence
Wild elephant sequence
Boa constrictor sequence

Chapter 5

Ideas for Television

Author's Note: The following ideas that Willis O'Brien devised for television were created by him during the 1950s and were never, to my knowledge, sold. Twelve drawings from "Preposterous Inventions" are missing, but the "Preface to the Sport of Boxing" appears to be complete, as do "Seeing it Through with a Champion," "A Visit with Our Boys," "A Preface to the Sport of Baseball" and "Understanding Rodeo."

O'Brien dabbled in most of these sports in his early days before entering the film industry, and it is possible that he may have designed other ideas that were sold. However, these are the only ones that appear to have survived.

The most interesting one of the group, "Preposterous Inventions," is the only one that shows O'Brien's sense of humor, similar in vein to *Mad* magazine. The other ideas—with the exception of "A Visit with Our Boys"—are straightforward demonstrations of various sports for proposed television programs. The idea for "A Visit with Our Boys" came from a newspaper clipping (which is included) dated December 25, 1951.

The following is part of an idea for a 15-minute TV show, "Preposterous Inventions." These inventions have actually been patented, and the papers can be found in the Patent office or library. Illustrated on the screen with animated drawings and accompanied by pseudo-serious commentary, these would be highly entertaining. The source of material for these inventions is practically inexhaustible and can

Title and sponsor's commercial.

The commentator explains that this invention can be constructed at home.

The commentator selects a paper from the pile on his desk, explaining that perhaps the efforts of our inventors to assist their fellow men with their problems has not been fully appreciated, etc., etc....

The commentator explains the adjustment of this contraption on the victim's back.

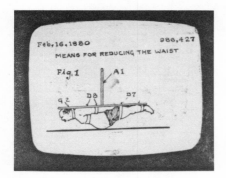

Close-up of an actual patent pacer.

The commentator warns of the danger of overbalancing.

An animated line drawing of a wife being thrown over as she pushes her husband forward onto his stomach.

An animated line drawing of a wife rocking her husband back and forth, becoming exhausted.

Close-up of the commentator suppressing a smile.

The commentator suggests the auxiliary power can be had by calling the kids in.

The commentator warns of the over-enthusiasm of children.

The commentator explains that we have a very able staff of scientific engineers who will work out ideas that anyone cares to send in and will demonstrate them on future shows.

be added to by request-
ing the public to submit
any ideas they may have
along these lines.

The following is an
idea for a 15-minute TV
show, "Preface to the
Sport of Boxing," in
which the viewers meet
the contestants and get
a line on their workouts.
It should stimulate in-
terest in the contest and
create anticipation in the
fans of the bout to come.

Seeing It Through with a Champion

(An idea for a 30-minute television show)

We meet a champion, hear about his background, his start in his pro-
fession and see him in a contest at his best. Then, with the aid of the
"Portarama," we see how his work appears *from his angle* and how it
would appear from the opponent's.

Use of the Portarama would remove the show from the class of an
ordinary interview and would assist greatly in keeping the action moving
and add interest to the interview. The view from the Portarama would
be intercut with the regular scenes. Use of the Portarama would give as
exciting an effect as Cinerama's scenic railway ride.

The sketches beginning on page 157 are based on the life of an imaginary champion, for the purpose of illustrating, approximately, what we
would see.

On page 161 is a list of a few experiences that should be thrilling
when shown in this manner:

Sponsor's commercial.

Narration explaining the process of bag punching.

The subject of the interview between the interrogator and the matchmaker is the backgrounds of boxers on the next show and the matchmaker's method of matching up contestants so the fights are not one-sided, etc. The matchmaker invites the interrogator to the gym to see the boxers.

Narration explaining the differences between bags, etc.

At the gym the interrogator meets the boxer and trainer.

Introduction of professional sparring partners. Narration explaining the abilities of each, etc.

A round of boxing (with narration).

Sponsor's commerical (while switching to opponent's camp).

A trainer instructs a boxer between rounds.

The interrogator meets the opponent. A short interview follows.

A round of boxing (with narration).

The opponent boxes a round (with narration and a final reminder of the date of the upcoming fight).

Background for the title: Bronco riding.

Competing in small rodeos.

Ten seconds to go...

Riding the bucker (rider's angle via Portarama).

Portarama camera mounted on a horse (packsaddle) at the proper height. Hinged body and neck, to give proper response to bucking (as would a human body).

Bronco riding	Boxing
Brahma bull riding	Wrestling
Football (carrying)	Ski jumps, Slaloms
Bullfighting	Bob sledding
Diving (Acapulco)	Ice hocky
Window washing (20 stories)	Lion taming
Trapeze performing	Horse racing
Sulky driving	Auto racing
Topping trees	Pole vaulting
Suicide (San Francisco Bridge)	Stunts (falls from a horse, etc.)

Possible Sponsors
Gillette
General Foods (Wheaties)
Marlborough cigarettes

Possible Sidelines
Syndicated Cartoon Strip
Illustrated book on champ's lives
Records, tapes, interviews
Color slides
Statuettes
Useful statuettes (ashtrays, etc.)

A Visit with Our Boys

Version 1

The following idea (storyboard begins on page 163) is for a 15-minute daily television program:

Bring our boys to the screen in their homes, showing enough of the country where they are stationed to make it interesting and covering every branch of the armed forces, including the navy. The boys will be photographed with sound, allowing them to say a few words of greeting to the folks back home. The commentator will announce their names and hometowns. The photographs will be carefully indexed and filed, so that anyone desiring them can have a blowup of their picture, which should become quite a business in itself and run for a long time. Also, once a month we would have enough material for a two-reel picture for theaters, blowing it up from 16mm Kodachrome to 35mm Technicolor.

Preface for Version 2

The following idea (storyboard begins on page 166) is for a 15-minute TV show, "A visit with our boys" wherever they are stationed, bringing them to the television

Fade in, over a slowly turning globe, the name of the sponsor—presenting ... "A Visit with Our Boys" (martial music)

Announcer: "Now we'll see who will visit us today. Among them may be your boy, sweetheart, brother, husband or just a friend."

"Around this old world we'll go...

The announcer will introduce the sponsor's products...

On the sea...

In the air...

Announcer: "A typical scene from the land where they are . . . a long, long way from home . . ."

On the ground...

Announcer: "Here they are . . . the best in the world."

A pin spotlight travels over the surface of the globe and stops on the peninsula of Korea. Announcer: "It's the boys in Korea..."

Announcer: "Permit me to introduce . . .

Announcer: "Jimmy Jones, Yreka, California; Bert Johnson, Phoenix, Arizona; and John Spencer, Great Falls, Montana. (Ad lib from the boys.)

Follow with introductions of as many boys as is possible, allowing them to ad lib a word or two to their loved ones . . . then . . .

Announcer: "And now your sponsor will continue to seek your boys, wherever they may be and bring them to you Monday through Friday . . .

screens at home just to smile and wave and say a brief "Hello" to Mom or Mary and the folks. To add interest and drama, a little of the country where they are stationed can be shown and yet allow approximately 150 or 200 boys to appear on the screen. I have the assurance of someone now in government service that we will receive full cooperation and our cameramen will receive the same consideration as war correspondents.

This show could easily sustain 15 minutes, three times a week, and the source of material is practically inexhaustible, since we would continually take in all branches of the military service. I believe that this type of show would be a natural for a sponsor, such as a cigarette company. A sideline could be the enlargement of the boys' pictures, at cost, for their families and friends, upon request, or perhaps, a box top.

The title appears over a revolving globe.

in the air, or . . .

After the sponsor's commercial, the commentator explains that this is "A Visit with Our Boys," bringing them to the screens at home from wherever they may be . . .

on the ground.

On the sea . . .

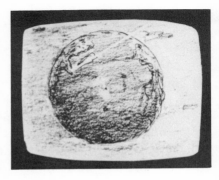

A pinpoint of light moves along the globe, stopping at . . . Korea!

A view of boys coming back from the front.

A view of Korean countryside and natives.

A view of mechanized troops in Korean countryside.

A brief interview with a few boys.

The commentator announces the names and addresses of the boys, who appear in close-up, greeting some loved one at home.

The commentator explains that enlargements of any of the boys' pictures that have just appeared on the show may be obtained, etc.

A Preface to
the Sport of
Baseball

   The following is an idea for a 15-minute TV show, "A Preface to the Sport of Baseball," explaining a few of the fine points of the game and introducing the players.
   This should stimulate interest in the game and create anticipation in the fans, especially the "kid" players, and enable the "once-in-a-whilers" to enjoy it more. The eight teams of the Coast League should furnish plenty of material, in conjunction with animated diagrams and high-speed shots showing the actual plays in slow motion, such as sliding into base, and the ball curving over home plate.
   I suggest a good sports writer or an ex–ball player for the interviewer.

The title and sponsor's commercial over a baseball and bat.

Long shot of the team at practice.

The commentator meets the manager of the team. A brief interview follows.

A close-up of the first and second basemen being interviewed.

The commentator and manager discuss the players.

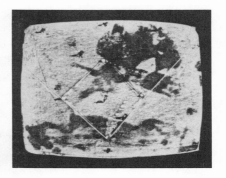

An animated diagram (with cuts of players) illustrating several tricky plays.

The first and second basemen meet the commentator.

The first baseman illustrating how a long reach can make an out.

The manager promises more such shots of the work of the shortstop and third baseman tomorrow...

Understanding Rodeo

The following is an idea for a 15-minute TV show, "Understanding Rodeo," for, as in everything else, you miss a lot if you do not understand the tricks and rules of the game. Here we get the dope first hand from the "champs" themselves and see them in action!

There is material here for a series of, at least, 15 exciting shows.

The title and sponsor's commercial over the background shot.

Ten seconds are added to the roper's time if he breaks before the flag drops.

Interview with the champion calf roper.

"When seconds count" . . . The roper is off the horse as soon as the rope is on the calf.

Tense moments before the calf is released.

The horse also must be a champion.

Some calves are tough to pull over and can cause the roper to lose out if he doesn't understand the technique.

When three legs are tied, the time is stopped.

Following the rodeo circuit keeps the roper on the go . . .

Part III. Collaborators

Chapter 6

Producers, Directors, and Fellow Technicians

Like many successful filmmakers, O'Brien had his regular team of collaborators — some who worked with him, some who worked for him and some he worked for. In the latter department, and top of the list is Merian C. Cooper. Without doubt, Cooper was one of the most important influences in O'Brien's life. It is interesting to speculate what would have happened to O'Brien had there been no Kong — a character created by Cooper. Likewise, it would have been unlikely that Cooper could have made the film without O'Brien's genius. Their talents complemented each other to create a bold classic of the cinema. Cooper's character was reflected in all the work he did: a brave, courageous man who would rise to the challenge — be it film or war — a great showman who had imagination and foresight.

Ernest B. Schoedsack was the other key collaborator with O'Brien, directing four of their films and involved with two others ("War Eagles" and *This Is Cinerama*). A tough, cynical hard worker, Schoedsack had a rather sparse film career, and there are indications that he may have been involved in other film projects that were aborted for some reason. An example is "Uncrowned King," which is not listed in any of his filmographies.

Other than the films that Marcel Delgado worked on with O'Brien and a few others that I managed to find, I do not know Delgado's other film work. George Lofgren worked on both "War Eagles" and *Mighty Joe Young*. I know nothing else about him. Cameraman Bert Willis worked on *The Lost World* (1925), *King Kong, The Last Days of Pompeii* and *Mighty Joe Young*; he died on December 23, 1985, at age 91.

From *The Lost World* (1925) onward, O'Brien had assistants to help him with the actual animation on all his films. On *King Kong*, he worked with Buzz Gibson, who started as a grip on *Creation* and animated much of *Son of Kong*; Gibson died in February 1985, at age 88. Orvill Goldner also worked on the animation of *Kong*; he died on February 28, 1985, at age 78. For *Mighty Joe Young*, O'Brien had help from Ray Harryhausen, Peter Peterson and Marcel Delgado. Both Harryhausen and Peterson worked on two other projects each with O'Brien. The last animator to work with O'Brien was Jim Danforth, on *It's a Mad, Mad, Mad, Mad World*. Another important collaborator was Linwood G. Dunn, who did optical work on five projects, with O'Brien.

Director Harry O. Hoyt joined O'Brien on two projects (*Creation* and *The Lost World*, 1925). As with many other associates and collaborators of O'Brien, information on Hoyt's life and work was difficult to obtain. Likewise, the Nassour Brothers. If they did more films after *The Beast of Hollow Mountain*, I don't know them.

Steve Archer: Born August 1, 1957

Steve Archer collaborated on two versions of "The Last of the Oso Si-Papu," which was left to him by the late Darlyne O'Brien in 1985. Born and educated in England, he entered the film industry in 1975 as assistant to Cliff Culley in the matte department at Pinewood Studios. In 1980, he worked as an animator and assistant to Ray Harryhausen on *Clash of the Titans*. Since then, he has worked on several feature films, TV commercials and TV series as an animator, camera operator, cameraman, editor and codirector of animation sequences. He won the D & AD Silver award for the most outstanding special effects for his work on the "Reed Employment" TV commercial.

Films

1976   *The Pink Panther Strikes Again*. Uncredited work as effects assistant.
        Candleshoe. Uncredited work as effects assistant.
        Escape from the Dark. Uncredited work as effects assistant.

1980   *Clash of the Titans*. Assistant animator to Ray Harryhausen.

1982   *Krull*. Animator of the "Crystal Spider" for the "Widow of the Web" sequence under Special Effects Supervisor Derek Meddings.

1984   *The Neverending Story.* Animator of "Falkor the Luck Dragon" for
       Special Effects Supervisor Brian Johnson.
       "Force of the Trojans." Aborted Charles H. Schneer/Ray Harry-
       hausen project.

1986   "Deity." Script by Stephen J. Stirling based on O'Brien's "The
       Last of the Oso Si-Papu." Set during the 1940s.

1988   *The Adventures of Baron Munchausen.* Uncredited animator.

1990   *The Gate 2.* Animator for Special Visual Effects Director Randy
       Cook.
       "Spiderman the Movie." Screenplay by Barney Cohen, Ted
       Newson and John Brancato. Rewrite by Joseph Goldman.
       Shelved project. Archer, Robert Ryan and the Light and Mo-
       tion Corporation were to create the effects.

1991   "The Creator." Treatment by Deirdra Baldwin and Steve Archer
       incorporating O'Brien's "The Last of the Oso Si-Papu." A
       modern-day version of the story.

1992   "Three Months' Fun." Steve Archer's documentary project about
       the making of Errol Flynn's film, *William Tell*.

TV Series

1988   "Mr. Majeika." Uncredited animator.
       "Spitting Image: The Reagan Years." Animator of "Mount Rush-
       more" and "Reagan's brain" animation sequences.
       "Spitting Image Series." Animator of "Camberwick Greenbelt,"
       "Butterman," "Cher: I Got Bits of You, Babe" and "Royal Bank
       Job" animation sequences. Also photographed and edited. Co-
       directed these sequences with Steve Bendelack.

1990   "Winjin' Pom." Directed by Steve Bendelack.

TV Commercials

Numerous commercials between 1984 and 1988, including

1986   "Royal Bank of Scotland: Shoes." Directed by Gerry Anderson.
       "Royal Bank of Scotland: Hat." Directed by Gerry Anderson.

1988   "Reed Employment: Get Out of the Office." Directed by Steve
       Baron. Steve Archer received the silver D & AD award for the
       most outstanding special effects.

Merian C. Cooper:
Born October 24, 1893; Died April 21, 1973

Merian Caldwell Cooper was born in Jacksonville, Florida. O'Brien worked on eight Cooper projects; *King Kong, The Son of Kong, The Last Days of Pompeii,* "War Eagles," *Mighty Joe Young,* "Food of the Gods," *This Is Cinerama* and "The Elephant Rustlers." Cooper had a distinguished career, both in films and in war. He attended Lawrenceville School and Annapolis Naval Academy, from which he resigned in 1915. In 1917, he graduated from the Georgia School of Technology and then served in World War I in the air force, becoming a captain, and spent time as a prisoner of war in Germany.

After the war in 1919, he resigned from the air force and joined the Polish army to fight against the communists. As lieutenant colonel with the Kosciusko Flying Squadron, he met Ernest B. Schoedsack in Poland, and in 1920, he was shot down, captured and falsely reported killed. With Schoedsack, he codirected two successful documentaries, *Grass* (1925) and *Chang* (1927). From 1930 to 1932, he was director of Pan American Airways. In 1931, he joined RKO and became David O. Selznick's executive assistant in 1932. After Selznick left RKO, Cooper became head of production at both RKO and Pathé Studios. In 1933 he created Pioneer Pictures with Jock Whitney and C. V. Whitney.

Cooper became executive director of Pioneer in 1935, which merged with Selznick-International. He left Selznick-International in 1937 to form Argosy Pictures with John Ford. He also started producing for MGM from 1937. During World War II, he served as colonel with the U.S. Army Air Corps and was chief of staff to General Claire Chennault in China with the Flying Tigers in 1942. In 1950, he became brigadier general in the U.S. Air Force Reserve. In 1952, he was production head of Cinerama and received a special Academy Award "for his many innovations and contributions to the art of motion pictures." In 1954, he left Cinerama and formed C. V. Whitney Productions which he left in 1956 to retire.

His last public appearance was in Hollywood on December 30, 1971, when he delivered the eulogy at the funeral services for Max Steiner, composer of the *King Kong* music score. Two months before Cooper's death from cancer, he was working with Ronald Haver on a book about the making of *King Kong*; the book was never finished.

Books

1924   *The Sea Gypsy*, with Edward A. Salisbury.

1925   *Grass.*

1927   *Things Men Die For.*

1932   *King Kong* with Edgar Wallace; novelization by Delos W. Love-
       lace.

19??   *Under the White Eagle.*

Films

1924   *The Lost Empire/In Quest of the Golden Prince*, released in 1929.
       Cooper is credited as editor, writer and titler on this film, but
       Cooper denied it, although he was associated with the film's
       producer, Edward A. Salisbury.

1925   *Grass/Grass: A Nation's Battle for Life/Grass: The Epic of a Lost
       Tribe.* Coproducer and codirecter with Ernest B. Schoedsack
       and Marguerite Harrison and cophotographer with Schoed-
       sack; personal appearances by Cooper and Schoedsack.

1927   *Chang.* Coproducer and codirector with Schoedsack.

1928   *Gow, the Head Hunter.* Cooper is credited as cophotographer, but
       as with *Lost Empire*, he denied it.

1929   *The Four Feathers.* Codirected by Shoedsack and Lothar Mendes.

1932   *Roar of the Dragon.* Story by Cooper and Jane Bigelow (an RKO
       film).
       The Most Dangerous Game/Hounds of Zaroff. Associate producer
       (RKO film).
       The Phantom of Crestwood. Associate producer (RKO film).
       Monkey's Paw. Executive producer of this troubled RKO produc-
       tion, which had additional scenes directed by Shoedsack.

1933   *King Kong.* Cowriter and codirector with Schoedsack. This was
       Obie's first film for Cooper.
       Lucky Devils. Assistant producer (RKO film).
       Diplomaniacs. According to *The RKO Story* by Jewell and Harbin,
       Cooper received his first credit as executive producer on this
       Wheeler and Woolsey comedy (RKO film).
       The Silver Cord. Executive producer (RKO film).

Professional Sweetheart. Executive producer (RKO film).
Melody Cruise. Executive producer (RKO film).
Bed of Roses. Producer (RKO film).
Double Harness. Executive producer (RKO film).
Morning Glory. Executive producer (RKO film).
Ann Vickers. Executive producer (RKO film).
Ace of Aces. Executive producer (RKO film).
Chance of Heaven. Executive producer (RKO film).
After Tonight/Sealed Lips. Executive producer (RKO film).
Little Women. Executive producer (RKO film).
The Big Romance. Executive producer (RKO film).
Flying Down to Rio. Executive producer (RKO film).
The Son of Kong. Executive producer. O'Brien as technical creator. Directed by Schoedsack (RKO film).

1934   *The Lost Patrol.* Executive producer (RKO film, directed by John Ford).
Spitfire. Executive producer (RKO film).
Sing and Like It. Executive producer (RKO film).
Success at Any Price. Executive producer (RKO film).
Finishing School. Executive producer (RKO film).
Stingaree. Executive producer (RKO film).
La Cucaracha. Cooper's story, for his company, Pioneer.
Red Morning. According to Jewell and Harbin's *The RKO Story*, this film includes beautiful footage of New Guinea photographed for a Merian C. Cooper picture that was never completed. Which film, though?
The Crime Doctor. Executive producer or producer?

1935   *Becky Sharp.* First film made in three-strip technicolor for Cooper's company, Pioneer.
She. Producer. Directed by Irving Pichel and Lansing C. Holden (RKO film).
The Last Days of Pompeii. Producer. Directed by Schoedsack with O'Brien as chief technician (RKO film).

1936   *The Dancing Pirate.* Made for Cooper's company, Pioneer, with photographic effects by O'Brien.

1938   *The Toy Wife/Frou Frou.* Producer (MGM film).

1939   "War Eagles"/"White Eagle"/"The War Eagle." Aborted project for MGM. O'Brien was to supervise the effects on this film.

Stagecoach. Uncredited preproduction work on this John Ford film.

1940   *The Long Voyage Home.* Made for Cooper's company, Argosy, directed by John Ford.

1942   *The Jungle Book.* Uncredited preproduction work on this Arthur Lubin film.

1947   *The Fugitive.* Coproducer with John Ford. This was the first joint feature film for RKO and Argosy pictures.

1948   *Fort Apache.* Coproducer with John Ford (Argosy/RKO film). *Three Godfathers.* Coproducer with Ford (Argosy/MGM film).

1949   *Mighty Joe Young.* Coproducer with Ford, with O'Brien as technical creator (Arko film, distributed by RKO). *She Wore a Yellow Ribbon.* Coproducer with Ford (Argosy/RKO film).

1950   *Rio Grande.* Coproducer with Ford (Argosy/RKO film). *Wagonmaster.* Coproducer with Ford (Argosy/RKO film). "Food of the Gods." Cooper developed many concepts and studio artists did illustrations for animation sequences, with O'Brien as chief technician, but the project was abandoned because of script problems.

1952   *The Quiet Man.* Coproducer with Ford (Argosy/RKO film). "The New Adventures of King Kong." Cooper wrote a story treatment and hoped to make the film in Cinerama and hired O'Brien to investigate the animation equipment needed, but the man who was developing the special animation projectors died, and the project was abandoned. *This Is Cinerama.* Coproducer and supervisor of "Cypress Gardens of Florida" and "Beautiful America" sequences. O'Brien worked on the film as an artist.

1953   *The Sun Shines Bright.* Coproducer with Ford (Argosy film).

1955   *The Seven Wonders of the World.* Cooper received credit for his advice on this Cinerama film.

1956   *The Searchers.* Executive producer for his company C. V. Whitney Productions on this film directed by John Ford.

1960   "The Elephant Rustlers." Unmade story idea by O'Brien.

1963   *The Best of Cinerama.* Coproducer on this Cinerama compilation film, including scenes from "This Is Cinerama," "Cinerama Holiday," "The Seven Wonders of the World," "Search for Paradise" and "Cinerama South Seas Adventure."

Jim Danforth: Born circa 1940

Jim Danforth was born in Ohio and grew up primarily in Illinois, near Chicago. When he was 12, his parents moved to California, first near San Francisco and six months later, to the Los Angeles area. He started in the film industry as assistant to Art Clokey, did titles and sequences for TV show "The Dinah Shore Show," and then worked as assistant on film *The Time Machine*. He has been nominated twice for an Academy Award for best visual effects for his work on *The Seven Faces of Dr. Lao* and *When Dinosaurs Ruled the Earth*. He has worked as a model animator, matte painter, optical effects man and model maker and has written scripts and directed. He was an animator on O'Brien's last assignment, *It's a Mad, Mad, Mad, Mad World*.

Films

1958   "The Princess of Mars." Unrealized Danforth project. No script, but many drawings and paintings. George Pal helped him stage a presentation at MGM for Hulbert Burroughs and ERB Inc., Attorneys.

1959   *The Time Machine.* Special effects assistant on this George Pal film (MGM).

1960   *Goliath and the Dragon.* Animator.
       Jack the Giant Killer. Animator.

1962   *The Wonderful World of the Brothers Grimm.* Animator (Cinerama film).
       It's a Mad, Mad, Mad, Mad World. Animator (with Willis O'Brien as consultant and director of animation).

1964   *The Seven Faces of Dr. Lao.* Animator and miniature effects supervisor. Nominated for an Academy Award for best visual effects.

1965   "At the Earth's Core." Unmade Danforth script.

1970   *Willie Wonka and the Chocolate Factory.* Animator.

1971   *When Dinosaurs Ruled the Earth.* Special effects, animation and second unit direction. Nominated for an Academy Award for best visual effects.

1974   *Flesh Gordon*. Animator and matter painter. He animated the "Beetlemen" (originally, one of Peter Peterson's Beetlemen figures). Only the armature was used; George Barr redesigned the exterior covering. The "Great God Porno" animation model was also originally the "Las Vegas Monster" model.

1976   "Thongor in the Valley of the Demons." Danforth was to be director and effects creator on this unmade fantasy project for producer Milton Subotsky.
       "The Legend of King Kong." Aborted remake for Universal from a script by Bo Goldman, based on the Delos W. Lovelace novel. Director: Joseph Sargent, producers: Hunt Stromberg, Jr., and Joe Kirby. In Sensurround process. Danforth was to do the animation, but Paramount's version was made instead.

1978   *Planet of the Dinosaurs*. Matte painter.

1979   "Timegate." Aborted feature film to have been directed and coproduced by Danforth from his screenplay.

1981   *Caveman*. Special effects designs and second unit direction.
       Clash of the Titans. Assistant animator to Ray Harryhausen (MGM).

1983   *Twilight Zone: The Movie*. Matte painter.

1984   *The Neverending Story*. Matter painter.

1985   "Willybu." Unrealized Danforth script.

1988   *They Live*. Photographic effects and matte paintings.

1990   *The Neverending Story: The Next Chapter*. This film used his matte paintings from the 1984 film.

1991   *Memoirs of an Invisible Man*. Matte paintings.
       West of Kashmire—A Sherlock Holmes Adventure. A live action project, with animation and matte paintings. Danforth is producing a seven-minute trailer with his wife that contains an elaborate reconstruction of 221B Baker Street and locations where *Gunga Din* and *Lives of a Bengal Lancer* were filmed.

Marcel Delgado: Born 1890, Died circa 1976

Marcel Delgado worked on nine O'Brien projects: *The Lost World* (1925), *King Kong, The Son of Kong, The Last Days of Pompeii*, "War

Eagles," "Gwangi," *Mighty Joe Young* and *It's a Mad, Mad, Mad, Mad World*
as a model maker and miniature maker. He grew up in his native village
of La Parrita, Mexico, and at six years old was sculpting toys. His family
moved to California in 1909. In 1911, his father died, forcing him to leave
school and find a full-time job. After World War I, he received training
at an art institute. His first feature film work was on *The Lost World*. After
that, he worked on many films, creating models and miniatures.

Films

1925   *The Lost World*. Model maker for O'Brien.

1930   *Creation*. Model maker for O'Brien.

1933   *King Kong*. Model maker for O'Brien, on the technical staff.
        The Son of Kong. Model maker for O'Brien, on the technical staff.

1935   *She*. Miniature maker.
        The Last Days of Pompeii. Miniature maker.

1938   "War Eagles." Built several animated miniatures of Viking men
        and finished the eagle models for this project with O'Brien.

1941   "Gwangi." Built an allosaurus animation armature and prototype
        for this aborted project with O'Brien.

1949   *Mighty Joe Young*. Built the animation models on this film for
        O'Brien.

1955   *The Beast of Hollow Mountain*. This film used his animation arma-
        ture from "Gwangi."

1960   *The Wonderful World of the Brothers Grimm*. Built a large dragon
        head with his brother Victor.
        Dinosaurus! Model maker.

1961   *Jack the Giant Killer*. Miniature maker with brother Victor.

1962   *It's a Mad, Mad, Mad, Mad World*. Created the miniature anima-
        tion figures, animated by Jim Danforth. O'Brien's last film.

1966   *Fantastic Voyage*. Model maker.

Linwood G. Dunn, ASC: Born December 27, 1904

Linwood C. Dunn did optical work on four of O'Brien's films: *King
Kong, The Son of Kong, Mighty Joe Young* and *It's a Mad, Mad, Mad,*

Mad World and was in charge of photographic effects on the latter. He was born and raised in Brooklyn and had little formal training. By 1925, he and his brother and sister were playing in a band at resorts in the Catskills (he learned to play the saxophone from George Eberle). In 1923, he became a projectionist for the American Motion Picture Corporation in New York, carrying a portable projector (35mm) from schools to churches. At that time, he intended to pursue a musical career, but when he was offered a job as camera assistant in 1925 on the serial *The Green Archer*, he took it. In 1926, he graduated to second cameraman.

By 1929, he had become first cameraman (today that would be director of photography). He joined RKO as assistant in the photographic effects department, where he stayed for 28 years, photographing miniatures and the earliest back projection shots and created his own zoom lens. In 1942, Eastman Kodak commissioned him to design and manufacture a special effects optical printer. In 1944, he was given the Academy Technical Achievement Award for "the design and construction of the Acme-Dunn Optical prnter." In 1946, he formed the Film Effects of Hollywood. From 1976 to 1982, he was a member of the Board of Governors of the Academy of Motion Picture Arts and Sciences, and from 1977 to 1979, he was chairman of the academy's Cinematography Executive Committee and Special Effects Award Committee. He received the Herbert T. Kalmus Gold Medal Award in 1971 and a Special Citation of the SMPTE in 1978. In 1979, he was honored with a special Academy Award for Outstanding Service and Dedication, and in 1981, the academy upgraded his 1944 Academy Award for "basic achievements which have a definite influence upon the advancement of the industry." He was president of the American Society of Cinematographers in 1977 and 1979, was treasurer of the ASC until 1985, and served on the ASC's Board of Governors and Editorial Advisory Committee. In 1985, he received the Golden Hugo Award and an honorary Doctor of Fine Arts degree from the San Francisco Art Institute. He is currently on the Publications Advisory Committee of the *American Cinematographer* magazine.

Films

1925   *The Green Archer*. Assistant cameraman.

1926   *Snowed In*. Assistant cameraman.

1927   *Hawk of the Hills*. Second cameraman.

1929   *Queen of the Northwoods*. First cameraman.

Flight. Operative cameraman. This Frank Capra film may have been released in another year.

Ringside. Matte shot (RKO film).

1930   *Cimarron.* Cameraman (RKO film).

The Case of Sergeant Grischa. Photographed miniatures on this RKO film.

Danger Lights. A 63.5mm early widefilm made in the Natural Vision Process (RKO film).

1933   *So This Is Harris.* Created optical wipes (RKO film).

Melody Cruise. Optical wipes (RKO film).

Hips, Hips Horray. Optical wipes (RKO film).

King Kong. Optical effects (O'Brien film for RKO).

The Son of Kong. Optical effects (O'Brien film for RKO).

Lucky Devils. Optical effects (RKO film).

The Phantom of Crestwood. Optical effects (RKO film).

Before Dawn. Optical effects (RKO film).

Ace of Aces. Optical effects (RKO film).

1934   *Down to Their Last Yacht.* Retouching (RKO film).

Anne of Green Gables. Optical effects (RKO film).

1938   *Bringing Up Baby.* Optical composites (RKO film).

1939   *The Hunchback of Notre Dame.* Optical work (RKO film).

1940   *Flicker Flashbacks.* Optical restoration of old films made in 1912 (RKO film).

Citizen Kane. Optical composites and recomposing of scenes (RKO film).

1942   *The Cat People.* Optical work; dissolves and duplicating of shots (RKO film).

1949   *Mighty Joe Young.* Opticals (O'Brien film for RKO).

1951   *The Thing.* Electrical effects at end (RKO film).

1953   *The Narrow Margin.* Skip-framed fight scene at climax, to "give it a little zip" (RKO film).

1954   *The French Line.* He added diffusion and shadows on Jane Russell's "bazooms" (RKO film).

1961   *West Side Story.* Created and supervised the photographic effects and title sequence.

Journey of the Stars. Film effects of Hollywood; designed and created special optical equipment for this Cinerama-Boeing 70mm Spacearium film.

1962   55 *Days at Peking*. Special photographic effects consultant.
        Circus. Special photographic effects consultant on this Frank Capra 70mm film (Ultra Panavision).
        It's a Mad, Mad, Mad, Mad World. Photographic effects.

Linwood Dunn did special effects work on the following films, but the exact type of work is not known.

1964   *My Fair Lady*.

1965   *The Great Race*.

1966   *Hawaii*. Academy Award nomination.
        The Bible.

1967   *Tobruk*.
        A Place to Stand. 70mm Expo '67 film.

1970   *Darling Lili*.
        Airport.

1979   *The Shape of Things to Come*.

Ray Harryhausen: Born June 29, 1920

Ray Harryhausen collaborated with O'Brien on three feature film projects: *Mighty Joe Young, The Valley of the Mist* and *The Animal World*. Educated in southern California at the Audubon Junior High School and Manual Arts High School, he developed a hobby of reconstructing prehistoric animals and later filming them in 16mm. He also attended City College in Los Angeles, where he studied dramatics, photography and sculpture, and the University of Southern California, where he studied art direction and film. His first commercial work was for producer George Pal, animating "Puppetoons" for Paramount. He then joined the Frank Capra Unit of the Signal Corps during World War II. In 1947, he was first assistant to O'Brien on *Mighty Joe Young*, released in 1949. From 1946 to 1953, he made his own puppet animation fairy tale films on 16mm and created the technical effects on his first solo feature film in 1952. From 1953 to 1961, he worked as technical effects creator, forming a partnership with producer Charles H. Schneer on a series of films for Columbia. From 1963 until 1981, he worked as creator of special visual effects and associate producer. He appeared as an actor in a cameo role for *Spies Like Us* in 1984 and retired from the business in 1987. His *Film Fantasy Scrapbook* was published in 1972 and reissued and enlarged in 1974, 1981 and 1989. He was awarded a special award in 1992.

Films

1938   "Evolution." Uncompleted 16mm documentary.

1940   *Dipsy Gypsy*. Animator. Puppetoon short for George Pal productions. (All Puppetoon shorts were made for Pal).
        Jasper and the Scarecrow. Animator. Puppetoon.
        Hoola Boola. Animator. Puppetoon.
        Western Daze. Animator. Puppetoon.
        Jasper and the Watermelons. Animator. Puppetoon.
        Sleeping Beauty. Animator. Puppetoon.
        Tulips Shall Grow. Shooting title: "Nuts and Bolts." Animator. Puppetoon. O'Brien also worked on this film.

1946   *Mother Goose Stories*. 16mm fairy tale.

1949   *Mighty Joe Young*. First technician to O'Brien.

1950   "The Valley of the Mist." Aborted O'Brien project.
        Little Red Riding Hood. 16mm fairy tale.
        "Baron Munchausen." Aborted 16mm fairy tale.

1951   *Hansel and Gretel*. 16mm fairy tale.

1952   *The Story of Rapunzel*. 16mm fairy tale.
        The Beast from 20,000 Fathoms. Technical effects.
        "The Elementals." Created the story idea and shot test footage, shown to producer Jack Dietz, coproducer of *The Beast from 20,000 Fathoms* and *The Black Scorpion*. A script was written, but the project went no further.

1953   *It Came from Beneath the Sea*. Technical effects credit.
        The Story of King Midas. 16mm fairy tale.
        "The Tortoise and the Hare." Uncompleted 16mm fairy tale.

1956   *Earth vs. the Flying Saucers*. Technical effects credit.
        The Animal World. Animation credit. O'Brien was the supervising animator.

1957   *20 Million Miles to Earth*. Technical effects credit.

1958   *The 7th Voyage of Sinbad*. Visual effects credit. In Technicolor and Dynamation.

1959   *The Three Worlds of Gulliver.* Visual effects credit. In Super-Dynamation.

1960   "Tarzan and the Ant Men." Unrealized project.

1961   "Food of the Gods." Unrealized project.
        Mysterious Island. Visual effects credit. In SuperDynamation.

1963   *Jason and the Argonauts.* Originally known as "Jason and the Golden Fleece." Associate producer with Charles H. Schneer and creator of special effects.

1964   *First Men in the Moon.* Associate producer with Schneer and creator of special visual effects. In Panavision and Lunacolor.

1966   *One Million Years B.C.* Special visual effects credit. Special processes: Giant Panamation.

1969   *The Valley of Gwangi.* Associate producer and creator of special visual effects.

1973   *The Golden Voyage of Sinbad.* Coproducer with Schneer, creator of visual effects and credit for cocreating the story. In Dynarama.

1977   *Sinbad and the Eye of the Tiger.* Coproducer with Schneer, creator of special visual effects and credit for cocreating the story. In Dynarama.

1981   *Clash of the Titans.* Coproducer with Schneer and creator of special visual effects.
        "Sinbad and the Seven Wonders of the World." Aborted project written by Beverly Cross.
        "Sinbad on Mars." Aborted project scripted by Kenneth Kolb. Space rocket designs were made by an artist for this idea.

1983   "People of the Mist." Aborted project based on the novel by H. Rider Haggard of *She* fame. Michael Winner was to be the director.

1984   "Force of the Trojans." Aborted Charles H. Schneer project, written by Beverly Cross. The art director was Michael Stringer; Andrew V. Maclagen was to direct. Harryhausen did designs for the "Scylla" and "Charybdis" sequences. Jim Danforth, David Allen and Steve Archer were asked to do animation on it.
        "Skin and Bones." Harryhausen did an illustration and wrote a story treatment based on this story by Thorn Smith, author of

Topper. His wife Diana suggested the idea to him, and it was submitted through a friend to Woody Allen.

1987   *The Puppetoon Movie*. Compilation film that contains animation from *Hoola Boola, Sleeping Beauty* and *Tulips Shall Grow* (the latter with O'Brien).

Harry O. Hoyt:
Born August 6, 1891 or 1885, Died 1961

Harry O. Hoyt collaborated with O'Brien on two projects: *The Lost World* and *Creation*. He was born in Minneapolis and educated at the University of Minnesota, Columbia University, and Yale University. He started writing stories for the screen while a student at Yale and worked as an actor, scriptwriter and director. He also wrote short stories, novels and motion picture adaptions for 15 years. Around 1916, he appeared to have been a scenario editor at Fox, then moved to Metro, where he worked in the scenario department.

Films

1912   *The New York Hat*. Hoyt is supposed to have written for this D. W. Griffith film, which Anita Loos also claimed to have written.

1915   *Courage of Two*.[105] Author.
        Road to France. Author.
        Queen of Hearts. Author.
        Beloved Blackmailer. Author.
        By Hook or Crook. Author.
        Just Silvia. Author.
        I Want to Forget. Author.
        The Sea Waif. Author.
        Free Air. Director.

1916   *Notorious Gallagher*. Actor, playing a Sing-Sing warder.

1919   *The Invisible Hand*. Director.
        Through the Toils. Director.
        Broadway Saint. Director.
        The Forest Rivals. Director.

1921   *The Rider of the King Log/Rider of the King Log*. Director.

The Curse of Drink. Director and scriptwriter.

1922 *That Woman.* Director.

1924 *The Woman of the Jury.* Director.
The Law Demands. Director.
Fangs of the Wolf. Director.
Sundown. Codirector with Laurent Trimble.
The Radio Flyer. Director.
The Fatal Plunge. Director.

1925 *When Love Grows Cold.* Director and scriptwriter.
The Lost World. Director. Effects by O'Brien.
The Primrose Path. Director.
The Untamed Woman. Director.

1926 *The Belle of Broadway.* Director.

1927 *Bitter Apples.* Director and scriptwriter.
The Return of Boston Blackie. Director.

1928 *The Passion Song.* Director.

1930 *Darkened Skies.* Codirector with Harry Webb.
"Creation." Aborted project with Willis O'Brien (RKO).

1933 *Jungle Bride.* Codirector with Albert Kelly.

1938 "Lost Atlantis." Aborted attempt to use the "Creation" storyline,
in collaboration with producer Trem Carr and special effects
man Fred Jackman (from "Lost World"). Jackman photographed
two reels of animation for the project before the film's sponsor
Harry Cohn halted the production. The project was restarted
two years later using new dinosaur models created by Walter
Lantz and Edward Nassour. Columbia withdrew its support
from the film, and it was never completed.

1943 *The Avenging Rider.* Hoyt wrote the script, based on his story,
"The Five of Spades."

Peter Peterson: Birthdate unknown, Died 1961

Little is known about Peter Peterson except that he was an ex-grip
and worked with Obie on three feature films. He suffered from mul-
tiple sclerosis for the last 10 or so years of his life. He died of kidney
cancer.

Films

1933   *King Kong*. It is rumored that he worked as a grip on this film.

1949   *Mighty Joe Young*. Second technician, with O'Brien as technical creator (RKO film).

1957   *The Black Scorpion*. Special effects by Willis O'Brien and Peter Peterson (Warner Brothers).

1958   "The Las Vegas Monster." Animation by Peterson on *Black Scorpion* sets for his unrealized film project.

1959   *The Giant Behemoth/Behemoth the Sea Monster*. Animator, with Willis O'Brien as animation supervisor (Allied Artists film).

1960   "The Beetlemen." Color animation tests shot by Peterson for his unrealized film project.

Ernest B. Schoedsack:
Born June 8, 1893, Died December 23, 1979

Ernest Beaumont Schoedsack, also known as "Shorty" and "Monty," was director of four O'Brien projects: *King Kong, The Son of Kong, The Last Days of Pompeii* and *Mighty Joe Young*. He also worked uncredited on *This Is Cinerama*, as did O'Brien. He began in films as a cameraman for Mack Sennet at Keystone in 1914. During World War I, he was a captain in the Signal Corps, and after Amistice Day, November 11, 1918, he joined the Red Cross relief mission, helping Polish refugees escape from Russian-occupied territories. In Vienna, he met Merian C. Cooper at the railroad station. He remained in the war to its end, driving ambulances, shooting movies for the Red Cross and helping Polish refugees from the Russian oil fields; he captured the withdrawal at Kiev on film and was the last man to cross the great Dnieper River Bridge. Later, he joined the Near East Relief and became involved in the Greco-Turkish War of 1921–22. He was awarded the distinguished Service Medal "for humanitarian work in Smyrna and the refugee camps of the Near East." In September 1922, he joined Cooper to make such films as *Grass* and *Chang* with Ruth Rose, later his wife, whom he married around 1927. In 1928, he went with Cooper to Paramount Pictures. In 1931, he made *Rango* by himself, and in 1932, he shot location footage for *Lives of a Bengal Lancer*, which was not used in the final film. Later in 1932 he joined Cooper at RKO, directing films at that studio until the late 1930s. While testing photographic equipment at high altitudes for the U.S. Air Force during World War II, he severely damaged his eyes when he dropped his face mask. He had several operations on his eyes that did not cure the problem. Partially blind, he worked on only two other films.

Films

1925   *Grass/Grass: A Nation's Battle for Life/Grass: The Epic of a Lost Tribe.* Codirector, coproducer, coscriptwriter and cophotographer with Cooper.

1927   *Chang.* Codirector and coproducer with Cooper.

1929   *The Four Feathers.* Codirector with Cooper and Lothar Mendes and coproducer with Cooper.

1931   *Rango.* Director and producer (Paramount film).

1932   *The Lives of a Bengal Lancer.* Schoedsack went to India and shot location footage for this film. The footage was never used because it had apparently deteriorated. Originally he was assigned to direct the film with John Cronwell, But Schoedsack obtained a release from his contract and joined Cooper at RKO. The film was finally made without him by Henry Hathaway in 1935.

   The Most Dangerous Game/Hounds of Zaroff. Codirector with Irving Pichel and coproducer with Cooper (RKO film).

   Monkey's Paw. Directed additional scenes on this RKO film.

1933   "Uncrowned King." *Film Weekly*, March 17, 1933, said that "the adventures of Colonel T. E. Lawrence in Arabia are the subject of 'Uncrowned King,' which Ernest B. Schoedsack is directing for Radio. Exterior scenes have already been filmed in Mesopotamia." What happened to the film is unknown.

   King Kong. Codirector and coproducer with Cooper. O'Brien was the chief technician (RKO film).

   Blind Adventure. Director. Written by his wife Ruth Rose (RKO film).

   The Son of Kong. Director, with O'Brien as chief technician (RKO film).

1934   *Long Lost Father.* Director.

1935   *The Last Days of Pompeii.* Director, with O'Brien as chief techni-
        cian (RKO film).
        Outlaws of the Orient. Director (Columbia film).

1938   "War Eagles"/"White Eagle"/"The War Eagles." An aborted
        Cooper project that Schoedsack may have been involved in.

1940   *Doctor Cyclops.* Director (Paramount film).

1949   *Mighty Joe Young.* Director, with O'Brien as technical creator
        (RKO film).

1952   *This Is Cinerama.* Prologue by Schoedsack, written by Ruth Rose
        and Schoedsack, both uncredited. O'Brien also worked un-
        credited on this film.

Willis O'Brien Filmography

The information for these films is as complete as I can make them, having been drawn from a variety of sources. *The Dinosaur and the Missing Link, Prehistoric Poultry, Ghost of Slumber Mountain, R.F.D. 10,000 B.C., Morpheus Mike, The Lost World* and the test animation footage from "Creation" are available in 16mm and VHS and Beta video formats from Glenn Photo Supply, 6924 Canby Avenue, Suite 103, Reseda, CA 91335. This company also has a selection of photographs from O'Brien's films and watercolor artwork for sale.

The Dinosaur and the Missing Link (1915), one reel. Producer: Herman Wobber. Direction, story, photography, special effects and animation: Willis O'Brien. Distributed by Edison (reissued three months later as *The Dinosaur and the Baboon.*

The Birth of a Flivver (1916), one reel. Direction, story, photography, special effects and animation: Willis O'Brien. Distributor: Edison.

R.F.D., 10,000 B.C. (1917), one reel. Direction, story, photography, special effects and animation: Willis O'Brien. Distributor: Edison.

Morpheus Mike (1917), one reel. Direction, story, photography, special effects and animation: Willis O'Brien. Distributor: Edison .

Prehistoric Poultry (1917), one reel. Direction, story, photography, special effects and animation: Willis O'Brien. Distributor: Edison.

"Curious Pets of Our Ancestors" (1917).

"In the Villain's Power" (1917).

"The Puzzling Billboard" (1917), from the series, "Sam Loyd's Famous Puzzles."

Mickey's Naughty Nightmares (1917), an animated series containing footage of a real boy.

The Ghost of Slumber Mountain (1919)

Credits

Direction, story, special effects, animation and photography: Willis H. O'Brien. Producer: Herbert M. Dawley. Distributors: Cinema Distributing Corporation and World Film Corporation.

195

The Cast

Willis H. O'Brien .... Mad Dick

The Lost World (1925)

They sought a virgin world, and even there found
love!—Catchline for the film.

Credits

Production company: First National. Trade review running-time footage, March 2,
1925: 9,209 feet. (According to *Monthly Film Bulletin* [1971], the footage was 9,700
feet.) Black and white. Running time: 75 minutes. Note: A complete print of the
original version, screened in 1925, does not appear to exist, although present-day versions are representative of the original movie and contain most of the original dinosaur
footage. However, footage of Alma Bennett and Virginia Brown Faire is missing, according to William K. Everson (1971).

Dramatic direction .... Harry O. Hoyt
Produced under the supervision of .... Earl Hudson
Scenario and editorial direction .... Marion Fairfax
Based on the story by .... Sir Arthur Conan Doyle
Directors of photography .... Arthur Edeson,
J. Devereaux Jennings and Homer Scott
Film editor .... George McGuire
Assistant director and director of settings and architecture .... Milton Menasco
Special effects .... Marcel Delgado and Ralph Hammeras
Makeup .... Cecil Holland
Chief technician .... Fred W. Jackman
Story by arrangement with .... Watterson R. Rothacker
Research and technical direction .... Willis H. O'Brien

The Cast

Paula White .... Bessie Love
Sir John Roxton .... Lewis Stone
Professor Challenger .... Wallace Beery
Ed Malone .... Lloyd Hughes
Gladys Hungerford .... Alma Bennett
Marquette .... Virginia Browne Faire
Professor Summerlee .... Arthur Hoty
Challenger .... Margaret McWade
Apeman .... Bull Montana
Austin .... Finch Smiles
Zambo .... Jules Cowles
Colin McArdle .... George Bunny
Major Hibbard .... Charles Wellesley
Jocko .... Jocko

Creation (1930–31)

Just a lot of animals walking around.—Merian C. Cooper's verdict on the "Creation" footage, from *The Making of King Kong* by Goldner and Turner (1975).

Credits

A shelved project for RKO Pictures.

Director .... Harry O. Hoyt
Scenario .... Willis O'Brien and Harry O. Hoyt
Producer .... Bertram Millhauser
Adaption and dialogue .... Beulah Marie Dix
Production artists .... Mario Larrinaga, Byron L. Crabbe, Ernest Smythe and Juan Larrinaga
Director of photography .... Eddie Linden
Animal supervision .... Olga Celeste
Technical staff .... Marcel Delgado, E. B. Gibson, Orville Goldner, Carroll Shepphird and Fred Reefe
Chief technician and animator .... Willis O'Brien

The Cast

Hallett .... Ralf Harodle
Snooky .... The chimpanzee

King Kong (1933)

Holy mackerel, what a show!—Robert Armstrong as Carl Denham in *King Kong*.

Credits

A Cooper-Schoedsack Production for RKO Pictures. Length: 8,930 feet. Running time: 100 minutes. Originally given the "H" for Horrific certificate when shown in 1936 in England, later changed to an "A" certificate. Reissued in 1947 and 1952 and revived in London's West End cinema, the Cannon Premiere, on August 3, 1986, with the restored footage that was cut on the previous two reissues in a new print. Released on video in a restored colorized version in 1989 by the Turner Entertainment Company.

Producers and directors .... Merian C. Cooper and Ernest B. Schoedsack
Executive producer .... David O. Selznick
Screenplay by .... James A. Creelman and Ruth Rose
Idea conceived by .... Merian C. Cooper and Edgar Wallace
Chief technician .... Willis H. O'Brien
Technical staff .... E. B. "Buzz" Gibson, Marcel Delgado, Fred Reefe, Orville Goldner, Carroll Shepphird

Art technicians . . . . Mario Larrinaga and Byron L. Crabbe
Photographers . . . . Eddie Linden, Vernon Walker and J. O. Taylor
Music . . . . Max Steiner
Sound effects . . . . Murray Spivack
Settings . . . . Carroll Clark and Al Herman
Recorded by . . . . E. A. Wolcott
Film editor . . . . Ted Cheesman
Production assistants . . . . Archie S. Marshek and Walter Daniels
Scenario associate . . . . Horace McCoy
Operative cameramen . . . . . Eddie Henderson, Felix Schoedsack and Lee Davis
Assistant cameraman . . . . Bert Willis, William Reinhold,
William Clothier and Clifford Stine
Optical photography . . . . Linwood G. Dunn and William Ulm
Projection process . . . . Sidney Saunders
Dunning process supervision . . . . . Carroll H. Dunning and C. Dodge Dunning
Williams Matte supervision . . . . Frank Williams
Special effects . . . . Harry Redmond, Jr.
Sculptor . . . . John Cerisoli
Construction technician . . . . W. G. White
Technical artists . . . . Juan Larrinaga, Zachary Hoag and Victor Delgado
Associate, sound effects . . . . Walter G. Elliott
Makeup supervision . . . . Mel Burns
Set decorations . . . . Thomas Little
Supervising art director . . . . Van Nest Polglase
Costumes . . . . Walter Plunkett
Assistant to Merian C. Cooper . . . . Zoe Porter
Painting technician . . . . Peter Stich
Camera aircraft pilots . . . . Duke Krantz and George Weiss
Technical advisers . . . . Dr. J. W. Lytle, Dr. O. A. Paterson
and Dr. Harry C. Raven
Art titles . . . . Pacific Title Co.
Sound system . . . . RCA Photophone

The Cast

Ann Darrow . . . . Fay Wray
Carl Denham . . . . Robert Armstrong
Jack Driscoll . . . . Bruce Cabot
Captain Englehorn . . . . Frank Reicher
Charles Westson . . . . Sam Hardy
Native chief . . . . Noble Johnson
Witch king . . . . Steve Clemento
Second Mate Briggs . . . . James Flavin
Charlie . . . . Victor Wong
Socrates . . . . Paul Porcasi
Dock Watchman . . . . Russ Powell
Hotel victim . . . . Sandra Shaw
Sailor . . . . Ethan Laidlaw
Sailor . . . . Blackie Whiteford
Sailor . . . . Dick Curtis
Sailor . . . . Charles Sullivan
Sailor . . . . Harry Tenbrook

Sailor .... Gil Perkins
Theatre patron .... Vera Lewis
Theatre patron .... Leroy Mason
Reporter .... Frank Mills
Reporter .... Lynton Brent
Native dancer .... Jim Thorpe
Police captain .... George MacQuarrie
Handmaiden .... Madame Sul-te-wan
Native woman .... Etta MacDaniel
Native man .... Ray Turner
Girl .... Dorothy Gulliver
Girl .... Carlotta Monti
Navy pilot .... Barney Capehart
Navy pilot .... Bob Galloway
Navy pilot .... Eric Wood
Navy pilot .... Dusty Mitchell
Navy pilot .... Russ Rodgers
Engineer .... Reginald Barlow
Flight commander .... Merian C. Cooper
Chief observer .... Ernest B. Schoedsack
and
King Kong, the Eighth Wonder of the World

The Son of Kong (1933)

Well, if it isn't a little Kong!—Robert Armstrong as
Carl Denham in *The Son of Kong.*

Credits

Production Company: RKO. Length: 6,243 feet. Original running time: 68 minutes
(*The Making of King Kong* by Goldner and Turner [1975] lists the running time as 71
mintes). Release date in England: July 30, 1934. Certificate "A." The film was also
rereleased during the late 1930s with *Frankenstein* (1931) and *Dracula* (1931).

Executive producer .... Merian C. Cooper
Director .... Ernest B. Schoedsack
Associate producer .... Archie S. Marshek
Story by .... Ruth Rose
Photography .... Eddie Linden, Vernon L. Walker and J. O. Taylor
Music .... Max Steiner
Settings .... Van Nest Polglase and Al Herman
Sound effects .... Murray Spivack
Recorded by .... Earl A. Wolcott
Editor .... Ted Cheesman
Chief technician .... Willis O'Brien
Technical staff .... E. B. "Buzz" Gibson, Marcel Delgado,
                        Carroll Shepphird, Fred Reefe and W. G. White
Art technicians .... Mario Larrinaga and Byron L. Crabbe
Special effects .... Harry Redmond, Jr.

```
Associate, sound effects ............................ Walter G. Elliott
Cameramen ............................... Bert Willis, Linwood Dunn,
                                    Clifford Stine and Felix Schoedsack
Set decorations ...................................... Thomas Little
Costumes ......................................... Walter Plunkett
Makeup supervision ..................................... Mel Burns
Williams process supervision ......................... Frank Williams
Dunning process supervision ....... Carroll Dunning and C. Dodge Dunning
Recording process ........................... RCA Photophone System
```

The Cast

```
Carl Denham ..................................... Robert Armstrong
Hilda Peterson ...................................... Helen Mack
Captain Englehorn ................................... Frank Reicher
Helsrom ........................................... John Marston
Charlie ............................................. Victor Wong
Mickey ........................................... Lee Kohlmar
Peterson .......................................... Clarence Wilson
Mrs. Hudson ...................................... Katharine Ward
Red .................................................. Ed Brady
Journalist ......................................... Gertrude Short
Servant ........................................... Gertrude Sutton
Chinese vendor ................................... James B. Lelong
Native chief .................................... Noble Johnson
Magician ......................................... Steve Clemento
Bailiff ............................................ Frank O'Conner
Bill ........................................ Constantine Romanoff
Tommy .......................................... Harry Tenbrook
Dutch ........................................ Leo "Dutch" Hendrian
```

The Last Days of Pompeii (1935)

MORE than awe-inspiring spectacle; MORE than great human drama; MORE than inspiring entertainment ... EMOTIONAL DYNAMITE ... blasted from the living ashes of a past whose heart-call echoes through the walls of time.... A FLAMING PANORAMA OF EXCITEMENT HURLED TO THE SCREEN WITH A SURGING POWER THAT WILL STORM THE HEARTS OF THRILL-HUNGRY MILLIONS OF TODAY! Behold the wonders of the biggest show in 2,000 years!— trade advertisements for the film, 1935.

Credits

Production Company: RKO-Radio. Length: 8,550 feet. Running time: 92 minutes. Certificate "A." (*Film Daily* listed the running time as 96 minutes in 1936.)

Director .... Ernest B. Schoedsack
Producer .... Merian C. Cooper
Screenplay .... Ruth Rose
Collaboration on adaptation .... Boris Ingster
Original story .... Melville Baker and James A. Creelman
Production associate .... John Speaks
Music by .... Roy Webb
Photography .... J. Roy Hunt
Chief technician .... Willis O'Brien
Art direction .... Byron Crabbe
Photographic technician .... Eddie Linden
Photographic effects .... Vernon Walker
Special effects .... Harry Redmond
Sound effects .... Walter Elliot
Art director .... Van Nest Polglase
Associate .... Al Herman
Costumes .... Aline Bernstein
Set dressing .... Thomas Little
Recorded by .... Clem Portman
Music edited by .... P. J. Faulkner
Edited by .... Archie F. Marshek
Assistant director .... Ivan Thomas
Uncredited effects .... Marcel Delgado, Gus White and Carroll Shepphird

The Cast

Marcus .... Preston Foster
Burbix .... Alan Hale
Pontius Pilate .... Basil Rathbone
Flavius .... John Wood
Prefect .... Louis Calhern
Flavius as a boy .... David Holt
Clodia .... Dorothy Wilson
Cleon .... William V. Mong
Warder .... Henry Kolker

The Dancing Pirate (1936)

The first romantic musical in 100 percent new Technicolor! Made by that brilliant team who gave you that gem of a short production "La Cucaracha." — From the poster for the film.

Credits

Directed by .... Lloyd Corrigan
Executive producer .... Merian C. Cooper
Producer .... John Speaks
Designed in color by .... Robert Edmond Jones
From the story by .... Emma Lindsay Squier

Dance director .... Russell Lewis
Musical director .... Alfred Newman
Technicolor director .... Natalie Kalmus
Photographed by .... William V. Skall
Art director .... W. B. Ihnen
Photographic effects .... Willis O'Brien
Screenplay .... Ray Harris and Francis E. Farogoh
Adaption .... Jack Wagner and Boris Ingster
Musical lyrics .... Richard Hart and Lorenz Hart
Editor .... Archie Marshek

Production company: Pioneer. Technicolor. Length: 7,658 feet. Running time: 85 minutes. (The 1948 reissue gives a length of 6,902 feet.) Distributor: Radio Pictures, and presented by Pioneer Pictures by Merian C. Cooper. Certificate "U." Robert Benchley is also credited for the adaptation.

The Cast

Jonathan Pride .... Charles Collins
Alcalde .... Frank Morgan
Serafina .... Steffi Duna
Pamfilo .... Luis Alberni
Don Baltazar .... Victor Varconi
Chago .... Jack La Rue
Blanca .... Alma Real
Tecolote .... William V. Mong
Pirate chief .... Mitchell Lewis
Shepherd .... Julian Rivero
Mozo .... John Eberts
Royal Cansinos .... Cansino Family
Pirate cook .... Cy Kendall
Orville .... Harold Waldridge
Orville's mother .... Vera Lewis
Landlady .... Nora Cecil
Miss Ponsonby .... Ellen Lowe
Pirate mate .... Max Wagner
Sailor .... James Farley

War Eagles (1938–39)

Credits

An unrealized project for MGM, Loew's.

Directors-producers .... Merian C. Cooper and Ernest B. Schoedsack
Script .... Cyril Hume
Special effects .... Willis O'Brien, Marcel Delgado and George Lofgren
Drawings .... Duncan Gleason

Gwangi (1941)

This was a rodeo with a dinosaur, what the
hell!"—Ernest B. Schoedsack's comment on
"Gwangi."

Credits

RKO Pictures/Colonial Pictures. An aborted feature-film project.

Coproducers .... Willis O'Brien and John Speaks
Script .... Harold Lamb and Emily Barrye
Effects technician .... Marcel Delgado

The Cast

T.J.? .... Anne Shirley
Tuck Kirby? .... James Craig
Professor Bromley? .... Edgar Kennedy

Mighty Joe Young (1949)

Oh well! It was one of those things. You do it!—
Schoedsack on *Mighty Joe Young*.

Credits

Production company: ARKO. Distributor: RKO Radio Pictures. Length: 8,411 feet.
Running time: 93 minutes. Certificate "A." Release date: July 23, 1949. The
orphanage sequence was tinted red on the original release.

Director .... Ernest B. Schoedsack
Producers .... John Ford and Merian C. Cooper
Screenplay by .... Ruth Rose
Story by .... Merian C. Cooper
Photography .... J. Roy Hunt, ASC
Technical creator .... Willis O'Brien
First technician .... Ray Harryhausen
Second technician .... Peter Peterson
Technical staff .... Marcel Delgado, George Lofgren and Fitch Fulton
Art director .... James Basevi
Assistant art director .... Howard Richmond
Photographic effects .... Harold Stine and Bert Willis
Optical photography .... Linwood Dunn
Film editor .... Ted Cheesman
Sound editor .... Walter Elliott
Musical score .... Roy Webb
Musical director .... C. Bakaleinikoff
Unit production manager .... Lloyd Richards
Assistant director .... Samuel Ruman
Production effects .... Jack Cannon

Costumes .... Adele Balkan
Set dressing .... George Altwils
Sound .... John L. Cass and Clem Portman

The Cast

Jill Young .... Terry Moore
Greg Johnson .... Ben Johnson
Max O'Hara .... Robert Armstrong
Mr. Joseph Young .... Mr. Joseph Young
Windy .... Frank McHugh
Jones .... Douglas Fowley
Crawford .... Dennis Green
Smith .... Paul Guilfoyle
Brown .... Nestor Paiva
Mr. Young .... Regis Toomey
Jill, aged 7 .... Lora Lee Michel
Schultz .... James Flavin
and Primo Carnero, Man Mountain Dean and the Swedish Angel

The Valley of the Mist (1950)

Credits

Unrealized feature film project for Jesse L. Lasky.

Producer .... Jesse L. Laskey, Sr.
Associate producer .... William Lasky
Screenplay .... Jesse Lasky, Jr.
Based on the story .... "Emilio and Guloso"
Original story idea by .... Willis O'Brien and Darlyne O'Brien
Special effects .... Willis O'Brien and Ray Harryhausen
Additional scriptwriter .... Richard Landau

This Is Cinerama (1952)

The film that puts YOU in the picture! — Publicity
blurb for the film.

Credits

Released on September 30, 1952, by Cinerama Productions Corporation. Six-track magnetic Cinerama Stereophonic Sound System. Prints by Technicolor. Running time: 135 minutes. (In *Wide Screen Movies* Carr and Hayes list the running time as 120 minutes plus an intermission.) The film was reissued in England in October 1973 with a running time of 135 minutes and 133 minutes, and was rereleased in the United States in 1971 by the Cinerama Releasing Corporation and Film Effects of Hollywood, which did the optical conversion to 70mm Super Cinerama. Filmed in Cinerama.

Wide Screen Movies also noted that the film never had an actual title on the release prints and was referred to as "Cinerama" for the first two years of its release.

Executive producers .... Lowell Thomas, Michael Todd, Louis B. Mayer
Producers .... Merian C. Cooper and Robert L. Bendick
The "Atom Smasher" Roller Coaster Ride,
"Folk-dancing Festival in Salzburg," "The Edinburgh Tattoo"
and "The Canals of Venice" sequences .... Michael Todd, Jr.
"Vienna Boys Choir" and "The Temple Dance"
finale in the "La Scala" sequences supervised by .... Michael Todd
Prologue supervisor .... Walter Thompson
Prologue written by .... Ernest B. Schoedsack and Ruth Rose
"Beautiful America" sequence supervised by .... Fred Rickey
                                                    and Merian C. Cooper
"Cypress Gardens, Florida sequence .... Merian C. Cooper
Pilot .... A. Paul Mantz, air speed record holder
Additional sequence supervisors .... Merian C. Cooper and Michael Todd
Production executive .... Louis B. Mayer
Associate producer .... Michael Todd
Musical director .... Louis Forbes
Additional music (uncredited) .... Max Steiner
Cameraman .... Harry Squire
Assistant cameraman .... Jack Priestley
Camera technician .... Coleman Thomas Conroy, Jr.
Grip .... Marty Philbin
Sound .... Richard J. Pietschmann, Jr.
Sound assistant .... Fred Bosch
Film editors .... Bill Henry and Milton Shifman
Paintings .... Mario Larrinago and Willis O'Brien (uncredited)
Sound effects .... Reeves Sound Studio
Set design .... Leo Kerz
Music .... Cinerama Philharmonic Orchestra, Salt Lake City
                                Tabernacle Choir, Vienna Philharmonic,
                        Vienna Boys Choir, Long Island Choral Society
Business manager .... Frank Smith
Creator of Cinerama process .... Fred Waller
Technical development .... Hazard E. Reeves
Technical assistants .... Wentworth Fling, William R. Latady,
        Richard Babish, Frank Richmond, Robert Dresser and Walter R. Hicks
Cinerama research and development .... Fred Waller, Hazard E. Reeves,
                Walter Hicks, Wentworth Fling, Karl Vogel, Dr. Ernest Hare,
            Fred Koppler, Michael Chitty, Ernest Franck, Norman Prisament,
                Otto Popelka, Emil Neroda, Richard Vorisek, Ed Schmidt,
                Richard J. Pietschmann, Jr., C. Robert Fine, Larry Davee,
                    Lyman Wiggins, S. J. (Joe) Begun, Richard Ranger
Cinerama sound .... Reeves Soundcraft Corporation
Projectors .... Century Projection Corporation
Advertising .... Peter Schaeffer and McCann-Erickson
Publicist .... Lynn Farnol
"America the Beautiful" music and lyrics by .... Katharine Lee Bates
                                                    and Samuel A. Ward
Film stock .... Eastman Kodak Company

Filmed in New York City and Niagara Falls, New York; Cypress Gardens, Florida; Rockaway Beach, Scotland; Spain; Salzburg, Austria; Venice, Italy; and La Scala Opera House, Milan, Italy.

Host and narrator .... Lowell Thomas

The Animal World (1956)

Should not be missed by anyone! Most unusual in drama, suspense and excitement! — *Showman's Trade Review.*

Credits

Production company: Windsor. Distributor: Warner Brothers. Length: 7,253 feet. Running time: 80 minutes (there is also a running time of 82 minutes). Color by Technicolor. Certificate "U."

Writer, producer and director .... Irwin Allen
Production associate .... George E. Swink
Music composed and conducted by .... Paul Sawtell
Photographed by .... Harold Wellman, ASC, and naturalist photographers throughout the world
Art director .... Bert Tuttle
Film editors .... Gene Palmer and Robert A. Belcher
Sound effects editors .... Henry L. DeMond, MPSE, and Walter Elliott, MPSE
Music editor .... Richard Harris
Supervising animator .... Willis O'Brien
Animation .... Ray Harryhausen
Special effects by .... Arthur S. Rhoades
Narrators .... Theodore Von Eltz and John Storm

The Beast of Hollow Mountain (1956)

From the dawn of history ... A monster beyond belief! — From the film poster for the film.

Credits

Distributor: United Artists. Producers: William and Edward Nassour. Length: 6,907 feet. Running times: Great Britain, 77 minutes; United States, 81 minutes. CinemaScope. Color by DeLuxe. Certificate "A."

Directors .... Edward Nassour and Ismael Rodriguez
Screenplay by .... Robert Hill
Additional dialogue .... Jack DeWitt
Based on the original story by .... Willis O'Brien

Camera (DeLuxe Color) .... Jorge Stahl, Jr.
Special effects .... Henry Sharpe
Music .... Raul La Vista
Editors .... Holbrook Todd and Maury Wright

The Cast

Jimmy Ryan .... Guy Madison
Sarita .... Patricia Medina
Enrique Rios .... Eduardo Noriega
Felipe Sanchez .... Carlos Rivas
Panchito .... Mario Navarro
Pancho .... Pascual Garcia Pena
Don Pedre .... Julio Villareal
Margarita .... Lupe Carriles
Martinez .... Manuel Arvida
Manuel .... Jose Chavez
Jose .... Magarito Luna
Carlos .... Roberto Contreras
Jorge .... Lobo Negro
(Guillermo Hernandez)
Shopkeeper .... Jorge Trevino
Employee .... Armando Guitierrez

The Black Scorpion (1957)

Shown uncut! Every terror exactly as filmed!—
Advertisement for the film.

Credits

Distributor: Warner Brothers. Aspect ratio: 1.85. Length: 7,896 feet. Running time: Records vary from 86 to 87 to 88 minutes, indicating that the film may have been cut for British release. Certificate "X."

Director .... Edward Ludwig
Script .... David Duncan and Robert Blees
Based on the story by .... Paul Yawitz
Special effects .... Willis O'Brien and Peter Peterson
Cinematography .... Lionel Lindon, ASC
Art director .... Edward Fitzgerald
Music composed and conducted by .... Paul Sawtell
Orchestrations .... Bert Shefter
Electronic music .... Jack Cookerly
Film editor .... Richard Van Enger, ACE
Producers .... Jack Dietz and Frank Melford
Assistant directors .... Jaimie Contreras and Ray Heinze

The Cast

Henry "Hank" Scott .... Richard Denning
Teresa Alvarez .... Mara Corday

Arturo Ramos .... Carlos Rivas
Juanito .... Mario Navarro
Dr. Velazco .... Carlos Muzquiz
Jose De La Cruz .... Pascual Pena
Florentina .... Fanny Schiller
Father Delgado .... Pedro Galvan
Major Cosio .... Arturo Martinez

The Giant Behemoth (U.S. Title) (1959)
Behemoth, the Sea Monster (British Title)

Out of the sea, burning like fire . . . Behemoth! —
From the press handout for the film.

Credits

Distributors: Allied Artists (United States), Eros (Great Britain). Length: 6,272 feet. Running time: 70 minutes. Quota length and running time: 5,811 feet, 64 minutes. An 80-minute running time is listed in *Focus on Film*'s filmography of O'Brien. Certificate "X."

Directors .... Douglas Hickox and Eugene Lourie
Producer .... David Diamond (Ted Lloyd)
Script by .... Eugene Lourie
Story by .... Robert Abel and Allen Adler
Special effects .... Willis O'Brien, Peter Peterson,
                           Jack Rabin, Irving Block and Louis DeWitt
Photography .... Ken Hodges
Art director .... Harry White
Music .... Ted Astley
Editor .... Lee Doig
Sound .... Sid Wiles

The Cast

Steven Karnes .... Gene Evans
Professor James Bickford .... Andre Morell
Jeannie MacDougall .... Leigh Madison
Tom .... Henry Vidon
John .... John Turner
Dr. Sampson .... Jack MacGowran
Submarine Officer .... Maurice Kaufmann
Scientist .... Leonard Sachs

The Lost World (1960)

See the death-battle of the Jurassic dinosaurs!
70-foot Brontosaurus goes wild! Tyrannosaurus

hatches baby monster! Sea-serpent of the lava lake appears from the depths! Flesh-eating vegetable traps explorers!—Trade advertisements for the film.

Credits

Production Company: Saratoga Production. Distributor: 20th Century–Fox. Length: 8,730 feet. Running time: 97 minutes. CinemaScope, DeLuxe color. Release dates: August 29, 1960 (England), July 13, 1960 (United States).

Producer and director .... Irwin Allen
Screenplay by .... Irwin Allen and Charles Bennett
Music by .... Bert Shefter and Paul Sawtell
Director of photography .... Winton Hoch, ASC
Art directors .... Duncan Cramer and Walter M. Simonds
Set direction .... Walter M. Scott, Joseph Kish and John Sturtevant
Special photographic effects .... L. B. Abbott, ASC,
James B. Gordon, ASC, and Emil Kosa, Jr.
Film editor .... Hugh S. Fowler, ACE
Assistant director .... Ad Schaumer
Technical adviser .... Henry E. Lester
Costume designer .... Paul Zastupnevitch
Makeup by .... Ben Nye
Hair styles by .... Helen Turpin, CHS
Effects technician .... Willis O'Brien
Production illustrator .... Maurice Zuberano
Sound .... E. Clayton Ward and Harry M. Leonard
Orchestration .... Howard Jackson and Sid Cuttnar

The Cast

Lord Roxton .... Michael Rennie
Jennifer Holmes .... Jill St. John
Ed Malone .... David Hedison
Professor Challenger .... Claude Rains
Gomez .... Fernando Lamas
Professor Summerlee .... Richard Haydn
David .... Ray Stricklyn
Costa .... Jay Novello
Native Girl .... Vitina Marcus
Burton White .... Ian Wolfe
Stuart Homes .... John Graham
Professor Waldron .... Colin Campbell

It's a Mad, Mad, Mad, Mad World (1963)

For the first time ... the revolutionary new Cinerama single lens process!—Publicity blurb announcing the change from the three-lens to the single-lens 70mm format.

Credits

Distributor: United Artists. Production company: Kramer. A Casey Productions,
Filmed in Ultra Panavision 70, presented in 70mm Super Cinerama. Technicolor.
Westrex six-track magnetic stereophonic sound. Length: 21,675 feet. Running time:
192 minutes. (Original running time was 210 minutes, including an 8-minute overture
and a 16-minute intermission. When it was released in 70mm, it was reedited to 162
minutes plus the overture and intermission. The 35mm version runs at 154 minutes
without the overture and the intermission; this is the same running time as the current home video version.) Winner of the Academy Award for best sound effects in
1964.

Producer and director .... Stanley Kramer
Story and screenplay by .... William and Tania Rose
Assistant to the director .... Ivan Volkman
Cinematography .... Ernest Laszlo
Production designer .... Rudolph Sternad
Music .... Ernest Gold
Title song .... Ernest Gold and Mack David
Film editor .... Fred Knudtson
Sound .... John Kean
Production manager .... Clem Beauchamp
Stunt supervisor .... Carey Loftin
Art director .... Gordon Gurnee
Costume design .... Bill Thomas
Costume supervision .... Joseph King
Assistant directors .... Charles Scott, Jr., Bert Chervin
                                             and George Batcheller
Location manager .... William Mull
Special effects .... Danny Lee
Photographic effects .... Linwood G. Dunn, ASC, James B. Gordon, ASC

Film Effect of Hollywood staff:
Director of photography .... James B. Gordon, ASC
Production manager .... Don Weed
Matte artist .... Howard Fisher
Consultant and director of animation .... Willis O'Brien
Supervisor of miniatures .... Howard Lydecker
Animator .... James Danforth
Cinematographic specialists .... Cecil Love and Bill Reinhold
Model maker .... Marcel Delgado
Process photography .... Farciot Edouart, ASC
Title designer .... Saul Bass
Casting .... Stalmaster-Lister Co.
Additional film editors .... Gene Fowler, Jr., and Robert C. Jones
Music editor .... Art Dunham
Sound recording .... Samuel Goldwyn Studios
Sound supervision .... Gordon E. Sawyer
Sound engineer .... James Keene
Rerecording .... Clem Portman, Vinton Vernon and Roy Granville
Sound editor .... Walter G. Elliott
Assistant to the producer .... Anne Kramer

```
Property master ........................................... Art Cole
Set director ........................................... Joseph Kish
Construction coordinator ......................... Arnold "Bud" Pine
Aerial photography ................................. Albert Wetzel
Additional photography ................ Irmin Roberts and Hal A. McAlpin
Camera operator ................................. Charles F. Wheeler
Camera assistant ................................. Richard Johnson
Chief gaffer ................................... Joseph Edesa
Company grip ................................... Morris Rosen
Assistant company grip ......................... Martin Kaschuk
Script supervisor ............................... Marshall Scholm
Makeup ............... George Lane, Lynn Reynold and Dick Smith
Hair stylist ................................... Connie Nichols
Music recording ............................... William Britton
Orchestration ................................. Albert Woodbury
Music production assistant ....................... Bobby Helfer
Titles ....................................... Playhouse Pictures
Title producer ............................... Bill Melendez
Title animation photography ..................... Allen Childs
Title editor ................................. Hugh Kelley
Studio security ............................... Vance Boyd
```
Songs

"It's a Mad, Mad, Mad, Mad World," "31 Flavors" and "You Satisfy My Soul":
```
Dance music singers ........................... The Shirelles
Players ..................................... The Four Mads
```

Filmed at Revue Studios (Universal City Studios) and on location in Colorado and in Santa Rosita Beach State Park, San Diego, Agoura, Long Beach, Malibu, Palm Springs (Palos Verdes Estates), San Pedro, Santa Ana, Santa Barbara, Santa Monica, 29 Palms and Yucca Valley, California.

The Cast

```
Captain T. G. Culpepper ......................... Spencer Tracy
J. Russell Finch ............................... Milton Berle
Melville Crump ............................... Sid Caesar
Benjy Benjamin ............................... Buddy Hackett
Mrs. Marcus ................................. Ethel Merman
Ding Bell ................................... Mickey Rooney
Sylvester Marcus ............................. Dick Shawn
Otto Meyer ................................. Phil Silvers
Lieutenant Colonel J. Algernon Hawthorne ......... Terry-Thomas
Lennie Pike ................................. Jonathan Winters
Monica Crump ............................... Edie Adams
Emmeline Finch ............................. Dorothy Provine
First cab driver ................... Eddie "Rochester" Anderson
Tyler Fitzgerald ............................. Jim Backus
Airplane pilot ............................... Ben Blue
Police sergeant ............................. Alan Carney
Mrs. Halliburton ............................. Barrie Chase
Chief of police ............................. William Demarest
Second cab driver ........................... Peter Falk
```

Colonel Wilberforce .... Paul Ford
Third cab driver .... Leo Gorcey
Dinckler .... Edward Everett Horton
Jimmy, the Crook .... Buster Keaton
Nervous man .... Don Knotts
Airport tower controller .... Carl Reiner
Airport firemen .... The Three Stooges
              (Moe Howard, Larry Fine and Curly Joe De Rita)
Union official .... Joe E. Brown
Sheriff Mason .... Andy Devine
City fire chief .... Sterling Holloway
Irwin .... Marvin Kaplan
Airport manager .... Charles Lane
Lieutenant Matthews .... Charles McGraw
Gertie, the switchboard operator .... ZaSu Pitts
Schwartz, the police secretary .... Madlyn Rhue
Ray .... Arnold Stang
Airport tower radio operator .... Jesse White
City mayor .... Lloyd Corrigan
Voice of Ginger Culpepper .... Selma Diamond
Deputy sheriff .... Stan Freberg
Voice of Billie Sue Culpepper .... Louise Glenn
George, the steward .... Ben Lessy
Biplane pilot's wife .... Bobo Lewis
Miner .... Mike Mazurki
Negro truck driver .... Nick Stewart
Chinese laundryman .... Sammee Tong
First detective .... Norman Fell
Second detective .... Nicholas Georgiade
Smiler Grogan .... Jimmy Durante
Detective .... Stanley Clements
Police officer .... Allan Jenkins
Police radio operator .... Harry Lauter
Dinckler's store salesman .... Doodles Weaver
Traffic officer .... Tom Kennedy
Airport tower radioman .... Eddie Ryder
Helicopter observer .... Don C. Harvey
Patrolman .... Roy Engel
Patrolman .... Paul Birch
Helpful motorist .... Jack Benny
Motor joker .... Jerry Lewis
Airport officer .... Howard Da Silva
Bit parts (cut from the shorter versions of the film): Chick Chandler, Barbara Pepper, Cliff Norton, and Roy Roberts
Stuntmen (cut from the shorter versions of the film): Dale Van Sickel, Harvey Parry, Max Balchowski and Cary Loftin.

Credited Work

Following is the most complete list of films on which O'Brien worked that he received credit for:

1917   *The Dinosaur and the Missing Link*
       The Birth of a Flivver
       RFD 10,000 BC
       Morpheus Mike
       Prehistoric Poultry
       Curious Pets of Our Ancestors
       In the Villain's Power
       The Puzzling Billboard
       Mickey's Naughty Nightmares

1919   *The Ghost of Slumber Mountain*

1925   *The Lost World*

1933   *King Kong*
       The Son of Kong

1935   *The Last Days of Pompeii*

1936   *The Dancing Pirate*

1940   *Tulips Shall Grow* (Note: O'Brien may have worked on other Puppetoons.
       There is a photograph of him and Ray Harryhausen at work on *Nuts
       and Bolts*, which may have been the working title of *Tulips Shall
       Grow*.)

1949   *Mighty Joe Young*

1956   *The Animal World*
       The Beast of Hollow Mountain

1957   *The Black Scorpion*

1959   *The Giant Behemoth/Behemoth, the Sea Monster*

1960   *The Lost World*

1987   *The Puppetoon Movie*

Uncredited Work

O'Brien worked on all the following films except *The Brave One, King Kong vs. Godzilla, King Kong Escapes, The Valley of Gwangi* and *Trog*, which were derived from
projects or ideas that he worked on or was connected with originally.

1930   *Just Imagine*

1942   *The Miracle of the Bells*
       The Bells of St. Mary's
       Going My Way

1952   *This Is Cinerama*

1956   *The Brave One* (script derived from O'Brien's "Emilio and Guloso" story
       idea).

1963   *It's a Mad, Mad, Mad, Mad World*
       King Kong vs. Godzilla (the script derived from O'Brien's "King Kong
       vs. Frankenstein" story idea that he presented to producer John
       Beck).

1967   *King Kong Escapes* (many situations in this film are similar to ideas O'Brien created for "King Kong vs. Frankenstein")
1969   *The Valley of Gwangi* (derived from O'Brien's 1941 "Gwangi" project)
1970   *Trog* (contains animation from *The Animal World* by O'Brien and Harryhausen)

Aborted Film Projects

The following projects that O'Brien was connected with were in various stages of development when they were canceled or abandoned. More information on them can be found in Don Shay's *Cinefex* article on O'Brien.

1927   "Atlantis"
1928   "Frankenstein"
1930   "Creation"
1938   "War Eagles"
1941   "Gwangi"
1950   "The Valley of the Mist" (based on "The Story of Emilio and Guloso")
1952   "The New Adventures of King Kong (referred to as the Cinerama remake of King Kong)
1960   "The Elephant Rustlers"

Unmade Story Ideas
Sold to the Nassour Brothers

The following story ideas, all circa the 1950s, were sold to the Nassour Brothers and never developed into films, except for *The Beast of Hollow Mountain*. The storylines for each of the titles can be found in Don Shay's *Cinefex* article on O'Brien.

"The Last of the Labyrinthodons"
"Below the Bottom"
"The Vines of Ceres"
"The Devil's Slide"

Unsold Story Ideas

Except for "Triple Assignment," "King Kong vs. Frankenstein," "The Leviathan" and "The Pelican," the following story ideas were unsold and left to me at the time of Darlyne O'Brien's death in 1984. "Triple Assignment," "King Kong vs. Frankenstein" and "The Pelican" are mentioned in Don Shay's *Cinefex* article on O'Brien.

1950   "Triple Assignment"
       "The Bubbles"

"Bounty"

"The Eagle" (no illustrations survived).

"Matilda or the Isle of Women" (This also started life as "The Pelican" [no illustrations survived].)

"The Last of the Oso Si-Papu" (Storyboards and an animation model were created for this idea.)

"Baboon—a Tale About a Yeti" (storyboards included).

"Umbah" (only a few drawings survived).

1960 "King Kong vs. Frankenstein" (The idea was used as the basis for "King Kong vs. Godzilla," but the story of "King Kong Escapes" also contains some similarities.)

1950s "The Leviathan" (mentioned in the book, *From the Land Beyond, Beyond* by Jeff Rovin, and could be another title for "The Last of the Labrynthodons).

Unsold Ideas for Television

All these ideas were written during the 1950s and were handed over to me by Donald E. Hughes after the death of Darlyne O'Brien:

1950s "The Westernettes"

"A Preface to the Sport of Baseball"

"A Preface to the Sport of Boxing"

"Seeing It Through with a Champion"

"Understanding Rodeo"

"Preposterous Inventions"

"A Visit with Our Boys"

Unsold Theme-park Ideas

O'Brien made watercolor illustrations for these two ideas. What has happened to them is unknown.

1950s "The Westernettes"

"Trip to the Moon" (adopted title)

Wetback Material

Three unfinished variations of the same idea which could be further developments of the Mexican theme used for "The Story of Emilio and Guloso."

1959 "The Littlest Torero"

1959 "The Littlest Wetback"

1959 "The Little Wetback"

Notes

1. Ernest B. Schoedsack, "Kicking the Kong Around," *Film Pictorial*, April 29, 1933, pp. 18 and 29.
2. After "War Eagles," there was a brief highlight of *Mighty Joe Young*, which resulted in an Academy Award for Obie.
3. Some footage of the trading post and savages no longer survives in present-day prints of the film.
4. *Bioscope*, March 5, 1925.
5. Jose Lederer in *Kine Weekly*, March 5, 1925.
6. *Picturegoer*, April 1925.
7. Geoff Brown in *Monthly Film Bulletin*, June 1976 (Retrospective).
8. According to William K. Everson, 1971.
9. Interview with Don Shay, 1965.
10. Ray Harryhausen, *Film Fantasy Scrapbook*, 1972, 1974 and 1989.
11. Orville Goldner and George E. Turner, *The Making of King Kong*, chap. 5.
12. April 12, 1933. BFI Information department, source unknown.
13. April 17, 1933. BFI Information department, source unknown.
14. *Photoplay*, May 1933, p. 46.
15. May 1933. BFI Information department, source unknown.
16. May 1933. BFI Information department, source unknown.
17. The length of the running time given in this review was 8,952 feet. The film also had a British "A" film certificate.
18. *American Cinematographer* 64 (August 1983), pp. 48, 49–97, 101.
19. Victoria Mather, *Daily Telegraph*, August 1, 1986.
20. Iain Johnstone, *Sunday Times*, August 10, 1986.
21. David J. Hogan, *Who's Who of Horrors and Other Fantasy Films*, 1981, p. 176.
22. Interview with Kevin Brownlow, circa 1970.
23. From a letter to Mike Hankin from Darlyne O'Brien, dated March 16, 1982.
24. From a letter to Don Shay, November 1963.
25. Darylne O'Brien, interview Kevin Brownlow, circa 1970.
26. Richard B. Jewell and Vernon Harbin, *The RKO Story* (Octopus Books, 1982).
27. *Kine Weekly*, November 7, 1935.
28. *Motion Picture Herald*, October 12, 1935.
29. *Film Daily*, October 3, 1935.
30. *Film Weekly*, February 15, 1936.
31. Ibid.
32. Darlyne O'Brien, interview with Kevin Brownlow, circa 1970 in Los Angeles.

33. Jewell and Harbin, *The RKO Story*.
34. Brian Coe, *The History of Movie Photography*, chap. 7, pp. 112–139.
35. *Picturegoer Weekly*, November 28, 1936.
36. *Film Weekly*, October 17, 1936.
37. *Monthly Film Bulletin*, 1936.
38. *Kine Weekly* (July 31, 1936).
39. Jewell and Harbin, *The RKO Story*.
40. O'Brien's work for *The Dancing Pirate* is discussed in more detail in Don Shay's excellent biographical article, "Willis O'Brien — Creator of the Impossible," which gives a more detailed account of O'Brien than is possible here.
41. According to "Willis O'Brien — Creator of the Impossible," "Merian C. Cooper reenlisted in the U.S. Army Air Corps and 'War Eagles' slipped quietly into limbo," *Cinefex 7* (January 1982), p. 52; the book also gives more details about the test reel and the project itself.
42. Dan Ford, *The Unquiet Man — The Life of John Ford* (William Kimber & Co. 1982). In this period, Cooper was planning "War Eagles" at MGM. According to Jewell and Harbin's *The RKO Story*, he had all ready left, yet Ford's book says he had left them in 1940. It is possible that Cooper was still connected with RKO at this point.
43. "War Eagles," had several scripts written for it that included different events in the Valley of the Ancients section of the film; one event detailed an encounter between Naru and apemen in an arena.
44. Interview with Marcel Delgado, April 6, 1973, and letter from Delgado to Don Shay, December 12, 1963, courtesy of Don Shay. Quote is edited from both interview and letter.
45. Ray Harryhausen, interview with Steve Archer and Mike Hankin, 1985. Regarding Cooper being called into the armed forces, other sources state that he enlisted. A "War Eagle" armature does exist today in the collection of animator Jim Danforth.
46. A more detailed account of "Gwangi" can be found in Shay's "Willis O'Brien — Creator of the Impossible," which gives the story synopsis, production history and O'Brien's storyboards with Delgado's allosaurus model.
47. Ray Harryhausen, interview with Steve Archer and Mike Hankin, 1985. "Gwangi" finally made it to the screen in 1969, under the title *The Valley of Gwangi*, with special effects by Harryhausen, who gives an account of how this happened in his *Film Fantasy Scrapbook*.
48. Jewell and Harbin, *The RKO Story*, p. 240.
49. *To-Day's Cinema*, October 14, 1949.
50. Paul Dehn, October 14, 1949.
51. Leonard Mosley, *Daily Express*, October 14, 1949.
52. *London Times*, October 17, 1949.
53. Fred Majalany, *Daily Mail* (London), October 14, 1949.
54. *Motion Picture Herald*, October 15, 1949.
55. Ray Harryhausen, interview with Steve Archer and Mike Hankin, 1985.
56. Ray Harryhausen, interview with the author, 1990.
57. Information from Kevin Brownlow.
58. Interview courtesy of Kevin Brownlow. Harryhausen was also called "Harry" by MGM executives on his last film, *Clash of the Titans*.
59. Marcel Delgado, interview courtesy of Don Shay.
60. Interview with Darlyne O'Brien, conducted by Kevin Brownlow, circa 1970.
61. Ray Harryhausen, interview with Steve Archer and Mike Hankin, 1985.
62. Ephraim Katz, *The International Film Encyclopedia*, 1980, pp. 1151–52.
63. Jewell and Harbin, *The RKO Story*.

64. Art Cohn, "Roller Coaster Ride," *The Nine Lives of Mike Todd* (1959), p. 252.

65. Information on the Kong/Cinerama project is from Kevin Brownlow.

66. According to Don Shay, Obie did the caveman artwork. See Shay, "Willis O'Brien—Creator of the Impossible," *Focus on Film* 16 (Antumn 1973).

67. G. Bowman, *Evening News* (London), September 29, 1954.

68. Opening narration from the film.

69. *Motion Picture Herald*, April 21, 1956.

70. *Variety*, April 18, 1956. The film previewed April 6, with a running time of 81 mintues.

71. Warner Press Information, undated, from the BFI reference library.

72. Ray Harryhausen, interviewed by Steve Archer and Mike Hankin, 1985.

73. Paul Mandell, "Of Beasts and Behemoths," *Fantastic Films* 2 (March 1980).

74. Katz, *The International Film Encyclopedia.*

75. From the "Black Scorpion" script that includes some details not found in the finished film.

76. John Brosnan, *Future Tense.*

77. *Monthly Film Bulletin* (December 1958), p. 44.

78. *Hollywood Reporter*, September 20, 1957.

79. *Motion Picture Herald*, September 9, 1957.

80. *Kinematograph Weekly*, February 20, 1958.

81. Interview with Kevin Brownlow, circa 1970.

82. Jim Danforth, interviewed by Steve Archer, 1985.

83. *Variety*, March 18, 1959.

84. *Variety* (London), November 3, 1959.

85. Ibid.

86. *The Daily Cinema*, October 30, 1959.

87. *Monthly Film Bulletin* (December 1959), p. 311.

88. *Variety*, March 18, 1959, and *Film Daily*, March 23, 1959.

89. Phil Kellison, interview used by kind permission of Paul Mandell from his "Of Beasts and Behemoths," *Fantastic Films* 2 (March 1980).

90. Irving Block, interview, from Robert and Dennis Skotak "Special Effects Designed and Created by Jack Rabin and Irving Block," in *Fantascene* 1 (Summer 1976).

91. *Variety*, July 6, 1960.

92. *Motion Picture Herald*, July 9, 1960.

93. *The Daily Cinema*, August 3, 1960.

94. Patrick Gibbs, *Daily Telegraph* (London), August 6, 1960.

95. *Kinematograph Weekly*, July 28, 1960.

96. Quoted in Ezra Goodman, *The Fifty-Year Decline and Fall of Hollywood*, pp. 320–21.

97. Jim Danforth, interviewed by Steve Archer, 1985.

98. Darlyne O'Brien, interview with Kevin Brownlow, circa 1970.

99. Donald E. Hughes, interview with Steve Archer and Stephen Pickard, 1985.

100. Linwood G. Dunn, ASC, "The Mad, Mad, World of Special Effects," *American Cinematographer* (March 1965).

101. Don Shay, "Willis O'Brien—Creator of the Impossible."

102. Jim Danforth, interviewed by Steve Archer, 1985.

103. Darlyne O'Brien, interview with Kevin Brownlow, circa 1970.

104. Registered (No. 26775) with the Screen Writers Guild.

105. The films may have been made during the period 1912–15.

Bibliography

I found the following sources useful in my research on the life and work of Willis O'Brien and his fellow collaborators:

Books and Periodicals

Ackerman, Forrest J. "Famous Monsters of Filmland" O'Brien obituary c. 1962.

Boyle, John. "And now . . . Cinerama." *American Cinematographer* (November 1952).

Brosnan, John. *Future Tense*. London: MacDonald and Jane's, 1978, pp. 129, 142 and 167.

Carr, Robert E. and R. M. Hayes. "The Multiple-Film and Deep Curved Screen Processes." *Wide Screen Movies*. Jefferson: McFarland & Co., 1988, pp. 11–40.

Coe, Brian. "All the Hues of Nature." *The History of Movie Photography*. New York: Zoetrope, 1982.

Cohn, Art. "Roller Coaster Ride." *The Nine Lives of Mike Todd*. Hutchinson, 1959. (The biography was published posthumously in 1959. Both Todd and Cohn were killed together the previous year in a tragic airplane crash.)

Dunn, Linwood G. "The Mad, Mad, Mad, Mad World of Special Effects." *American Cinematographer* (March 1965).

Ford, Dan. *The Unquiet Man—The Life of John Ford*. William Kimber & Co. (1982).

Goldner, Orville and Turner, George E. *The Making of Kong*. San Diego: A. S. Barnes & Co., 1975.

Goodman, Ezra. *The Fifty-Year Decline and Fall of Hollywood*. New York: Simon & Schuster, 1961.

Hart, Henry. "Cinerama." *Films in Review* (December 1952).

Harryhausen, Ray. *Film Fantasy Scrapbook*. Rev. ed. San Diego: A. S. Barnes & Co., 1981.

Hogan, David J. *Who's Who of Horrors and Other Fantasy Films*. San Diego: A. S. Barnes & Co.

Jewell, Richard B., and Vernon Harbin. *The RKO Story*. New York: Octopus Books, 1982.

Katz, Ephraim. *The International Film Encyclopedia*. New York: Macmillan Press, 1980.

Kimble, Greg. "How the West was Won . . . in Cinerama." *American Cinematographer* (October 1983).

Mandell, Paul. "Of Beasts and Behemoths." *Fantastic Films* (March 1980) pp. 34–38, 55, 57, 60 and 62.

Murcury, Miron. "Willis O'Brien: The Oaklander Who Created King Kong." *The Moniclarion* (p. 16) and exhibition brochure of the same title (1984).

Reemes, Dana M. "A Lost World." *Directed by Jack Arnold*. Jefferson: McFarland & Co., 1988.

Rovin, Jeff. *From the Land, Beyond, Beyond*. New York: Berkley Windhover Books, 1977.

Shay, Don. "Willis O'Brien—Creator of the Impossible." *Focus on Film* 16 (Autumn 1973), pp. 18–48. Revised and updated in *Cinefex*, January 1982.

Skotak, Robert, and Dennis Skotak. "Special Effects Designed and Created by Jack Rabin and Irving Block." *Fantascene* (Summer 1976).

Additional Articles, Authors Unknown

"*King Kong* 50th Anniversary Celebrations." *American Cinematographer* (August 1983), pp. 49–97 and 101.

"Universal Victorious in 'King Kong' Battle." *Hollywood Reporter* (September 14, 1976), p. 13.

Louis B. Mayer announcement regarding Cinerama films. *Film Daily* 15 (October 1952), p. 11.

"Footage from 'Mad, Mad, Mad, Mad World' Shows Potential of Cinerama Single Lens." *Motion Picture Herald* (June 26, 1963).

Interviews

Merian C. Cooper, Ernest B.Schoedsack & Darlyne O'Brien interviewed by Kevin Brownlow and Ronald Haver, circa 1970.

Ray Harryhausen, interviewed by Steve Archer and Mike Hankin in 1985 and 1990.

Jim Danforth, interviewed by Steve Archer in 1985.

Donald E. Hughes, interviewed by Steve Archer and Stephen Pickard in 1985.

Phil Kellison, interview from Paul Mandell's "Of Beasts and Behemoths," 1980.

Index